CLASH OF FLESH AND METAL

CLASH OF FLESH AND METAL

ALICIA ELLIS

CLASH OF FLESH AND METAL

This is a work of fiction. All characters, organizations, and events portrayed in this book are products of the imagination or are used fictitiously.

Cover design by J Caleb Design

Published by Figmented Ink in Atlanta
First Publication, April 2021
Trade Paperback ISBN: 978-1-939452-56-6

Library of Congress Control Number: 2021906492

1

"This won't hurt. It just looks like it does." The technician held my metal arm out to one side and flicked on the laser.

Two weeks after removing all unauthorized data from my artificial intelligence, CyberCorp—otherwise known as my parents—had granted me the skin I wanted. Then it took only twelve minutes to custom cut a skin sheet and fit fingernails to the fingers. It felt like a lifetime.

"Almost done," the tech said.

I willed my feet to stop their nervous taps beneath my chair.

Mounted from the ceiling, the laser emitted a red light as the tech guided it down my arm. Its heat warmed my face. When he reached my fingertips, the bright light went off, immediately cooling the room and my nerves.

The tech released me. "Well?" He shifted in his seat before setting his hands down in his lap. "Are you happy?"

When I flexed both hands, they bent in unison. Matching light-brown fingers, wrists, elbows. The new one was perfect—except for being artificially intelligent. "It's good."

"I followed all your parents' instructions exactly." He reached for the laser. "But we can redo it if you want."

"It's great. Thank you."

His shoulders relaxed. "You're good to go unless there's anything else I can do for you."

I hopped to my feet. The skin moved with me as if it had always been there.

That meant I could get out of here. I could run to the elevator and out the front doors while waving both middle fingers in farewell to CyberCorp Tower.

But then I'd be all over the news again, and I'd never hear the end of it from my mother. So instead, I thanked him again and left at a reasonable pace.

"Lena, how are you?"

I jumped when the voice assaulted me from the side as soon as I stepped into the hallway.

Dr. Athena Fisher fell into step on my left. Her blond hair was pulled into a bun with a pen sticking out of it, and her long legs moved more slowly than mine to match my pace. "Everything go okay?"

"I have skin." My tone was flat. I stepped onto the moving walkway that stretched down the middle of the hallway.

"And that's what you wanted."

What I wanted was my original arm back, but this would do—as long as I could keep people from hacking into it to make me sleepwalk and strangle my friends. "Yes," was all I said though. "That's what I wanted."

"Good." She beamed. "You have a second chance—a new start that not a lot of people with injuries like yours would get." She was keeping up fine even off the automated walkway. Still, she stepped onto it next to me and squeezed in close so we fit side by side. "And you and I have a second chance to become friends."

Once upon a time, the doctor wanted nothing to do with me, preferring to spend her time perfecting the Model One androids. But life-threatening situations tended to bond people.

As we reached the set of three elevators and stepped off the walkway, I waved my left wrist in front of a small black plate on the wall. A soft beep confirmed the scanner read my ID chip.

"You had them install your chip." It was a statement with a question behind it.

I turned to meet her eyes. "I need to know where I am at all times." It would be a ridiculous thing to say for most people. But for a deadly sleepwalker, it made perfect sense.

With the chip embedded in my arm, I could use a chip-tracking application to make sure I stayed in bed when I was supposed to. The alternative of *not* knowing where I was—that was worse.

Technology wasn't the only devil. Humanity was full of monsters too.

Dr. Fisher nodded, but her gaze went over my head. I could tell she'd gone to the dark place. I went there myself when I thought about what happened. It was better *not* to think about it, but for better or worse, thoughts were one thing CyberCorp had not yet developed a machine to control.

"I needed it to—" I started.

A too-familiar sound of metal clomping against tile issued behind me, and I whirled, every muscle in my body winding up to spring. A Model One had just stepped into the hall. Its humanoid shape was designed to look like us, but its metal form reflected the white lights shining down from the ceiling. Red eyes stared straight ahead.

An automatic door opened on the opposite side of the hallway, and the android's metal feet clanged as it stepped through. The door hissed shut behind it.

"You were saying?" Dr. Fisher asked.

"It just made sense." I kept my focus down the hall, just in case that thing came back out. The elevator door next to us closed, and I hadn't even noticed it had opened. I waved my wrist to call another one.

"I wanted to apologize for how I treated you and thank you for saving me after that android went crazy when . . ." Broad-shouldered and six feet tall in flat shoes, Dr. Fisher tended to intimidate on first meetings. But now, uncertainty pinched her features. She licked her lips as she reached for more words.

"It's nothing. We're good." The elevator opened again, and I got in. One step closer to leaving CyberCorp Tower.

After a pause, Dr. Fisher stepped inside too. "It wasn't your fault that you needed help, and Ron . . . you saved me and—"

"I have a lot to account for." To the elevator, I added,

"Lobby." Then I raised my hands, palms out. "Whether I meant to or not, these hands killed three people. One life is a start, but that's all it is."

"Speaking as someone whose life you saved, I think it's plenty." She placed a heavy hand on my shoulder. "Give yourself a break. No good can come from dwelling on past actions that you had no control over."

The elevator doors slid open, and I slipped out from under her grasp and into the lobby. Dr. Fisher's footsteps followed me, slower than mine but eating up more space with each step.

In the afternoon sun that streamed through a wall of windows, the white-and-silver tile floor of the lobby shone as if it had just been cleaned. I hurried across the tiles to the single elevator that would take me down to the VIP parking garage.

Around me, people stood in small clusters around invisible displays that I couldn't see. The displays were virtual, presenting CyberCorp's most exciting new tech as virtual objects on top of the real world.

I didn't have the networked contact lenses needed to see them. Technically, the chip in my head was capable of displaying virtual objects to me, but I'd made them turn that feature off.

Movement in the corner of my vision made me turn my head, and my gaze locked on a dark-skinned man with closely cropped hair and a straight back. Detective Johnson.

I stopped.

Dr. Fisher stepped on my heel.

"Oh, I'm so sorry." She followed that with a string of profuse apologies that I blocked out.

The detective stood next to another man and a small kid, facing what I assumed was a virtual display. But while the dad and kid were smiling and waving their arms to interact with whatever they were seeing, the detective watched me.

His arms stayed folded over his chest. His eyes narrowed, and his mouth pressed into a tight line. He wasn't wearing the chest holster he'd worn the last time I saw him, but the bulk near his hip told me he was still carrying a gun.

"You know him?" Dr. Fisher asked.

"Detective Johnson. He's one of the detectives who tried to arrest me." I cringed. "I slammed him pretty hard in the shin."

"Your arm was reacting in a moment of stress, thanks in part to all the data Ron loaded onto you." She paused. "He looks pissed. Maybe I should talk to him."

Before I could answer, she was striding in that direction, and the detective's attention switched from me to the large blonde woman. He dropped his arms to his sides and stood up straighter, although he wasn't much taller than she was.

I hurried for the garage elevator. When I peeked over my shoulder, Dr. Fisher was gesturing wildly while Johnson watched me.

But he didn't make a move to follow. Crisis averted.

For now.

2

IN THE VIP GARAGE UNDER CYBERCORP TOWER, OLIVIA and Claire waited on opposite sides of my car. Modern vehicles tended to look like bullets with sleek, uninterrupted curves. Mine was not one of those.

As far as I was concerned, though, my cherry-red sedan found its beauty in its lack of high-tech features. No automated doors that slid upward. No rotating front seats. And most importantly, no auto-drive.

Liv stood on the driver's side with her face tilted upward and away from Claire. She'd given up the cropped blue hairstyle, and today, she had it plaited into two long cornrows that extended halfway down her back.

Claire stood on the other side of the vehicle, both hands on top of it, shooting a glare so sharp it threatened to slice Liv in two. She towered several inches above the other girl, and her short dark hair showed off cheekbones so defined they could cut.

"You waited?" I said. "I told you I'd call when I got done."

"We were leaving—" Liv started, her voice loud and abrupt.

"She wouldn't stop arguing with me." Claire jabbed a finger in Liv's direction.

My attention jumped back and forth between them. "You couldn't drive and argue?"

"You don't have auto-drive," Claire said. "That makes it harder."

"To drive and argue?"

"I told her to drive," Claire continued.

Liv spun on her. "You don't tell me what to do!"

"I see." I waved my left hand at the back door of the car, and the locks clicked on all four doors. "You've been out here arguing for twenty minutes." I pulled it open and gestured for Liv to get inside. Then I opened the driver's side and dropped into my seat before beckoning Claire inside as well.

Claire opened the passenger door and ducked in beside me.

"I'm not a chauffeur," Liv said, still standing outside behind my seat.

I tapped the steering wheel. Sensing my ID chip, the lights on the dashboard lit as the car started in complete silence. More modern electric vehicles had an artificial hum added by the manufacturers to warn pedestrians. But since my model was introduced early in the era of electrics, its engine ran in silence.

"Are we going or what?" I shouted.

Liv finally got in.

I backed out of the parking space and directed the car to the exit. At the edge of the garage, a metal gate rolled to the side as we approached, and I drove into the Thursday afternoon sun.

After a minute of silence, Claire shifted to face me. "Which boy do you like?"

"Excuse me?" I braked at a red light. My gaze flicked from the road to Claire and then to Liv in the rearview mirror. Liv leaned forward in her seat. I returned my attention to the road.

"Jackson has basically been your boyfriend since you were six," Claire said.

"That's . . . not true. I've just known him that long."

"I said *basically*."

"How often is someone's first love also their true love, though?" Liv said, nodding with each word, as though what she was saying should be obvious.

"Not often?"

"Like never."

"My parents have been a couple since they were fifteen," Claire said. "They always talk about loyalty being what kept them together. You have to give people second chances when they've had your back forever."

"You don't just keep people around because they've *been* around," Liv said. "People change and grow apart. You have to know who you can trust right now, not when you were six."

"What is this about?" I asked.

"Jackson!" Claire said.

At the same time, Liv shouted, "Hunter!"

"Uh-huh."

"You can't leave him on the hook like this," Liv said. "He's a great guy. He was your shoulder to cry on right after the accident."

"If we're getting technical, I don't think I ever cried on his—"

"He listened to all your rants about Jackson and the sleep-walking."

"Well, he—"

"But you were wrong about Jackson never listening to you and about him expecting you to run CyberCorp," Claire cut in.

"Can y'all just stop?" I shouted.

In front of us, the traffic light turned green, and I rotated the wheel toward my house. Both girls continued to stare at me, Claire from beside me and Liv in the rearview mirror.

"It's only been a couple months since I lost an entire arm and had it replaced with a robot. And—"

"It looks great, by the way," Claire said, but she clamped her mouth shut when I glared at her.

"Someone hacked into my brain and forced me to kill people—and I may or may not have contributed to that by hating CyberCorp and the Model Ones to begin with."

"You didn't," they said in unison.

"I was an easy target, though, because of how I felt. Either way, believe it or not, deciding which boy I like better is not at the top of my priority list. Mostly, I'm just trying to stay upright."

Claire turned toward the front of the vehicle and mumbled something I couldn't hear. Liv muffled a giggle and then slapped her on the shoulder.

"Glad y'all are getting along at my expense."

I turned the car into a posh area of town where shops lined both sides of the street. As per architectural regulation in this neighborhood, the building facades sported white-toned stone that matched sidewalks so bright they might have just been poured. Flowering trees marked the walkways on the street side.

"Hold on." Claire tapped the back of her ear to activate her micro-comm, a small device that sat right behind it. "Yeah?" Her gaze went blank as she listened to someone on the other end of the connection. "I really can't right now." She stole a quick glance at me. "Because I don't want to."

"Is everything okay?" I whispered.

Claire shifted away from me. "Fine. Give me ten minutes." She tapped her ear again.

"What's up?" I asked.

"I'm sorry. I still want to hang out, but I have to do something for my parents first. Drop me home?"

"You can't," Liv said. "We have the . . . thing."

"What thing?" I asked. When no one answered, I asked, "Are you coming by when you're done?"

"Definitely." She turned in her seat to look at Liv. "I'll be there."

"What's going on?" My friends were the least subtle people on the planet.

"Lena's car," Claire said, her tone overly cheerful, "navigate to Claire's house."

"Navigating," came the reply through the speakers in a low feminine voice. A map appeared on the screen of the dashboard to redirect me.

"I know where you live." I pointed at the steering wheel with one hand. "And I'm driving manually. The car doesn't need to know the way."

"Right." She raised her voice. "Lena's car, end navigation." She lowered it again. "I don't know why you don't just use auto-drive."

"How long will you be?" I tried to keep the disappointment out of my voice. I had been looking forward to a return to ordinary life. Or at least an imitation of it. Three friends hanging out after school seemed like a perfect start.

"Less than an hour—probably only half that. I promise."

I took the next right and circled back the way we came. Five minutes later, we pulled into a tree-lined neighborhood with sidewalks that curved lazily up both sides of the street. Claire's neighborhood fancied itself high-end traditional. Each house had its own character—one light yellow, the next blue, then gray, then pale green. But manicured trees and bushes fronted each one, not a single leaf out of place.

I eased the car to a stop at the end of Claire's driveway.

"I'll see you at your place. I won't be long." She stepped out, slammed my door, and ran to her front porch.

Liv opened her door as well and switched to the passenger side.

As we took off back the way we came, Liv crossed her arms over her chest. "She just bailed on us."

"You don't even like her."

"I don't dislike her. But that's not the point. We had a plan. You don't bail on plans."

I fixed my face into a false smile because, as disappointed as I was, it was important that Claire and Liv be friends. My dance card wasn't exactly overflowing these days, thanks to three murders and having broken up with Jackson. In their own ways, these two had stuck with me, and they were going to love each other if it killed all of us.

"She'll be right back," I said, my tone so bright that Liv narrowed her eyes at me.

"What do you think that was all about?"

I shrugged. "Dunno. Girlfriend stuff maybe. I haven't seen Brianna lately. I hope they're okay."

Liv smirked. "Oh, she has problems in her relationship, so she has to meddle in yours."

I stared at her until she took my point.

"I'm not meddling. You're already with Hunter. I'm not the one trying to blow up your thing to relive ancient relationship history."

"I am *not* with Hunter."

"So Jacks—"

"I'm not with anyone. I lost my arm, had someone control me in my sleep, and then killed three people. I'm . . . on hiatus." I slowed the car as we approached our next turn.

"Does Hunter know that?"

I jerked the wheel too far. Liv stared at me as I straightened up and set my car in the right traffic lane. "I'll tell him next time we talk."

Outside, the city rolled past my window. We'd gone to CyberCorp right after school, but now, rush hour was picking up. Cars packed the road on both sides, and the occasional drone whizzed overhead carrying packages and messages across the city.

Since it was February and the days were short, the sun crept below the horizon, streaking the sky in yellows and oranges. Digital billboards flashed to life on the sides of buildings and mounted on stands to tower high above.

"It wasn't your fault, you know," Liv said.

"I know." We drove past a building whose side sported a billboard showing me, a light-skinned biracial black girl with untameable dark curls, wearing a pair of red platform heels. The digital version of me skipped across the building in a way that I definitely would not if I wore anything that high. The real me would have face-planted on step two.

"Lena?"

I recited the mantra I'd been telling myself—and everyone else had been telling me—for the past two weeks. "I know it wasn't my fault."

It sounded more robotic than my arm. My fault or not, Debbie was still dead. And Kevin. And Harmony. Debbie's face remained a grotesque image seared in my memory.

Maybe I hadn't chosen to kill them, but I'd allowed it to happen. I'd refused to let my car take me home on auto-drive the night of my accident. I was fiddling with the controls instead of watching the road, and it cost me my arm. After the arm, I didn't work hard enough to discover the source of my sleepwalking and to stay awake when I suspected myself.

Ron programmed my AI to kill, but I opened all the doors and windows and invited him in.

This was on me.

"Lena?"

Somehow, I'd stopped at a light, and it was now green. I eased my foot onto the accelerator and put the car back in motion.

We rode in comfortable silence for half the remaining ride home before I put her on the spot. "What's the deal with Ron?"

Liv's body went rigid.

"You don't have to talk about it." I held my breath because, yes, she did have to talk about.

She stared straight ahead through the windshield. Her left knee started a steady bounce. "He made bail."

"What!" My foot fell too hard on the accelerator, and I had to will myself to ease off so I wouldn't ram the car in front of us.

Liv kept her attention on the road, even though I was the one driving. Her knee picked up speed like she was winding up for takeoff.

I softened my tone. "Who paid it? He's not exactly rolling in money."

"We always suspected he had a backer, right? Someone else provided the equipment he used. Outside of Cyber-Corp, he didn't have access to a machine powerful enough to hack the EyeNet to send you the data that made you do what you did. Inside CyberCorp, it would have been too risky since everything is logged."

"Everything except my arm." For privacy and because

my arm wasn't exactly part of their standard manufacturing chain, my parents and doctors had stored its log only on the chip embedded at the base of my skull. Lucky for Ron, though, he was on my team and had access to everything he needed. "He contacted you?"

"Do we have to talk about this?" Liv's voice was high-pitched with more than a hint of whine. But one glance at my face—which was as neutral as I could make it—and she continued in a mutter. "He called me."

"He's allowed a phone?"

"He said he dug up an old one. Just a standard smartphone. He can't have anything high-tech. Definitely no computers. But his counsel insisted he be allowed a low-tech phone to facilitate his defense."

"His defense!" Again, I had to calm myself with long breaths. "What defense could he possibly have?" I kept my tone low even though my nerves were stretched so thin and tight they'd snap at any minute.

She shrugged.

My hand-screen buzzed from the inside of my jacket. I stopped at a light and extracted it to check the new notification. It said Philip Pollock was streaming live audio.

Liv peeked at my hand and wrinkled her nose. "You're still listening to him? I thought you were over that."

"If you mean I no longer think tech is the source of all our problems—yes. But in the wrong hands . . . people died, and I still think Pollock was the money behind Ron."

"Have they found him?"

"He's long gone—more proof that he's guilty. I keep hoping he'll give something about his location away when he broadcasts. The police can't get a warrant to track his ID chip because there's no real evidence. It's just speculation."

Since my hand-screen was already paired with my vehicle, Pollock's voice burst through the car speakers as I streamed the audio.

"They are so threatened by me—by our movement against their machines—that they have conspired to bring me down. Make no mistake: they don't want you to hear the truth."

"Can you tell where he is?" I leaned toward the speakers, trying to pick out any distinctive background noise. There was a slight static, but that was normal in his broadcasts.

The audio volume dipped as my car detected conversation.

"I can't—" Liv started.

"Shh. I need to hear this."

The audio rose again. "They prefer you smiling and nodding and integrating each new piece of technology into your lives so they can know you better, track you better. Your lives are not your own. They belong to CyberCorp . . ."

Even when I closed my eyes and strained my ears, nothing in the background noise gave any hints about where he might be. This was hopeless.

"You're not still into him, right?" I asked Liv. "Ron, I mean." The audio volume dipped again, but Pollock continued his rant.

Liv didn't answer.

"Please tell me you're not."

"I'm not." Her mouth stayed open as if there were more to say.

I held my breath and waited for her to speak on her own terms.

"I feel sorry for him." Her words tumbled out into the open in a rush now. "All of this was because of what Cyber-Corp did to his family. His father just died. He already lost his mother. You and I have these perfect families with two parents and siblings, and everyone loves each other."

I couldn't argue with that. My parents betrayed me by replacing my arm, but they did it because they thought it was their best option at the time. That was more than a lot of people had. "A rough life is not an excuse for murder."

She chewed her lower lip. "I know that."

After a few seconds without talking, the audio volume increased automatically again, and by now Pollock was on a roll.

"You may think these machines are good for humanity. They're convenient. They make life easier. Perhaps. But with each new product launch, they grip more tightly onto your lives. With each new product, you lose touch with other people. You make a phone call instead of visiting. Then you text instead of calling . . . Soon, you will just have a Model One stand in for the people you love. Eventually, there will be no point in loving at all. Your entire life will be automated without human contact."

His voice struck a discordant note right in my chest, sending my entire body vibrating off-key. I used to hang on this man's every word. He believed his teachings, and so had I. I still did in a lot of ways. But his existence was too convenient—too aligned with everything that happened.

He was the perfect backer for Ron. Moneyed. Passionate. Driven.

We couldn't pin any of it on him. There were no contact records between him and Ron, and of course he had an alibi for every murder. Why wouldn't he, since I'd been the unwitting assassin?

As Pollock's voice rose in passion and volume, my fists clenched, and my teeth ground together.

"Lena?" Liv was staring at me, her face close to mine, her brows pinched together.

"Sorry, what?"

She tipped her head toward the windshield, and somehow, I'd managed to get us to my house. One hand still gripped the steering wheel, but I'd stopped the car at the end of the long driveway.

"Oh."

She jabbed a finger down at my left hand, which held my hand-screen. The point right under my thumb was bent, and I was clutching it like it was a lifeline.

"Crap." I pulled the two halves of the hand-screen apart, and the center screen snapped together into a larger display like it was designed to. Good, not broken. I closed it and set it on top of my dashboard.

Pollock's voice stopped abruptly, but soft static continued to come through the speakers.

"I'll be in touch," he said, before the static stopped.

Silence filled the car where Pollock's voice had been, and my blood pressure dived back to a semi-normal level.

Liv tapped my shoulder. "You're spacing out a lot these days."

"I'm fine."

Mine was the only home sitting at the end of this cul-de-sac, since my parents bought up two lots on each side of us to ensure privacy and security. A sidewalk split off toward the top of the driveway and led up to a pair of doors that extended at least two people high. The solid-wood entry was stained deep red, contrasting with the white facade and wrought-iron accents.

Today, cars blocked the garage where I usually parked. They filled the driveway from the top of the small slope on which my house stood, all the way down to the street. I'd parked just behind an oversized black sport utility vehicle that was shaped like most other cars here but with one large back door in addition to the usual two side ones.

"I didn't realize my mom had an event tonight," I told Liv. "We can go to your place instead."

"This is good." Liv popped her door open and stepped out before I could put the car into reverse.

She beckoned for me to join her, so I opened my door and stepped onto the driveway.

She came around the car and gave me a quick hug. "Can we try to enjoy ourselves?" Then she spun and walked to the front door, with me hurrying behind her.

"What's going on?"

"It's a party. Try to relax."

I hadn't relaxed in months, and I doubted I would start now. Still, I followed Liv up the driveway and into the house for whatever torture my mother had planned.

3

A loud *bang* sounded as I stepped into the two-story foyer. I grabbed the back of Liv's shirt and flung her behind me.

My arms were up in front of me, hands balled into fists, before I registered the crowd of people standing in the large foyer and even spilling into the sitting room beyond.

"Surprise!" Balloons released from hands. A plastic-and-helium wave of purple, metallic white, and gold floated upward to slide across the wrought-iron chandelier and dance on the thirty-foot ceiling above.

The decorator would have a hell of a time fetching those down later.

In the middle of it all, my mother stood in a pair of black pencil-leg pants that stopped at the ankle to frame bright-pink pumps with pointed toes. Her silky mauve blouse contrasted against her dark skin, adding a touch of softness to the businesslike look. Today, she'd worked product into her hair, and it poofed around her head in tight, kinky curls.

"What's this?" I asked.

"It's a party, honey." My mother hurried toward me, her brow tight with concern. Before I could tell her I was fine and just startled, she was past me and pulling Liv to her feet. "Lena, you have to be more careful."

"I'm so sorry." I grabbed Liv's other arm and helped to haul her up. "I still don't know my own strength."

My mother's attention flitted across our crowd of guests. There were about thirty of them, wearing a mix of expectant looks and concerned frowns. Through a too-tight smile, she whispered, "Do we need to reevaluate your strength variables?"

"I'm fine," I told her, my face holding a smile so carefully manufactured that I hoped it matched hers. Louder, I added to everyone. "What's going on? I mean, this is amazing but . . . What is it?"

"It's a skin party," a familiar voice called. "A celebration of skin." At the sound of his voice, delicious tingles inched up my spine and settled at the base of my neck until I shook them away. I scanned the crowd until I found him. Hunter.

Today, a plain black shirt hugged his lean muscle—the physical therapy was treating him well. His hair fell a touch too long across his forehead, and by now, I had to assume he cut it that way on purpose. It worked. The dark color brought out the light-green flecks in his mostly brown eyes.

My breath caught, and I physically worked to get it

moving again. "Hey. I didn't know you'd be here."

What a stupid thing to say about a surprise party. When had I turned into a rambling idiot, and where was my off switch?

In my peripheral vision, my mother wrapped an arm around Liv's shoulders. "It's good to see you. Your shirt is torn, dear."

"It's—what?" Liv looked down at her collar, and it was indeed split down the middle, just low enough to show cleavage. "Aw." She fingered the tear. "I liked this one."

"Oh no!" I said, my voice way more dramatic than intended. "Let's get you something else to wear." I grasped her wrist and tried to drag her in the direction of our curved staircase—anything to get away from this "party."

I'd been here two minutes, and so far, I'd thrown my friend to the ground and embarrassed myself in front of a cute boy I was already conflicted about.

Our housekeeper and nanny, Marcy, appeared out of nowhere and pulled Liv from my grip before embracing her in a tight hug. Today, Marcy's white-blond hair was pulled back into a dignified French twist held in place with a matching white plastic comb. Her sixty-year-old face was just beginning to show age lines around the mouth and eyes, where it scrunched most when she smiled.

Liv's expression brightened by a hundred watts. "Ms. Marcy!" Although she and I first became friends back in middle school, we went on a long hiatus for the past few years. She hadn't seen Marcy since freshman year. Liv had two amazing dads, but Marcy was the one she'd gone to about things like bras and first periods.

"I missed you too, dear. Let's go upstairs and find something of Lena's for you to wear." To me, she added in a whisper, "It's just a party. This, too, shall pass."

She missed the pleading in my eyes that begged for her to take me with her. I really needed to work on my telepathy.

Liv and Marcy chatted excitedly with animated faces as they walked side by side up the stairs—leaving me stranded in this sea of staring people.

My mother's smile was impenetrable—a veritable weapon of war. "Let's all give Lena a moment to recover," she called in a voice both loud and sweet. Two sharp claps had everyone following her out of the foyer and into the space past the staircase.

We called it a *sitting room*, but it was more like a miniature ballroom. The ivory tile of the floor gleamed as if freshly waxed. Hanging from the high-domed ceiling, the large wrought-iron chandelier was turned on today. Each of its three overlapping circles gave off a ring of white light. Combined with the rays streaming in from a circular skylight above, it created a halo around the room.

For the festivities, our furniture had been replaced with high-top cocktail tables covered in white cloths with just enough metallic threads to catch the light. A long table spanned the far wall, and at one end, plates entirely too small for food sat next to silver forks.

A server appeared out of nowhere and offered me a tray of drinks in champagne flutes. He pointed at the three clustered on one side. "Sparkling cider, Miss Hayes."

I started to reach for a glass on the other side. He

chuckled and ducked away before I could grasp a flute of actual champagne.

When everyone else was safely out of earshot, my mother turned back toward me. Her tone softened. "How did it go?"

"It's fine." I held my left arm behind me, angled away from her. We would not be making any more changes to it except on my say-so.

She searched my face. "Please don't keep things from me, Lena. I thought I'd proven to you that, despite my many imperfections, all I want is for you to be alive and well."

"And happy?"

"That was implied. Speaking of which . . ." She grasped my wrist before I could get away. "Your father and I think it's time we gave you more responsibility. Someday, we hope you'll be a partner at CyberCorp, so it's important that we start now with garnering one another's trust."

I narrowed my eyes.

She tipped back her head and laughed. When she stopped, the edges of her mouth still danced upward. "Don't be so suspicious. Your father and I understand that we had some responsibility in what happened, and we want you to feel you can talk to us without judgment. In return, we will trust you to make good decisions and not to hide things or lie to us."

"And more responsibility means what?"

"For starters, we'll be away for the long holiday week-end, starting tomorrow. It's Presidents' Day, and officially, the company will be closed. Marcy will be here, but we expect you'll take care of your sister as much as needed."

"I'm always here for Allie. That's not new."

She licked her lips. "Also, moving forward, we will never track your ID chip without permission."

"Okay . . ." I waited for more because a promise not to violate my privacy didn't amount to much either.

"We will never control or track your car or other devices that are yours."

"Thank you."

"And you'll have nearly the same access to CyberCorp Tower as your father and I do. After all, you will be a partial owner come your twenty-fifth birthday, so you might as well get used to the responsibilities that come with that."

"Seriously?" I took a step backward. "You mean I don't have to check in at reception anymore?"

"You do not."

"I can go up to see the Model Ones on the seventieth floor whenever I want?"

"I'm not sure why you'd want to, but yes, if you like."

"I can see the new inventions on the draft floors?"

"Of course."

"And . . ." I searched my mind for what else I might want to do. "I can eat lunch in your office with my feet on the desk?"

Her lips curled. "Please do not."

"Can I streak through the hallways?"

Her eyes widened.

"How about just the lobby?"

She dropped her head and covered her face with one hand.

"I'll take that as a maybe."

The kitchen door opened to my right, and a line of servers stepped through and headed to the long table on the far wall. Each carried a metal tray of food. One by one, they set their trays down and spun on their heels like soldiers before marching back to the kitchen.

"When did you do this?" I asked my mother.

I'd been in school all day and gone to CyberCorp Tower to get my skin right afterward. My parents left the house before I did in the mornings and returned much later. They'd been working even longer hours lately due to the Model One launch.

She kissed me on the cheek. "I will always find time for my babies." She started to turn away but stopped mid-movement. "I almost forgot. I need to introduce you to someone."

Hunter caught my attention from across the room. Now, he sat in a window seat in the corner, sipping from a glass of soda. He kept glancing toward the front door, and I could empathize a hundred percent with the desire to escape one of my mother's parties.

"Can you give me three minutes, and then we can do the whole social thing?"

My mom nodded and then whirled away, a beaming smile on her face as she went to greet her guests.

I recognized most people here as acquaintances from school and—I was guessing—their parents. My guidance counselor sipped a glass of champagne while intensely nodding while a parent spoke.

Upward of twenty people filled our sitting room right now, and I didn't have nearly that many real friends. My mother's events were like that—it wouldn't be a party without network opportunities.

I took a step in Hunter's direction and realized he was the only one of my close friends here. Claire had said she would catch up. Liv was upstairs. Melody wasn't talking to me at the moment—not that I blamed her. And Jackson . . .

I fished my hand-screen from my jacket pocket and placed a call. The line rang once, twice, three times. I was just about to end the call when it connected.

"Hey." Jackson's voice was low and quick. "What's up?"

"Are you okay?"

"Yeah. What's up?"

"My mom's having this party." What was my point? "And you're not here." I didn't know what else to say. I didn't even know why I'd called him. To ask him to come? To ask him why he hadn't? My mom must have invited him —the fact that we broke up would never stop her from bowing to social niceties, and Jackson's family's old money meant he got invitations everywhere.

"I didn't think you'd want me there. Do you?"

"I . . ." My breath was short, and so was my capacity for words apparently. "I just thought you would be."

"Give me ten, maybe fifteen minutes. Can't wait to see you." The call disconnected, leaving my mouth hanging agape on a dead line.

As I slipped my hand-screen back in my pocket, my mother caught my eye and beckoned with one finger. Next to her stood a girl about my age with olive skin and dark hair that fell to her shoulder blades in luxurious waves.

"This is Nina Ortiz."

Nina stuck out a hand with long fingers that looked like they belonged playing piano. The move was so natural that it made it seem totally normal for teenagers to shake hands. So I did.

"Nina's family moved here five months ago. Hanover didn't have space for her in your class at the time, but we've made room. She'll start next week."

"There are three months left in the school year."

"And then Nina will be a Hanover graduate, with all the privileges that come with that diploma."

Nina flashed me a smile of mauve lips around perfectly aligned white teeth. Nina might be a lovely person, but introducing her to everyone in the room was not at the top of my want-to-do list right now.

I faced my mom fully. "Can we not do this right now?"

Her lips pressed together, and I could see her brain cogs turning, trying to decide whether to spoil the mood. She smiled, but her eyes were dead. "Why don't you and Nina"—she placed a hand on the girl's back and pushed her toward me—"go greet your guests."

Obediently, I fixed my best business smile on my face and led Nina away.

I steered her in the direction opposite Hunter, offering him a wave and a shrug as I jerked my head toward the new girl. I'd much rather be talking to him, but if I led Nina over there, my mother would come right over and drag us away.

Hunter and I needed to have a real conversation anyway, not one in a room full of people I half knew.

I needed to tell him that everything had changed now —that I wasn't the girl who was angry about the new arm but still in possession a whole soul. Now, I was the broken girl, the one who woke up over corpses.

That was not what he signed on for.

Luckily, Nina was everything I wasn't, and she carried the conversation with a tall boy and his mother whose names I couldn't recall. I'd seen him at sporting events, so likely, the boy went to a high school in the same athletic league as mine.

With Nina occupied and my mother busying herself with straightening food trays into perfect alignment, I escaped to Hunter's corner of the room. He looked up from his soda when I approached, and his face cracked into that perfectly imperfect smile with one side higher than the other.

"Hey." His voice was low and gruff, like liquid chocolate.

"Hey."

He pulled me into a warm hug that smelled like spring-time soap. For a split second, I remembered what it felt like to have *little* problems—like an English essay that required an all-nighter. Little problems like my parents tracking my location. Little problems like CyberCorp hospital and physical therapy. And Hunter—there to make it all better.

Unfortunately, my little problems had grown legs and arms and sharp teeth.

The sort that made you wonder if you were the person you thought you were. The sort that changed you. The sort that broke you.

I stepped back from his embrace and straightened up.

"I called you this morning. I wanted to wish you luck." He gestured toward the room. "And warn you."

I laughed and held out my metal arm, now fully encased in skin the same light brown as the rest of me. "Mission accomplished." I gestured toward the room. "And I wouldn't have been able to escape anyway."

He laughed. "Your mom is a force of nature. How did she even get my number?"

I pointed at his knee, which CyberCorp had rebuilt. "She's got your records." My smile fell away after a few seconds, leaving silence in the space between us.

"So . . ." His gaze flitted around and landed back on my face. "I was thinking—"

My jacket pocket vibrated, and I fished my hand-screen out, expecting to see Jackson's name on the display. Instead, a message from Claire popped up. "Claire's on her way." I shifted my attention back to him. "Sorry, what were you saying?"

"We should hang out." He pointed back and forth between the two of us. "It's been weeks since we've been alone, and I thought we could catch up." His volume petered out toward the end, and I had to lean in to hear him.

"We should definitely talk. How about tomorrow after school?"

"I was thinking Sunday."

Now that we were making plans, I needed to have this conversation sooner rather than later. I didn't want to wait two extra days. "Friday would be better, please."

"That's great then. I'll pick you up here at six."

"Perfect."

The doorbell rang, and I bolted for it, realizing almost to the door that I was nearly running and had left Hunter at the mercy of party pleasantries.

I yanked it open without checking the live video from our doorbell camera. On the other side stood Detective Johnson.

"Miss Hayes." His voice was all southern drawl, and like earlier, he was dressed casually in a black T-shirt and blue jeans. The impression was different from how I remembered him from a couple weeks back—in a suit, his back straight, and accent minimized. This version of him came off as less controlled.

"What can I do for you, Detective Johnson?"

"It's Jermaine or Mr. Johnson while I'm on suspension." He stepped forward with a slight limp, favoring his right leg. I'd hit him in that leg the last time we met.

"What's this?" Hunter appeared behind me.

"Suspension?" I sidestepped in front of Hunter to block him from the conversation. I didn't need to drag him into another of my problems. He'd been my go-to for venting over the last few weeks, and he deserved a break.

"That's right. When they took my badge, they said

something about harassing the city's most important bene-factors." He gestured toward me. "I assume that means your family. Having a party?" Despite the casual words, the question under the question hung in the air.

Three people dead, and I was having a party?

"My mother is." The words were out of my mouth before I realized that didn't look any better. After all, I may have been the weapon, but the real perpetrator was a CyberCorp employee who manipulated a CyberCorp product.

He moved closer.

I swung the door toward its frame, leaving it open only a foot. I might be just a high school kid, but my family had multiple teams of lawyers, some of whom had been around since I was in diapers. I knew my rights. "Can I help you?"

He craned his neck to see deeper into the house. "Seems an odd time to celebrate."

I pushed the door to shut it.

It caught on his foot. He reached a hand through the remaining crack and held out a card with his name and contact information.

"Why would I want that?"

"You're just a kid. Maybe you want an easy way out of something bigger happening inside your parents' company. I take confessions." He shook the card at me. "Take it and I'll leave."

I snatched it from his hand and immediately crumpled it into a ball.

He withdrew his foot, and I slammed the door closed.

4

"You can't just slam the door in cops' faces." Hunter stared at me, mouth agape.

"Not multiple cops," I said. "Just the one."

Liv bounded down the stairs in a scoop-necked fuchsia top that looked amazing next to her brown skin. She stopped and looked back and forth between the two of us. "What?"

"Lena just slammed the door on a cop."

"*Former* cop."

"Did he have a warrant?"

"Nope." I gestured toward the closed door. "Hence, the door."

"Works for me. What did he want?"

"He's very upset that I hurt his leg and got him suspended. Now, he wants to make sure I'm brought to justice or something. It's all very cliché."

Hunter tried to reach around me for the door, but I blocked his path.

"Not a good idea."

The humor drained from Liv's face. "Did you tell your parents? Your mother was just here." She spun and searched the space.

"No!" I shouted. Luckily, all the other guests were too far away and too involved in their conversations to notice. "I don't want a hundred lawyers making this go away. I just . . . want it to go away on its own."

"Honey, I don't think it's going to work that way." Her voice had turned soothing, like how I'd imagine she'd sound if trying to reason with a crazy person.

"I prefer to live in complete denial."

To Hunter, she said, "Can you give us a minute? Girl talk."

He rolled his eyes and then retreated back to his corner. On the way, he grabbed a glass of soda from a server with a drink tray.

Liv started to speak again, but I cut her off before any words made it out.

"If Detective Johnson is still hanging around in a few days, I'll tell someone. I promise. I want to handle my own problems from now on. CyberCorp hasn't exactly fixed things for me lately."

"Your parents are not CyberCorp."

"That's an arguable point." I checked my hand-screen again. No new messages. It had been over fifteen minutes since Jackson said he was coming, and it wasn't like him to be unreliable. Cocky and needy and hard-headed—yes.

Unreliable—no. "Give me a second." I held up a finger toward Liv and shifted slightly so I wouldn't be staring right at her.

I placed the call, and it rang on the other end. Liv scooted closer to try to see my hand-screen, but I rotated to put her on my other side.

At the fourth ring, I disconnected with a growl.

Liv made a show of scanning the room. Hunter was here. Melody and I weren't exactly tight these days. That left two people I could be calling. "Tell me you're calling Claire."

"She's on her way."

"So you weren't calling her just now?"

"He's not picking up. He should be here by now."

"Lena!"

I peeked over Liv's shoulder to find everyone engaged in mingling. Nina's popularity had shot off like a nuclear-powered rocket, and she was now surrounded by two teenage boys I vaguely knew and an older woman, all of whom were leaning toward her as if she were magnetic.

Of everyone in the room, only Hunter stared this way. I waved at him.

Liv shot a glance that way and then back to me. "I wanted to talk to you about something else." She lowered her voice. "Did he ask you out?"

"We broke up."

"*Hunter.*" She tilted her head in that direction.

"We're going out tomorrow, but it's not a date. Just some alone time to talk."

"Not Sunday?"

I tucked my hand-screen away and finally looked her in the eye, sighing loudly and purposely because I didn't need to be drilled about my love life—or lack thereof. "Something wrong with Friday?"

"You do know that Sunday is Valentine's Day?"

I cursed. "Are you kidding me? That's why he asked to go out then?"

"And you suggested tomorrow."

"And now he thinks I'm going out of my way to avoid spending Valentine's with him."

"Are you?"

"No . . . not specifically."

"Then what specifically?"

"I'm not in a good place for him."

"What place are you in?"

"I don't even know, and that's kind of the point. I can't commit to anything until the world starts making sense again." I inhaled a long breath. "So it's probably a good thing we're meeting up tomorrow instead. I don't want to give him the wrong impression."

"You don't want to give him the wrong impression . . . and so you agreed to a date?"

"I agreed to some alone time to talk and hang out."

"You think that's what he meant?"

"I don't know what to tell you, Liv. Once again, I handled something badly. It's kind of what I do n—" The weight that lived in my chest pressed down harder. I gasped and let out a short, shallow breath before sucking in another long one. The room wobbled.

Liv's hand was on my shoulder. "Breathe." She took in

an audible breath and then released it, gesturing for me to do the same. "I'm sorry. I didn't realize that would upset you so much. Breathe, Lena."

The weight lessened, and after a few seconds, the room stood still.

"You don't have to make any decisions right now. Your mental health comes first."

My hand-screen vibrated against my waist. I ripped it from my jacket and answered without checking the display. "Hello? Jackson?"

No response.

"Hello?" I checked the display—a number my hand-screen didn't recognize.

"Who is this?" The line disconnected, and I lowered the device.

"What was that?" Liv asked.

"Unknown number." I shook my hand-screen at her. "Jackson said he would be here by now, and he's not answering."

"So what?"

"So I should go over there." My chest was tight with nerves. Maybe because of Detective Johnson or maybe because Jackson had never not called me back in all my years of knowing him—even post-breakup. But an alarm in the back of my head was banging like a gong.

Liv shot a glance across the room at Hunter and then back at me.

I couldn't leave him at the mercy of one of my mother's events, so I beckoned him over. The two of them followed me out. I hurried toward my car. My feet itched for a full-on sprint while my head knew I might be over-reacting.

Sometimes, people didn't return calls. They got caught up in other things.

But unfortunately, my life wasn't that lucky these days. I'd already almost lost Jackson in a car accident.

Just as I reached my car, Claire's sleek black vehicle pulled up behind it. She stepped out and waited as we hurried toward her.

I spun my finger at her to indicate she needed to turn around. "We're leaving."

"Why? What did I miss?"

"The cops were here—for starters," Liv said.

"The cops?"

"Just one cop." I tossed Johnson's card at her since I still had it in my hand. She caught it and uncrumpled it.

Liv shook her head. "You keep saying that like it makes things better."

"Jermaine Johnson?" Claire asked, reading from the card. She turned it over to see the blank back. The card had no logos, nothing official about it. Just his name and contact information. "This doesn't look very official."

"He's on suspension. I'll explain later." I yanked my car door open. "Right now, I'm worried about Jackson."

"Is he okay?" Claire asked, already moving back toward the door of her own vehicle.

"I have a bad feeling. That's all."

"Is that where we're going?" Hunter asked. He'd stopped behind me, and now he took two steps backward. "I'm out."

Liv shot me a wide-eyed glare, but I ignored it. I didn't have time to massage Hunter's ego right now. I jabbed my finger at her and then at my car. "You coming?"

She glanced back and forth between Hunter and me. "Please get in the car," she said to him as she climbed into the passenger seat.

He stared at her for a few seconds before reaching for the back door and getting in behind her.

Jackson's house was less than a ten-minute drive away, and for once, I wished I had auto-drive. My hands trembled on the steering while. Twice, Liv had to shout at me to get me to stop at red lights before accidentally blowing through them.

Despite being so close by, Jackson's neighborhood and mine were like different worlds. My parents were the new kind of rich, the contemporary kind that left their suit jackets open and opted not to wear ties. Jackson's money was older.

Houses near mine featured large blocks of white stone with black accents in straight lines while Jackson's was the picture of old money. The homes here took up acre-sized lots, and most sat back from the road with long driveways lined by landscaped trees or bushes.

There were no sidewalks, sending a clear message of exclusivity. This was not a place for visitors to take a stroll.

I wasn't sure whether all of that made it more pretentious than mine or less.

Jackson's house had a facade of whitewashed brick. Pendant lights hung from a steepled awning over the front door. A tall iron fence kept the world out, and on it perched a telltale white box that housed a chip scanner.

The scanner recognized me, and the gate swung open as my car approached, with Claire's right behind me.

We bounced as the car hit the cobblestone driveway without slowing down. It forked in one direction toward the eight-car garage. We veered the other way toward the main entrance. The heavy oak door held an oversized metal door knocker that was entirely for show.

"Lena?" Liv's nails dug into her leg as I kept up a steady speed.

I jammed my foot on the brake and stopped a few feet from the house. A second later, I was out and running for the door. Liv stayed close behind me. Like the gate, the tall oak door unlocked when it detected me, and I pushed it open.

"Jackson!" I shouted.

All the lights were off. In my house, the rooms brightened automatically when someone was present. But here, Mr. and Mrs. Watts liked to feel in control.

"Lights," I said, and they came on overhead.

They illuminated the marble floor of the three-story foyer. Crystals of the chandelier overhead shone as the light hit them. Two levels of balconies rose overhead, one for the second floor and another for the third. Gold-tinted iron railings fronted each balcony.

"Jackson!" Liv shouted, her tone steadier than mine.

"His room is up there." I pointed to the top balcony that marked the third floor and aimed my next shout in that direction. "Jacks!" A note of panic creeped into my voice, and it fueled the roil of energy in my gut.

Liv opened her mouth again. "Jacks—"

I shushed her and strained for any sounds. There was nothing except the faint hum of electricity.

A shout cut through the silence from above, followed by a thud. I ran for the stairs.

5

I took the steps two at a time. At the landing between the second and third floors, I didn't pause for a breath and bounded up the next flight. Liv stayed close on my heels. Her footsteps pounded after mine.

"Jackson!"

His room was the only one on the third floor, a large suite accessed by a door at the top of the stairs. The door now hung on a single hinge. Inside, steady grunts were followed by loud clanks that sounded like metal hitting something solid.

A silver android had Jackson pinned to the ground. Each time it punched, Jackson grunted and dodged his head to one side. Each fist whizzed past an ear and slammed into the hardwood floor.

Its red eyes glowed, emotionless, inhuman.

"Shit!" I lunged toward them and yanked the robot off him with my left hand.

It stumbled backward. While I had it off guard, I wrapped my arm around its neck and yanked it down to my height.

Jackson didn't miss a beat. He jumped to his feet and slammed his fist into the thing's gut. He wrenched out its battery cell, and the android slumped in my grasp.

I released it and let it slide to the floor. It landed with a clang and a clunk.

Its red eyes, now dark, stared up at us.

Jackson slumped to the ground beside it, his chest heaving and his breath thin. A purple bruise covered most of the left side of his face. His upper lip had split, revealing shining metal underneath.

"What just happened?" Liv asked. She stood outside the broken door, eyes wide as she glanced back and forth between the downed android and Jackson.

Hunter reached the landing behind her and surveyed the room.

"The Model Ones," I said, enunciating each word, "are dangerous."

"It's hard to disagree at the moment," Jackson said between pants. His tone held more humor than I could muster.

I offered Jackson my left hand and hauled him to his feet. "What happened?"

He turned a full circle to scan the space from the busted door to the disabled android to the brand-new cracks in the hardwood floor. "I heard it coming up the stairs, fast. Running. It sounds different from my parents." He pointed at his feet. "Metal."

I waved my hand to move the story along.

"I shouted through the door that it should go away. My parents have it doing chores and stuff, but I didn't need its help with anything right then."

"What about Kim?" Claire stepped around Hunter and into the room.

Kim was their housekeeper.

Jackson shrugged. "Not here."

Claire walked a circle around the Model One, shuddered, and then returned to the doorway.

I gritted my teeth because this was one of the problems with Model Ones—they replaced humans—*and* they were dangerous. Poor Kim, who'd enjoyed a job here for the past two years, was probably trying to figure out how to feed her kids.

"Does she have kids?" I asked.

"No, why?"

"Forget it. So then what?"

"It knocked the door off the hinges, which is such a waste because it was unlocked." He paused, as if I was meant to laugh.

I didn't.

"It froze at first after it got through the door. I thought it was busted, so I got closer, and the damn thing sucker-punched me."

"Why?" Liv asked.

"Who knows? We fought for maybe a minute or two before you guys got here."

The bruise on his cheek was already fading into its usual tan, and his split lip was in the process of knitting itself up. Fleshy strands reached out from one side of the cut and grabbed the other side, pulling itself together like a zipper.

"Maybe it was jealous that I'm higher tech than it." He grinned, revealing perfectly white teeth—half of which had been built by CyberCorp.

Liv's lip curled, but she couldn't keep her eyes off Jackson's face.

I refocused my attention on his bright-blue eyes, which were still all Jackson. The same ones I'd stared into on a very regular basis since we were small. Most of the rest of him had been upgraded, but I could always find him in the eyes. "Be serious, please. This isn't a joke."

"And it's impossible," Liv said. "Isn't it? The Model Ones are learning machines, but they're pre-programmed to learn specific tasks. Those don't include . . ." She gestured toward the entire room. "Right?" She looked to me for confirmation.

"They're programmed for self-defense." Jackson felt his still-healing lip, as if checking its progress.

"Did you attack it?" Hunter asked. He stepped through the door and into the room. "Or did you attack someone else? Who was it defending?"

"Were you listening at all?" Jackson glanced over at Hunter, irritation painting his features.

"To your bullshit story, yeah, I heard it. It doesn't make sense."

"You calling me a liar?"

"I'm just saying the facts don't add up."

"Can we not fight?" Claire said, stepping between the

boys, who had been steadily inching closer to each other—and definitely not for a hug.

"Maybe the truth is something in between," Liv said. She paused, and I could tell she was searching for a way to lower the temperature. "Maybe Jackson's upgrades prompted it."

Jackson tilted his head to the side. "It saw me as a threat?"

"I guess that's possible," Hunter said.

"Or," I said, "the Model Ones are dangerous and unpredictable. The only thing predictable about them is that, if you give a machine the ability to think but don't give it human empathy, it goes off the rails." I gestured toward the android still crumpled on the floor. "Like so."

Jackson waved a dismissive hand. "Liv's explanation makes sense though." He grinned, loving the idea of being the apex predator in the room, even above a human-sized robot. "And either way, no harm, no foul."

"I guess so." Liv's expression looked a lot more doubtful than her tone.

As if to make his point about the lack of harm, Jackson's lip was now fully healed. The bruise was long gone. His face was once again pristine.

"Yeah," I said. "I guess." Still, it wouldn't hurt to dig a little deeper. "Can you help me roll it onto its stomach? I want to check the log."

Jackson helped me roll the Model One over, and I popped the back cover to check the display underneath. I frowned when it didn't light up.

Jackson swept up the battery cell from the floor and waved it in front of me.

Right. I couldn't read its log if the android was dead.

"Can you power it?" I asked him.

"The charging plate is downstairs, but it has to stand on top of it."

I grimaced at the android, with its stomach open and metal guts falling out. "Can it stand?"

"I probably have a power cord we can use instead. More importantly, you want to turn that thing back on?"

I thought about it for a second and then grasped the android's right leg and yanked, twisting as I did. With a screech of metal that scratched against my eardrums, the leg tore free. I kept pulling until all the cables that connected it internally to the torso popped loose.

Jackson grabbed the other leg and did the same while I worked on an arm. As we dismembered the robot, Liv pressed her teeth together.

"It's not alive," I told her as I gripped the arm and yanked. The last of my words were drowned out by the screech of metal and the sound of the other arm clanking against the hardwood where Jackson tossed it.

She cringed again.

Jackson went to his desk and opened the bottom drawer, which was full of all kinds of controllers and cables —mostly for game systems he'd acquired and discarded over the years. He began rifling through its contents.

Farther into the room, a king-size bed sat on a low, black wooden platform. Although Jackson's parents preferred a traditional look, Jackson was all clean lines and contemporary, and his parents let him decorate his own room. Or technically, they let him work with their interior designer.

The pale blue wall behind the bed contrasted with the charcoal paint on the other walls. Over the bed, a modern black chandelier hung, composed of three black circles, growing smaller in a way that formed a triangle pointing to the center of his giant bed. A dark-gray comforter was folded down at the head to reveal ice-blue sheets.

"Hey." Hunter brushed up against me, his shoulder touching mine. "How are you?"

I breathed in deeply and let air stream out through my mouth. "I'm good. He's okay, so nothing to worry about?" I intoned my voice upward at the end like a question, and when I turned to Hunter, he nodded although his brow remained knitted.

Jackson closed the drawer he was searching and spun a circle before locking onto his closed closet door. He opened it and disappeared into the cavern where he stored his clothes.

"Got it!" Jackson shouted from the depths within and emerged with a long black cable raised above his head.

I grabbed one end and checked the plug. It was a standard CyberCorp power cable. "Is this going to work?"

"Let's see." He plugged it into the wall and then searched the back of the android before flipping up a small plastic cover and revealing a matching outlet for the other end. "Good old CyberCorp is still using the same power cords for every device."

Both he and I knelt next to it while Claire, Hunter, and Liv retreated to the doorway.

The android hummed to life. Its eye lights glowed, casting red onto the floor it faced. They flickered a couple times, and the robot's midsection sizzled and sparked. Jackson and I both leaned backward, wound up to spring and run away if this went wrong.

The android's midsection issued a series of clicks, and then the eyes went out. But a second later, they bloomed to life again, and the display on its back flickered on.

"Malfunction," it said as the slit acting as its mouth opened and closed. The torso rocked as if trying to move and stand, but its legs lay several feet away. "Malfunction."

Its eyelids clicked closed and then open. A stamp in the metal of its skull identified this particular android as M1A312.

"A312," I said.

Its head rotated toward me, and the torso rocked back and forth on the floor again.

"Stop moving."

"Not authorized," it said in an electronic voice.

I gestured toward Jackson.

"Don't move, Theo," he said, and the android froze.

"You named it?"

He shrugged. "You know how my parents are."

I leaned forward toward the display on the android's back. Lines of information filled the screen, and several rectangles acted as touch buttons at the bottom. And at the top—the version date. Before I could read anything, the display flickered.

The word *REVERTING* filled the screen for less than a second.

And then again, the text and touch buttons were back.

I blinked and pointed.

"What?" Jackson leaned over me. "This one is running software from a week and a half ago. That's after they fixed the EyeNet bug that caused . . ." He gestured toward me but didn't voice it. "Right?"

"That should be a good version. But did you see that a second ago—the *reverting* thing?"

"The *what* thing?"

I jabbed a finger at the display. "The screen cleared for an second, and the word *reverting* popped up, and then all of this came back."

He scratched his chin. "Are you sure?"

Liv inched her way closer and stared down at the android before sliding back to her spot by the door.

"No one else saw that?" I scanned the faces of my friends, but all of them looked as blank as Jackson's.

"If it reverted to an older version of its software—that doesn't even make sense. The newest version would be the best version. Why would it go back?"

"Malfunction," the android said again in its eerie electronic voice.

"Maybe because you guys tore off its arms and legs," Claire offered.

"Good point." Jackson held up one of the android's arms and waved it in my face. Its metal cables swung beneath it. They clacked against each other with each swing, as if to make his point. "It's not exactly in peak condition. Not everything is a conspiracy."

"It's just malfunctioning, Lena." Liv placed her arm on my shoulder as I continued to glare at the android's display. "That's why it attacked Jackson in the first place. It doesn't mean anything."

No one said it, but we all knew she meant it didn't mean someone had hacked this android the way I was hacked.

As far I was concerned, though, the Model Ones couldn't be trusted.

6

JACKSON FOLLOWED US BACK DOWN THE STAIRS. ON THE landing between the second and first floors, he grabbed my arm to slow me and let the others walk ahead. "You can stay if you want. My parents are both out."

I raised both brows.

His cheeks flushed. "I just mean we could talk."

"Talk about what?"

"About us." His eyes were so earnest and his tone so quiet that I wanted to fall into his arms and tell him it would all be okay. But unfortunately, my world didn't revolve around the two of us anymore. I wasn't that girl anymore.

The girl I was now could only surround herself with trustworthy people. History proved I'd been wrong to trust everyone who smiled at me.

"Where were you before?"

He gestured upward toward his room, where the Model One still lay in pieces.

I shook my head. "You said it came into your room just a minute or two before we got there. You were already late by then."

"I just got home from CyberCorp, and I was about to head back out to your place." When I didn't respond, he added, "Appointment. You still have those too, right?"

"Let's talk another time." I gave him a quick hug, so I wouldn't have to see the disappointment on his face. But still, when I pulled back, there it was in the droop of his lips. I hurried down the last of the steps and caught up with the others in the driveway.

Liv and Hunter were standing close together on the passenger side of my car, talking together in loud hisses. Claire leaned against her car, her face turned away from them and fixed into an expression of exaggerated boredom.

"Are we going to report this?" Claire asked when she saw us step out of the house.

"Of course. It's a serious equipment malfunction." Jackson looked at me when he answered, since apparently everyone else was willing to believe there was nothing to worry about here. "I'm sure CyberCorp will handle it professionally. They didn't get this far in business by letting things fall through the cracks."

I snorted.

Hunter said nothing but glanced toward my left arm.

"All cutting-edge technology has a few bugs at first," Jackson added.

"Mm-hmm." Hunter kept his attention on me. "So we're reporting this?"

I took two large steps away from both boys. I was not in the mood for a pissing match. If they wanted to pummel each other verbally, they could do that on their own time. I tapped the driver-side window of my car, and it automatically slid downward.

I reached inside and swept my hand-screen off the seat. The larger screen that was folded inside snapped together as I pulled the two sides of the device apart.

I navigated to my sleep log. In that log, I'd saved a record of my sleep patterns over the past two weeks—ever since everything came out about me, Ron, and the murders.

Each row of the log indicated when I went to sleep, what time I woke up, and any moments I happened to wake up during the night.

It didn't account for any sleepwalking because that had stopped, as far as I knew. But starting tonight, now that my chip was installed, I could check my tracked location against the sleep log to make sure.

If I was guilty of any sleep crimes, I wanted to know about it before it escalated.

Like last time.

Last night, I didn't wake up at all between when I lay down and when my alarm went off for school in the morning. My log said as much. The night before, I'd woken up once to get water and to go to the bathroom, but I'd woken up in bed—where I was supposed to be—and then returned to bed seven minutes later.

I skimmed down the records for the past weeks. No large gaps in time. No wakeups in odd places. Most likely, I had nothing to do with this little Model One malfunction.

"What's that?" Liv whispered in my ear.

I jumped and waved my palm over the display to make it go dark before snapping the two halves together to close the device.

"Was that a sleep journal?" When I didn't answer, she grabbed my wrist and raised my hand upward until the hand-screen detected my irises and lit up again.

"Yes." I yanked my hand away. "I need to know where I am at all times." Even as the words came out of my mouth, they sounded ridiculous—and necessary. My life was ridiculous, so I couldn't help but say ridiculous things.

"You have to stop this, Lena. You can't let what happened change your life."

That was how everyone talked about it—*what happened, the incidents, what Ron made you do*. No one ever said the actual words. "You mean I shouldn't obsess about my part in killing three people?"

She chewed her lower lip.

I let my face and voice soften because she was only trying to help. "I'm not okay right now, Liv, even though everyone wants me to be. This is the best therapy I can manage—outside of going back to CyberCorp's shrinks like my parents want—because that's definitely out of the question."

"This isn't healthy."

"Oh yeah? Killing people is much healthier."

"How could you even have anything to do with this?" Liv gestured toward Jackson's house.

I took a moment to make my face look exaggeratedly pensive. "Well, let's see. Someone might have hacked into the chip my parents put into my skull without my permission, uploaded data that would cause me to become violent and to hate CyberCorp even more, and then direct me to do things I don't know about in my sleep."

She frowned.

"Oh, was that rhetorical?"

"Lena." She waved her palm over the display of my hand-screen, and it went dark again. "You did not do this. Ron is not allowed anywhere near computers. Whoever he was working with is long gone and wouldn't risk getting caught at this point. And even more to the point, all your software has been fixed."

"But the Model One—"

"It's a machine that will always have bugs. You are a human being, and you're the main one telling people the difference between the two. You cannot be judged by the actions of that *thing*." She gestured toward the house again. "Or by actions that someone else programmed your body to do."

Her face was set and serious, so obediently, I reached back through the car window and returned my hand-screen to the seat.

She nodded.

"One more thing though." I swept the hand-screen back up and raised it to my face. The display lit up.

"Lena!"

"This isn't even about me—I promise. I'm setting an alert for every time there's a news report about a Model One going crazy, just in case this isn't a one-off." I added some keywords to my alert so my device would tell me if they appeared together in any article or video: *Model One* or *android* in combination with any of the words *dead*, *dying*, *die*, *murder*, or *kill*.

Liv watched over my shoulder as I typed every variation of killing someone I could think of. "That's not at all obsessive." Sarcasm oozed from her mouth, slicking every word.

With a satisfied flourish, I reached back through the window and set the hand-screen down. "All done."

Liv took a step away and then stopped.

"What? I said I was done."

"Can I sleep over tonight?"

My eyes narrowed. "I'm still going to log my sleep."

"You won't need to if I'm there. I can keep coming over until you convince yourself everything is fine."

"It's not—"

"Great. It's settled." She flashed a grin so wide that I couldn't help but laugh. "And as much as I hate to encourage you to spend another second of thought on this —you are going to report the android malfunction to your parents or someone, right?"

"I'll sleep alone. Thank you. And yes—"

"We are definitely reporting it," Jackson called from several feet away, where he and Claire were standing with Hunter nearby looking like he wanted to escape into the ground.

"Eavesdrop much?" I asked.

"We were just talking about that," he said.

"We should," I agreed, "but not to my parents. They're just going to freak out that I was involved. I know someone in quality control." I pointed back toward the house. "She'll want to see the Model One."

Jackson nodded and headed back toward the front door. I followed behind him, and the two of us took the stairs to his room.

Pieces of the android still lay scattered across the floor —a torso with a head attached, two legs, and two arms.

Jackson swept up the torso as if it were made of paper and then grabbed a leg with the other hand. He opened his mouth to say something but then snapped it shut, glaring at the doorway behind me.

I turned to find Hunter there.

Jackson brushed past him, hitting his shoulder harder than necessary so that Hunter stumbled to one side.

"Can I help?" Hunter gestured toward the remaining pieces.

I could support all of this with my left arm and balance it with my right, but I couldn't say no to the eager look on his face. I passed him both arms and grabbed the remaining leg.

We walked down the stairs side by side in silence.

"How are you?" I asked.

"Good." His mouth opened and closed and then opened again. "I should be asking you that."

My guffaw was so violent that I snorted.

"That good, huh?" As usual, his lopsided smile was so

authentically him. "You know I'm always here if you want to talk." He paused, and his next words tumbled out in a rush. "Just to talk. Doesn't have to be anything more than that."

"Thanks. I appreciate that."

When we reached the front door, Jackson was standing beside my car, still holding the other android parts. His gaze snapped toward us and locked. "Are we ready?"

"I'm going alone," I said. To Claire, I added, "Can you take everyone home?"

"I'm coming with you." Liv was already headed around to the passenger side. When she grabbed for the door handle, the car issued a clicking sound, and the door didn't budge.

Judging from what I'd seen of my friends this afternoon, none of them was as convinced as I was that this could be more than a simple malfunction. If I was going to make anyone at CyberCorp take this seriously, I needed to present a united front.

And that meant just me.

"I'm going alone," I repeated. "You know how finicky CyberCorp is about the public accessing anything above their lobby. It's just easier if I go alone."

I set the parts I was holding on the top of my car long enough to open the back door, and then Jackson, Hunter, and I loaded everything inside.

"You're my ride," Liv said, and Hunter raised his hand to cosign it.

"I can take you home," Claire volunteered. Her tone

was syrupy sweet, but Liv cut her gaze that way and then back at me with a pleading look.

"She's cool," I said. "I promise."

"You can even choose the radio station." Claire touched the driver-side door handle twice, and the doors on both sides slid smoothly upward, revealing two leather front seats on rotating stands and a curved backseat built for conversation. "I don't bite, and I can't exactly leave you stranded."

Liv shot another distressed look my way. When I didn't budge, she darted for the backseat.

Hunter tilted his head toward the passenger seat of my car in a silent question.

"I would really rather go alone," I said to everyone. "This will go more smoothly that way. No one over at the Tower is going to want to hear that a Model One flipped out, and it will be easier if the news comes from me."

He climbed into Claire's passenger seat. The vehicle rolled off the driveway and onto the street with an electronic hum. Three seconds later, the sound of muffled bickering reached me before the car zoomed out of earshot.

Without waiting a half second after they were out of view, Jackson grabbed for the driver-side handle of my car. My presence right next to him told the car that I was the one opening the door, so it unlocked automatically. He scooted across to the other side and leaned back in the passenger seat.

"Get out."

"I know you think you have to save the world from AI all by yourself, but I'm a witness. You need me."

"Please get out of the car."

He didn't need to hear me explain to Dr. Sophie Kim of CyberCorp that all the Model Ones needed to be recalled —and that was what I planned to say. It would take some convincing, and I definitely wouldn't win that fight with Jackson beside me disagreeing.

I ran around to his side and threw the door open. "Out!"

"Just let me—"

I grabbed him by the forearm and yanked until he stood and stumbled out, his jaw unhinged.

"Wow, they really cranked up the strength on that thing, huh?"

"Ron did that. It's the one thing I let them keep from my old programming." I scowled at him until he stepped far enough from the door to allow me to slam it. "Comes in handy."

I hurried around to the other side and climbed into my seat. "I'll call you."

Then I started the car and turned it in the direction of CyberCorp Tower.

7

I stormed into the lobby of CyberCorp Tower and, back as straight as a plank, strode toward the elevator bay.

"Miss," called a receptionist. She jumped to her feet and hurried toward me. "Miss, can I help you?"

Confidentiality was a big deal, and the receptionists knew everyone who worked here—why wouldn't they, given the hours employees stuck around? And they got paid well in return. It was going on six o'clock in the evening, and the long, black receptionist desk was still fully attended.

I spun toward the woman, prepared to tell her that I was going up whether she liked it or not.

"Miss Hayes." She skidded to a stop, and her face flushed red. "Please." She gestured toward the elevators. "My mistake. I believe your parents are in meetings though."

"Perfect."

If Dr. Kim was going to tell me all of this was a simple malfunction, then I didn't need my parents worrying about what mental state led me to jump to conclusions.

I waved my wrist at the scanner in the elevator bay, and one of the six pairs of doors clunked open. A soft whisper inside the car welcomed me by name. "Welcome, Lena Hayes."

"Seventy," I told it.

The doors closed, and the elevator shot upward. The high-tech elevators moved so smoothly that my only indication I was rising were the numbers displayed on a panel.

The Tower was pyramidal shaped over the top ten floors, each one smaller than the one beneath it. The seventieth was toward the top and, given its smaller size, wasn't segmented into multiple offices.

I stepped out into a space made of only two rooms— the large expanse that greeted me and a small office blocked off by two windowed walls in one corner. My steps made no sound on the black rubber floor.

To my left, a row of androids stood against a white wall.

In the middle of the room, on the floor, sat Dr. Sophie Kim. The petite Asian woman was the go-to for quality control of CyberCorp's androids.

Her bluntly cut, short black hair blocked most of her face as she bent over an android head, a screwdriver in one French-manicured hand. The remainder of the android was already disassembled next to her—two hands, two forearms, legs, knees, and various other silver parts neatly positioned where they'd fit together.

This was nothing like the carnage that Jackson and I

had brought on the android that attacked him. This was a methodical study.

"Dr. Kim?"

She shrieked and dropped the android head, which hit the rubber floor with a soft thud. She covered her chest with her hand. "That's what I get for working so intently." She picked up the head, turned it upside down, and went back to work with what looked like a miniature hand drill. "And I've told you to call me Sophie—or *Dr.* Sophie if you must."

"I want to report a quality control issue."

She looked up, narrowed her eyes, and then set the head down upright. Its dark-red eyes stared at me until I shifted my attention back to Dr. Sophie. "You know we have a web page for that."

"I don't want to make a big deal out of it."

"So you came here?"

"I don't want it on the record."

"Because?"

"I'm not sure it's really a malfunction. Maybe someone hacked it."

She gestured for me to continue.

"A Model One attacked a friend of mine. Jackson Watts —he's the one who had almost a complete rebuild."

"The young man who as in the accident with you, yes. Was he doing a self-defense simulation?"

"I don't think so."

"The Model Ones are configured for self-defense, but it's a feature that is enabled only on select devices— because of the obvious liability concerns. I would assume that the Watts were able to get that feature enabled given how high profile they are and given how"—she paused, as if to choose her words—"apologetic your parents were about the accident."

"And if that feature is enabled, then it could run a simulation without there being a real threat around."

"On request of an owner only, but yes, that's correct."

"He said it attacked him. It knocked the door down and slugged him."

"If I recall from the reports, he is your ex-boyfriend." One manicured eyebrow executed an expert arch upward before returning to its assigned spot. "Is that right?"

"What does that have to do with anything?"

Dr. Sophie squinted at me for a moment. "You brought me the android?"

I nodded. "In the car."

She hopped to her feet without even touching her hands to the floor. "Show me." She led me toward the elevator and then inside. "Lobby," she instructed it. "You're in the VIP lot?"

"Uh-huh."

The doors closed, and she tapped the back of her ear to activate her micro-comm. "Call reception." After a few seconds she added, "Could you send a couple athletic interns down to VIP parking for an android retrieval?"

We reached the lobby, and Dr. Sophie marched across the tile to the solo elevator leading down to the VIP parking lot one level down. We exited into the underground space, and already, a young man and woman who looked like linebackers were waiting.

"You're the interns?" Dr. Sophie asked.

"How can we help?"

She turned to me. "Which is yours?"

I pointed to the cherry-red vehicle in the corner of the lot.

"Why so far?"

I'd parked in a spot just inside the entrance from the street. Unfortunately, it was one of the farthest from the elevator. "So I can make a fast escape?" I answered, although in truth I'd been in a hurry to get to her and had parked in the first available spot I found.

She snapped her fingers and pointed, and the two interns hurried ahead of us. I opened the back door and gestured inside, where the dismembered android was thrown in pieces.

Dr. Sophie glanced inside and then glared at me.

"It was necessary." The weight of her judgment was too much, so I stepped back and let her concentrate on the interns.

She pointed at one of them and then inside at the robot. "Grab the torso for me."

Obediently, the woman reached inside and held the torso up, with the back facing Dr. Sophie.

The doctor reached into the pocket of her white coat and extracted a long, thin cable and a vid-screen about eight inches on one side. She attached one end of the cable to her device and the other to the power outlet on the android. The Model One's back screen lit up, and text scrolled from the top downward on the display until it hit the bottom and then stopped.

She skimmed the screen for three seconds and then disconnected the cable and her hand-screen before dropping both back into her pocket. "Grab the rest of it, and let's get it to my office."

The two interns collected the pieces of the android and made their way back to the private elevator that led up to the lobby.

"What do you think?" I asked her in a whisper as we followed.

"It's running a proper software version with all patches. It's possible there are bugs we haven't yet discovered."

"Bugs that could allow hacking." I didn't add the words *like what happened to me*, but we both knew what I meant.

"That's the reason there's always a limited release of a brand-new technology like this before it goes truly public. But this . . ." She gestured toward the two interns who now waited ahead of us at the elevator. "This is the sort of thing I get paid the big bucks to discover before any customers put their hands on a product. Even before a limited release like we have now."

"When will you know more?"

"Tuesday of next week, most likely. I'll be away for the long weekend, and I'm not sure I'll get to this before then."

"But you don't believe it's a bug? You think Jackson set me up to—what? Get my attention?"

"I don't know what's in your friend's head. At this point, my guess—and it's only a guess—is that this wasn't an accident."

8

WE TOOK THE PRIVATE ELEVATOR UP TO THE LOBBY FROM the garage. From there, we grabbed one of the main elevators.

"How can we find out what really happened?" I asked Dr. Sophie.

"Seventy," said one of the interns, to no one in particular. The doors slid closed, and we started our trip back toward the top.

"We'll have to go through the code function by function, test the hardware with various scenarios, try to recreate the problem."

"Jackson said he thinks it attacked him because he's a threat, because he has so many machine parts."

"That's an interesting theory." Her face remained stoic and her tone as flat as a billboard.

The elevator doors slid open. Dr. Sophie stayed put in

front of me until her two interns stepped out with their arms full of android parts.

"We have everything we need for now." She stepped out and turned to face me, still blocking my path onto the floor. "There's nothing else you can do here." She leaned forward to put her head back between the elevator doors. "Lobby."

I opened my mouth to argue, but she was right. I wasn't exactly an expert at Model Ones—even though I was part machine too.

"Have dinner. Do your homework. Try to relax," she said as the doors closed.

I couldn't remember the last time I relaxed.

Actually, I could. It was that night at the club, right before the car accident that started all this. That was the last time anything had felt remotely ordinary.

The elevator doors opened again, and I took a step forward before I realized this wasn't the lobby. I'd stopped on the fifty-fifth floor. In front of me, in the hall, stood Greg Miller. His blank eyes stared straight ahead.

It took him a second or two to focus on me. "Lena. How are you?" His tone wasn't cold, just empty, as though every breath was a chore.

"Could be better."

He nodded, but his gaze slipped away back to the spot above my head, and I wondered if he'd even heard my answer.

A loud throat-clearing drew my attention, and a redhead stepped out from behind Mr. Miller—Melody. A ponytail holder held her hair back, and in a rare instance, her face was free of makeup, revealing the smattering of freckles across her nose and cheeks.

"Hey." My voice came out low and scratchy. As usual, Melody looked exactly like her twin sister Harmony—whom I'd killed thanks to the programming Ron forced into my head. My breath caught, and I sucked in a deep breath to keep from tearing up. "How are you?"

"We'll wait for the next one." Melody grabbed the back of her father's shirt and pulled. He didn't move in either direction.

"No, no." Mr. Miller offered me a weak smile. "There's no need. Lena doesn't intend us any harm."

"I lost my sister." Her brown eyes narrowed to thin slits. "And my best friend. You took those from me."

"Claire is still here," I whispered.

"Claire was Harmony's best friend." She spat out each word as if they tasted poisonous. "You were mine."

"I'm still—"

"Don't." The venom in her voice cut my words short.

Mr. Miller grabbed her hand from off the back of his shirt and squeezed it. "Lena is as much a victim as we are."

"Last I checked, little Allison was still alive."

He spun toward her, wide eyed.

I couldn't blame Melody though. If my little sister *had* died, sharing an elevator with the person whose hands killed her would not be at the top of my bucket list.

Mr. Miller's expression turned firm, and with a sigh, Melody followed him into the elevator cab. I shifted to the side to give them as much room as possible.

On the way to see Dr. Sophie, I'd been impressed with

how fast and smooth the ride was, but now, we seemed to inch downward. Silence pressed in around me like old gasoline, sticky and suffocating.

"How are you?" I asked again when the floor number inside the elevator hit twenty.

Melody didn't answer, and I continued to drown in the silence until we slowed to a smooth stop, and the doors opened. Mr. Miller gave me an apologetic nod before following his daughter out.

I stood there watching their backs until the doors started to close again. Then I stuck my hand out to stop them and stepped out myself. Once upon a time, Melody and I were friends—best friends—and now that was gone.

Yet another example of how my life would never be what it used to be.

I returned to the VIP parking lot feeling no better than I had a half hour ago when I showed up.

Only now, I didn't know whether that Model One really attacked Jackson—in which case the Model Ones might have a dangerous flaw—or Jackson made the whole thing up—in which case there was nothing to worry about except my ex being a jerk. Or maybe it was a simple glitch, and I was overreacting.

Either the sky was falling or it wasn't.

Simple.

And once again, it was on me to figure it out.

Was it too much to ask that my life with this new arm be calm for more than the span of a week or two?

When I reached my car, the former Detective Johnson

was leaning against the driver-side door. His giddy grin seemed out of place next to his stiff posture.

"I just had that polished." I didn't even glance at him as I gestured for him to move so I could get in.

"And it's a classic. And a limited edition," he said, still leaning. "Only seven hundred fifty of these babies were made. I'd guess it's worth more than three times my annual salary." He slid out of the way, still leaning, but at least it was against my back door now.

I hesitated before reaching for the handle. I hadn't known that.

I'd asked my parents for a car without auto-drive—something low tech. And apparently, they'd bought me the most expensive one they could find. I gritted my teeth and threw the door open, seething on the inside. It was like they went out of their way to try to turn me into a trophy to their wealth and privilege.

I slammed the door closed and tapped the wheel twice in quick succession to start the engine. The interior lights came on to show me the odometer and other readings, so I knew the silent engine was on.

Detective Johnson didn't leave. He couldn't see me through the ultra-tinted glass, but still, he stared me right in the eyes until a shudder went through me.

"I'm going to file a complaint," I called loudly enough for him to hear, "for stalking and harassment."

He mimed tipping a cap to me as he walked away. "Have a good evening, Miss Hayes. Stay out of trouble."

I'd backed the car out of the spot by only a few feet

when a blinking red square on my windshield caught my eye. I stopped and squinted at it.

It blinked again—two times in succession, varying between red and completely invisible. When I reached for it and touched my windshield, my fingers felt only glass. I waited until Detective Johnson stepped into the elevator. Then I pushed my door open and stepped out.

About four inches on each side, the square material continued to blink red every few seconds. When I touched it, its texture was as slick and smooth as glass. I pried it up from my windshield and turned it over in my hand.

It wasn't sticky like adhesive, even though it had been stuck to the glass. When I brought it within a couple inches of my face, faint lines of circuitry became clear inside the sometimes-transparent material.

"Facial recognition." The material turned black, and white words flashed across what now seemed to be a display. *"Lena Hayes confirmed."* The text faded and a new line appeared.

There once was a girl named Hayes.

I blinked, so startled that I almost dropped the device. But the surface stuck to my hands as easily as it stuck to my windshield. The words faded, replaced by new ones.

Who always got her way.

"I do not," I muttered.

The note blanked out, and I waited, my breath on pause.

The story's not done.

The remaining message showed up one line at a time, each one vanishing before the next took its place.

I'm still having fun.

As the text disappeared, my heart danced a hurried rhythm.

Was this about what happened to Jackson with his Model One? *The story's not done.* Did it connect back to the three murders? *I'm still having fun.* Did they plan to kill more people?

Fear snatched my heart like a vise and squeezed until my breath stopped. I dropped the note as my head lightened. I flailed out to catch myself from falling into the abyss of panic and caught myself on the car. Both hands pressed down onto the hood, and I sucked in long breaths that did nothing to steady me.

New words appeared on the note now sitting on the hood between my hands.

This will follow you all of your days.

9

WHEN I FOUND MY COMPOSURE, I SPUN TO THE LEFT and then to the right. Someone left this note on my car. What if that someone was still here?

Maybe that's what Detective Johnson was doing here, and then when I caught him, he pretended he was waiting for me. It didn't seem like his style though. He was more straightforward.

I could find out easily enough. I ran back to the elevator with my head swinging in both directions. No one else was in this parking lot. Just me, but I wasn't sure whether that should put me at ease or make me more nervous.

I waved my wrist at the sensor, and the elevator doors opened. Seconds later, I burst into the lobby of CyberCorp Tower. I hurried toward to the receptionist who'd tried to stop me earlier.

Her brown eyes widened as I approached. "Miss Hayes, I'm sorry I—"

"Can you show me security footage from the VIP parking lot?"

"I . . . uh . . ." She shot a helpless glance at a young black woman beside her behind the oversized reception desk.

The other woman shrugged and looked away. She leaned into the vid-screen in front of her, now intently interested even though she'd been examining her fingernails a moment ago.

"Someone left something on my windshield without permission, and I need to know who."

"I don't think I can . . ." The wild look in the receptionist's eyes reminded me of an animal knowing it was destined for roadkill.

I dialed my volume down three notches. "I'm sorry. I don't mean to put you in a weird position. I just need to know who's been near my car. It's important."

"I'm not usually allowed to give out any footage." Her gaze darted around the lobby, from the far wall to the main elevator bay to the VIP elevator that had brought me here. "I'm not sure whether you're an exception."

"It's okay." I made my tone soothing. "Are my parents still here?"

"They left ten minutes ago. Should I call them?"

"I'll do it." I wanted to keep them out of whatever was going on with the Model Ones, but I could tell them about the note without revealing that. I fished my hand-screen from my jacket and called my mom. The line connected almost immediately, and I put the device to my ear.

"Hey, we're on our way home now," came my mother's voice. It sounded far away.

"Am I on speaker?"

"I'm with your father in the car. It's just us. Is everything okay?" Her voice tightened toward the end.

"I found a note on my car. I think it's related to . . . the murders." There was no graceful way to phrase that. "I'm at the Tower now, and I'm trying to get the footage from the VIP garage to see who left it."

"Was it a threat?"

"I'm not sure, but it was creepy."

"Are you in public?"

"I'm in the lobby."

"Hang up and come straight home."

"But I—"

"Lena, hang up. And come straight home." Her tone was firm. "We do not discuss such matters in public."

I gritted my teeth. "I want the footage."

My father's voice cut in. "We have access to all of that at home. Please do as your mother asks."

The receptionist was still staring at me.

I disconnected the call and tucked the hand-screen away. "I'm sorry to bother you." I headed back to the VIP elevator.

I broke the speed limit most of the way home, running through yellow lights and darting looks in my rearview and side mirrors. But nothing out of the ordinary happened. No one was following me as far as I could tell.

Soon, I pulled into the five-car garage at home, jumped out of the car, and burst through the interior door into the mudroom that led to the kitchen. My mother, Allie, and Marcy sat at the kitchen table, a solid oak one with six chairs surrounding it and a glass vase overflowing with multicolored tulips.

A sheaf of paper sat on the surface in front of my mom, and she held several pages in her hand. Despite being the co-head of one of the world's largest tech companies, she still insisted on printing documents to read and analyze. Plus, as she always told me, the most secure document was one that was printed and locked away instead of stored on a computer.

A bowl of untouched fish and rice sat on the table too. She held the fork in one hand but seemed to have forgotten it as she focused on the papers. She raised one finger as I approached, so I shifted my attention to Allie.

"Hey, squirt. It's almost bedtime."

"I'm not a squirt!" Her words came out slow and slurred as her eyelids drooped. She slid off her booster seat and took two steps toward me before Marcy's stern tone threw up a brick wall.

"Vegetables." Marcy pointed at the kitchen table, where Allie's plate now held nothing but a cream-colored sauce and a small pile of green beans.

Allie scowled and made a show of stomping back and scrambling into her booster seat.

"It's a little late for dinner, isn't it?" I gestured toward the food.

My mother finally lowered her finger and the sheaf of

papers in the same hand. She set down the fork as well and offered me a tired smile. "Not for me."

Marcy nodded toward Allie. "She refused to eat until someone else ate with her." Her tone held a hint of scolding. "She asked for you."

"But apparently, I'm a fair replacement," Mom said.

Allie grinned at me. "I didn't see you this morning before you left for school. You didn't wake me."

I picked her up and spun her around. "You were snoring so peacefully. I just kissed you on your forehead and let you sleep."

She glowered. "I don't snore."

"Of course you don't," I said with exaggerated agreement as I set her back into her seat. I tapped her plate. "Eat your food."

"I could say the same to you." My mother gestured to the swinging door that separated the kitchen from the rest of the house. "But it can wait. Your father is in his office with that footage you asked for."

"Lena," Marcy said, "Allie's been waiting for you."

I pointed at my four-year-old sister, who was now sagged to one side. "She's asleep." As if on cue, she started snoring.

Marcy sighed. "Go on then."

I bounded up the stairs and headed straight for my father's office. The door was cracked open, so I rapped on it and stepped inside without waiting.

My father's tan face was pensive as he scrubbed one hand through dark hair that was starting to gray. He was leaning back in a leather office chair, his feet propped on a solid-wood black desk that spanned a full ten feet across the room. The front two wheels of the chair were off the ground, and when he rocked, he looked a hairsbreadth from toppling over.

As I stepped deeper into the room, I could see what had his attention. The wall-sized screen to my right was playing a video of the VIP parking garage at CyberCorp Tower. The time readout in the upper left read 6:23 p.m.

My car was nowhere in view.

"You parked in a blind spot." He set his chair on the ground and pointed to the bottom right of the screen. A red dot appeared there and moved to mirror his finger movements. He spun his finger, and a red trail circled the far bottom-right corner. "This lot is highly restricted with a chip scanner at each entrance. We record the ID of everyone who goes in and out. So we didn't think it was crucial to cover every inch with cameras. We can see the entrance and the exit and about thirty-nine of the forty-two spaces. You picked one of the three out of view."

I grimaced. "I was in a hurry to park and get inside."

"You compromised your safety in favor of saving a minute." He lowered his hand, and the red dot disappeared from the screen. "There's a reason we've had all those talks with you about being aware of your surroundings and always staying in camera view. Not just because you're female, and men aren't all good, but also because you're a Hayes." His eyes narrowed at me.

"Yes, sir."

He gestured toward the chair in front of me, opposite him on the other side of his giant desk. It was a plain, black wooden chair with a charcoal-colored cushion. I sat and pressed my lips together.

"Explain."

"I found a note on my car." I pulled the note from my pocket and placed it in his outstretched hand.

He held it for only a second before setting the transparent square in front of him on his desk. He nodded for me to continue.

"It was a poem." I recited it back to him as best I could remember. Since it rhymed, that made it easier to reconstruct.

He listened, eyes narrowed and lips pressed into a tight line. "So it didn't threaten you directly?" he asked when I finished.

"Not directly, but I read it to mean that what happened to my classmates could maybe happen again. *The story's not done. I'm still having fun.* What if someone else still wants to use me to hurt people?"

He tapped the note two quick times in the corner. The square flashed black twice and then went clear again. "Hmm."

"What is it?"

"Dynamic paper. It's a technology we briefly toyed with and then discarded due to lack of a market. Basically, it's a flexible silicon screen with embedded circuitry. It's not good for much else than this." He gestured toward me. "Passing messages. Our market research showed that, between micro-comms and hand-screens and the EyeNet, there wasn't room in the market for another communication device. We toyed with integrating dynamic paper into hand-screens." A smile touched his lips. "But even those are becoming obsolete."

I recognized that for a dig, but I had other things on my mind besides launching into a rant about unnecessary technologies. Plus, my opinions had shifted since seeing how useful my arm was to me. Without it, I wouldn't have been able to keep that Model Two from hurting anyone else when it was running on the same data Ron had loaded onto me.

Still, while some devices were helpful to society, others threw up barriers that kept us separated. If you could buy an android to perform a job, why hire a person? If you could send a message with a touch of the finger and sit across from each other virtually, why even meet in person?

"Let me show you something else." Dad pointed at the screen again and rotated his hand counterclockwise, as if turning a knob. The footage rewound until my car entered the frame briefly and rolled backward out of the lot. He held his palm up and swiped to the right, and the video started from there at normal speed.

I frowned as I watched myself drive into the parking garage from the private entrance accessible by fewer than a hundred people in the whole world. My windshield was clear, no note. "So someone left it while I was in the lot, not before. That should narrow it down."

"The note is clear. That was the point when we developed it—something that would blend into any environment until it had a message to pass." He froze the video and pointed. The red dot that mirrored his hand appeared on my windshield. "We don't know whether the note was already there."

"So it could have been left there any time. Weeks ago."

My father waved a hand, and the video was replaced by a new one. My red car sat at the end of our driveway. But I could see only the back end of it at this angle. Most of the car was blocked by the giant, black SUV that I parked beside.

For several seconds, we watched the video in silence as nothing happened. Then a black vehicle drove up, and out stepped Nina, the girl Mom had introduced me to. She walked toward the front door, passing to the left of my car and the SUV. Her body was blocked entirely by the SUV for a few seconds as she passed.

I was one of the last people to arrive at the party, and I left after only half an hour. There couldn't be many others who'd passed my car during that time, but thanks to that monstrous SUV, we wouldn't be able to see who left the note—if they'd even done it there.

I muttered a curse under my breath.

"My sentiments exactly, but there's good news too." He rewound the video until my car rolled backward into the street. Then he froze it. "See this. The way the light's hitting your car and reflecting from the windshield?"

"So what?"

"This technology is photosensitive. It darkens several shades in bright sunlight. There wasn't enough sunlight during your entrance to the CyberCorp garage to be sure, but here it's clear." His red dot swung over to the time-stamp. "At 5:02 this evening, the note was not on your car. Where did you go after that?"

"Jackson's house, and then to CyberCorp." Without pausing for a breath, I added, "Can I have those videos?"

He spun his finger in a quick circle, and a file-shaped icon appeared on top of the red light. He swept it to the edge of the screen, where a column of his preferred contacts appeared. I was the second photo there. He dragged the file icon to my image and released it.

My hand-screen buzzed in my pocket, but I didn't reach for it. The video files would be there if I needed them later.

My dad spun his chair away from the screen and toward me. "Why were you at the Tower?"

"I heard Melody was there, and I wanted to get her to talk to me." The lie stung in my throat.

But my father nodded, threw his feet back on the desk, and tipped his chair back again.

"She didn't want to talk to me." At least that part was true. I sat upright. "Does she have access to the VIP parking lot?"

"Greg Miller does, yes. But Melody's ID chip was scanned separately when she entered the public guest lot earlier today. She doesn't have her own access. I reviewed the records of everyone who went in and out, but none of those people jumped out at me as relevant. Did you see anyone while you were there?"

Without meaning to, I glanced to the right and then back to my father's face.

He raised a brow. "Tell me."

"Detective Jermaine Johnson showed up."

My father's eyes narrowed. "Why?"

"You didn't see him in the records?"

"If the detective was in the garage, he must have piggy-backed on someone else's entry. What did he want?"

I shrugged. "I think he's trying to intimidate me into confessing to something."

My father's jaw tightened, and the fury in his expression made me shift in my seat. "I'll contact the department about that. Anyone else in the garage?"

I shook my head.

"Who did you see at Jackson's?"

"Besides Jackson? Hunter, Olivia, and Claire."

"From what you're telling me, more likely than not, this is one of your friends—probably a prank. The detective is out of line, but I don't think cryptic poetry is consistent with what I know of him."

He had a good point. I couldn't imagine the intense, straight-backed detective sitting around trying to come up with rhyming words for *Hayes*.

"In either case, I'll have someone follow up with his department." My dad peeled the dynamic paper from his desk and tucked it into his top drawer. "But I don't expect anything to come from this. You should have a chat with your friends to see where they stand. It's important to surround yourself with trustworthy people."

He gave me a warm grin that showed his teeth. Suddenly, CyberCorp owner Mr. Thomas Hayes was replaced by my dad. "Your arm looks great, honey."

"Thanks." I went around the desk and kissed him on

the forehead and pointed at the side of his temple. "You've got more gray coming in."

"Ouch." He clutched his chest in mock harm.

I headed for the door and closed it behind me so he could get back to work.

What bothered me most wasn't the fact that someone had left me a note. It was on the outside of my car, so it wasn't like anyone had broken in. No, what bothered me was the timing of it.

The story's not done. I'm still having fun.

Did it mean the attack on Jackson? The word *still* seemed to imply whoever left the note was involved in what had already happened and what was *still* happening. So the Model One's attack on Jackson was somehow connected to the murders—to Harmony?

I'd spent the last two weeks trying to put all of that behind me.

And I was still right in the middle of it.

10

I CALLED LIV AS SOON AS I HIT THE HALLWAY OUTSIDE my dad's office. "Are you coming over or what?"

A half hour later, we were arranging two sleeping bags on the floor of my bedroom. We hadn't had a sleepover in years, and Marcy had helped us locate them tucked in a closet in one of the guest bedrooms.

Now, we lounged on a mountain of pillows arranged on top of the sleeping bags. The last time we'd done this, freshman year, she had a set of purple pajamas that matched yellow ones I had. We'd outgrown them by now.

And that was probably a good thing.

Liv threw a pillow at me, and my left hand batted it out of the way with no effort from me.

"So why am I here?" she asked. "You didn't seem on board with me sleeping over earlier. And don't give me that nonsense again about how you spontaneously decided you miss our sleepovers."

"I thought it was pretty convincing."

"You're a terrible liar." She snapped and pointed to her palm with the opposite hand. "I'm gonna need that hand-screen, by the way. We're not logging our sleep tonight."

I snatched my hand-screen off the nightstand and tucked it under my pillow. "I didn't agree to that."

She pointed at her hand again. "Give it or I'm leaving."

Scowling, I extracted it from under my pillow and slapped it into her palm.

"Ow." She slipped it under her pillow and then shook her hand out. "You don't have to break me, you know. I'm just trying to help."

"Sorry. I still don't know my own strength."

"So . . ." She raised her brows. "What brings me to your little palace tonight?"

I told her about the note on my car, as well as about the security footage.

"It wasn't Hunter," was the first thing out of her mouth.

I raised a brow at her. "I would have thought you'd be trying to convince me it wasn't *you*."

"Obviously, it wasn't me. I didn't leave your side the entire time we were there."

I played back the events of the evening, and she was right. She'd arrived at my house with me and then left with me, and then she'd stayed close behind me on the way up the stairs at Jackson's. The only time we hadn't been in the same room was when Jackson and I were carrying the android parts—and then she was with everyone else in the driveway. "It wasn't you," I repeated back.

"Or Hunter."

"Hunter reached the third floor after you and me."

"Lena!"

I raised both hands, palms out. "I'm not saying he did it. I'm just saying that he *could* have. So could Claire for that matter."

"Or Jackson."

I chewed my lower lip. "You think so?"

"He waited by your car for you and Hunter to come down with the rest of the Model One parts. I wasn't watching him the whole time."

"And he wasn't watching *you* the whole time."

"*He* was leaning against the car," she snapped. She took a deep breath and then leveled her tone. "We've been friends a long time. I kind of expect your trust at this point."

"So has Jackson."

"Okay, but between the two of us, which one is more likely to feel snubbed right now? Me or him?"

"Fair point."

"And more importantly, he was the one leaning against your car. I couldn't have left the note without him seeing me do it. So again"—she pointed at her chest—"innocent."

"Okay, then back to Hunter. What's your argument for him?"

"He thinks CyberCorp is a great company that helps people. He's too new to your social circle. He didn't even know Harmony or Kevin or Debbie long enough to want to hurt them."

"He knew I knew them."

"So what—now you think he's some psycho stalker who murders people because you know them?"

"I didn't say he killed anyone."

"So he just leaves notes to taunt you with the deaths of your friends who he didn't know? What would be the point?"

It did sound ridiculous when she put it that way.

"He wants to date you. And he's pretty great, so I suggest you jump on that."

I raised one eyebrow.

"Not literally," she muttered.

"You think it was either Jackson or Claire?"

"It was Jackson. His Model One. His note. It all goes back to him. Maybe he did it to get your attention because you're with someone else now."

"I'm not with anyone. I'm with myself . . ." That had sounded less weird in my head. "I'm trying to sort things out right now. That's all."

Liv jumped to her feet, climbed out of the pile of pillows, and started pacing the length of the room. "It has to be Jackson. No one else had access to his Model One. That *total asshole*." She was shouting by the time she finished.

"Hey! My baby sister is trying to sleep thirty feet from where you're cursing at the top of your lungs."

"That asshole," she whispered and then tapped the back of her ear. "Call Jackson."

I jumped to my feet, but Liv dodged when I reached for her and darted to the other side of the room.

"Olivia Harris," I shouted, "if you don't end that call!"

"Make me." She raced to the other side of the room, and soon we were running circles around my bedroom, trying not to trip over stray pillows.

"Hey, Jackson. Lena wants to know why the h—"

I lunged and tackled her and then slapped my right palm against her ear.

"Hello . . . hello!" she said into her micro-comm and then glared at me. "Why did you do that?"

"You are not calling the boy I dated for three whole years to accuse him of tormenting me with fake Model One attacks and notes on my car."

She mimicked my words back to me in a high-pitched voice, and I tackled her again, sending us both to the floor in a fit of laughter.

I felt something vibrate under me, so I reached under the pillows and extracted my hand-screen. It was Jackson.

"Hey." I jumped free of the pillow pile and held the hand-screen to my ear.

"Are you okay? I just got a strange call from Liv."

"It's fine. It's nothing. We're having a sleepover, and she's being silly." Liv tried to snatch the hand-screen from me, but I jumped out of her reach. "Gotta go. See you tomorrow." I disconnected and threw my hand-screen on a pillow before tackling Liv again.

There was a tap at the door, and Liv and I froze with my right arm gripping her in a loose headlock.

"Who is it?" I called.

The knob turned, and Allie's face appeared in the crack of the door.

"Hey, pipsqueak." I released Liv and shoved her off me. "You remember Liv?"

She shook her head and took a step back.

Liv smoothed back some hair that had come loose from her braids and offered my little sister a bright smile. "I think you were two years old the last time I saw you. I used to help Lena and your mom feed you at night."

Allie glanced at me, back at Liv, and shook her head again.

I beckoned for her to come closer. "This is Liv. She's one of my very best friends."

Allie held out her hand. Her expression serious, Liv gave it a businesslike shake. Allie grinned and threw herself on top of the pillow pile beside me.

"Tell me about your day," she said. "What was the most interesting thing?"

I held out my left arm. "I got my skin back."

Allie held my wrist and contemplated the rest of the arm. "It's good."

"You don't sound too thrilled."

"It's an arm." She shrugged. "A lot of people have them."

Liv laughed, but Allie's face stayed serious.

She balled up her little fist and knocked on my shoulder so it emitted a hollow thunk. "It's still metal?"

"Yes, it just looks like it used to now."

"The metal looked cool. You looked like a superhero." She shrugged. "But this is good too."

"I agree," Liv said.

I swung my face toward her. "What?"

"It's like she said. A lot of people have arms. It looked special before."

I stared at her for a few seconds, but her serious expression didn't change. Then I shifted my attention back to Allie. "Now tell me what was interesting about *your* day."

"I made a new friend." She pointed at Liv, who grinned.

"You have good taste in friends." I stumbled my way out of the pillow pile to my feet and then lifted my sister into my arms. "Time for bed."

I carried her to her room, tucked her into bed, and read her a quick bedtime story.

By the time I got back to my room, Liv was buried deep in a sleeping bag, fast asleep. I inched my hand under her head and extracted my hand-screen from beneath her pillow.

The digital readout projected from my nightstand onto the wall behind it read 10:14 p.m. I entered the time into my digital sleep journal and tucked the device back under Liv's pillow.

11

MY ONLY CLASS OF THE DAY WITH JACKSON WAS MY LAST class. So on Friday at 2:24 p.m., six minutes before the start of last period, I waited in AP Chemistry for him to show up. He always sat in the back-right corner, and today, I'd arrived in time to beat the person who normally sat next to him.

I extracted my hand-screen from the small backpack that held the few schoolbooks I'd been able to find in print. Most of my books were digital only.

I shot off a quick message to Claire. *"Have you seen Jackson today?"*

Her response came right away. *"At his locker before first period, but not since."*

At Hanover, the students had lockers mostly because it was what schools had always done. But most of my schoolmates stored everything they needed digitally. I was one of the few who carried any kind of bag.

My hand-screen buzzed again. *"You could just call him, you know?"*

Instead of answering, I waved my palm over the screen to turn off the display.

Dr. Sophie's words had run on repeat in my head the entire night before: Model Ones did not just attack people —unless an owner instructed them to. Liv basically agreed with her. The only one who could have made that android attack Jackson was Jackson himself.

But why—to get my attention? He couldn't know I'd show up at his house just because he didn't come to my party?

Or maybe he could know. He'd known me long enough that I might be predictable by now.

But I couldn't imagine him trying to scare me by putting that note on my car. He might want to get my attention, but he did not want to hurt me.

He didn't.

Right?

Our instructor, Ms. Lincoln, entered the room and headed straight to the wall behind her desk. She picked up a stylus and began writing. Each sweep of her hand against the white wall left the wall completely unchanged in my view. I shook my head at the ridiculousness of writing absolutely nothing.

The blonde girl who normally sat in the seat I'd taken walked in, took a step toward me, lowered her head, and sat in my usual place in the second row center.

I shifted my hand-screen to the edge of my desk,

display up, with the tiny side camera facing the front of the room.

The virtual text Ms. Lincoln was writing appeared on my device as she wrote. Everyone else in the class had contact lenses that could tap into the EyeNet. Technically, the hardware installed in my head could access the EyeNet, but I'd had my doctors turn that functionality off. My hand-screen had access though.

It was 2:29. Class would start in less than a minute, and still no Jackson.

I couldn't sit here for an hour, listening to the instructor teach something I didn't care about—not without confronting him first.

In a single motion, I stood, swiped up my hand-screen and my backpack, and hurried for the door. While the instructor's back was turned, I slipped into the hallway just as the bell rang to start class.

A classmate brushed past to get into the room I'd just left, but it wasn't Jackson. Other students hurried on quick feet to get to their classrooms, and instructors stepped into the hallway briefly to close their doors.

I leaned against the wall and waited for the hall to clear.

"Don't you have class?" My math teacher, Ms. Ossoff, stood just outside her open classroom door and peered at me over the thin frames of her glasses. "I thought your free period was in the morning."

One of the downsides of being semi-famous at a small prep school was that everyone knew your business. "I'm not feeling well." I couldn't exactly find Jackson if she sent me back to class.

"I'm sorry to hear that. I was just heading in the nurse's direction." Behind her, her room was empty, so it appeared this was *her* free period. Just my luck. She gestured for me to walk with her.

Since it didn't look like I had a choice, I did.

"How are you acclimating to your new . . . situation?" she asked as we walked.

"It's fine."

"Of course." Her sigh was audible. "My students are all just *fine*."

Our footsteps echoed down the empty hallway. When we took a turn that put us in view of the nurse's office, I grabbed my left arm.

"Oh." My groan sounded ridiculously false, even to me. "My arm is throbbing." I nearly rolled my eyes at my own over-the-top dramatics.

Ms. Ossoff stopped, and her brows shot upward. "Is that what hurts?" Her voice had taken on a high-pitched note of panic.

Instead of answering, I offered another long groan. I really shouldn't have declined all my opportunities to take drama as an elective. Liv was right—I was an awful liar. Top-notch bad.

"Should we call your parents?"

"No!" I straightened up for a split second and then grabbed my arm again. "I should go to CyberCorp. The doctors there know how to deal with this."

She was already reaching for her ear to touch her micro-comm.

"My parents were very clear that the doctors at Cyber-Corp were supposed to handle any pains. Those were supposed to be handled *weeks* ago." I emphasized my words. "The last thing I would want is for one of them to get into trouble."

She bobbed her head up and down, eyes wide as her hand lowered from her ear. "I don't want anyone in trouble."

"I should just go." I headed back the way we came, leaving her bobbing and with her hand still half-raised.

I quickened my footsteps until I rounded the corner out of her view and was sure I was out of earshot. As I headed for the school's main entrance, I shifted my backpack around to my side and slipped my hand-screen out to call Jackson.

It rang.

"Please answer."

Ring. Ring.

Just before I would have disconnected, the ringing stopped. Heavy breathing filled the connection.

"Jackson?"

"Hey." He paused to take a breath. "Lena, what's up?"

"That's what I called to ask you. You're not in class."

He chuckled, still out of breath. "Neither are you."

"Only because I'm looking for you." The snap in my voice could have popped a rubber band. "Where are you?"

"At the Tower."

My breath hitched, and suddenly I was the one

breathing hard. "Is everything okay? You're not hurt or anything, are—"

"I'm good, babe." Humor coated every word. "But I love that you care."

"I do not." I pulled the hand-screen away from my mouth long enough to glare at it.

"I miss you."

"You saw me yesterday, in school and afterward. You could be seeing me in class right now, but instead you're scaring me to death."

"Aw, that's sweet." He paused, and there was a loud bang in the background, followed by a string of curse words from Jackson. "Can I call you back?"

"Wait! I wanted to ask you more about yesterday."

"I already told you everything. I have to—"

"Dr. Sophie Kim at CyberCorp said a Model One would only attack someone in a self-defense simulation initiated by its owner."

I could still hear breathing on the other end of the line, but he didn't speak for seconds. "You think I'm lying about what happened?"

"Is there any way it could have been a simulation? That's all I'm asking."

"If it was, I didn't initiate it." He paused, and then added, "Didn't you say you saw an alert that its software was reverting? You think I did that too?"

"I don't know what to think."

"For all I know, you could have made that thing attack me. You probably have higher security credentials than almost anyone else when it comes to CyberCorp."

"I didn't do it." My words sounded hollow though. This wouldn't be the first time I did something awful without knowing about it. Maybe I had added some kind of program to the Model One and then set it to delete after it completed its task. "I didn't do it," I repeated, more to myself than to Jackson.

He sighed. "I'm sorry. I shouldn't have said that. I trust you, and I know you didn't do this."

I didn't answer.

"Let's talk later. I have to go." The line disconnected before I could respond.

At some point, I'd stopped walking, and now I stood frozen just inside the school's main entrance, staring at my hand-screen.

I hurried through the door and down the stairs to my red car, which had a prime parking spot near the entrance. After closing myself inside, I opened my digital sleep journal.

Nothing had changed since the last time I checked, except that last night had been uneventful. I'd hit the bed at 10:14 and then woken up at 6:30 this morning when my alarm went off. Just like the last time I checked, nothing jumped out at me as odd about my sleep patterns over the last couple weeks.

Since my chip had been installed beneath my new skin yesterday, I checked my new chip-tracking log as well. It confirmed my sleep record from last night. I'd been inside my house from just before 7:30 p.m. until just after 7:30 this morning.

There was no way I could have done this—not in my

sleep and definitely not while I was awake.

Unless I set it up weeks ago—before the EyeNet patch was installed on the chip in my brain.

Between killing people, had I also been running around sabotaging Model Ones?

12

"I NEED TO SEE YOU." I SPOKE INTO MY HAND-SCREEN AS I ducked into my car in the school parking lot. "Please," I added.

"Of course." It was disconcerting to hear Dr. Fisher happy to hear from me, but I'd take my good luck where I found it these days.

I backed out of my parking space. "I'm on my way now. Is that okay?"

"You've got great timing. I should wrap up what I'm doing in about fifteen minutes, and I'll meet you in my office."

"See you soon." I disconnected and tucked the hand-screen into my bookbag before throwing both onto the seat beside me.

The bag vibrated as I turned from the school parking lot onto the street. Since the hand-screen was paired with my car, the dashboard screen displayed my caller identification. It didn't recognize the number as someone in my contacts, but it looked like the same one that had called me yesterday and then hung up.

Curiosity won out. "Answer call," I told my car. One of the few downsides of refusing to use a micro-comm *and* refusing to drive a car with auto-drive was that hands-free calling was a little more involved.

The car connected.

"Hi," I said. "I think you have the wrong numb—"

A familiar voice came through the speaker. "It's Ron. Don't hang up. I—"

"End call," I told the car, and just like that he was gone. If only I could get rid of his memory so easily.

My hand-screen vibrated again, rumbling my backpack across the passenger seat beside me. I itched to block the number, but my hands squeezed tighter and tighter around the steering wheel with each second the unknown number displayed on my dash.

"Answer call. What could you possibly want from me?"

There was a long pause and then a quiet voice. "Wow, I didn't think you'd answer."

"I regret it already. What do you want?" I spat out each word, and it was right on the tip of my tongue to end this call again.

"A second chance."

I guffawed, and my chest hurt. Not from laughter but from everything else. It hurt to imagine Harmony staring up at me as I strangled her. I had no memory of it, but I knew it happened. What had she been thinking in those last seconds? "Tell me who helped you. Who provided the equipment to hack the EyeNet?"

"I can't do that." His voice was still quiet, pleading. I had to strain to make out the words.

"You're wasting my time. End c—"

"Wait! Hear me out. Don't you believe in second chances?"

Of course I believed in second chances. How else would I keep waking up in the morning after what I'd done? After killing one of my best friends. After waking up over Debbie's body. After being too blind to see that I was being used by someone I considered a friend. *This* someone.

"Let me explain. Give me a chance to earn your forgiveness."

"You think I'd believe anything you have to say?"

"I never lied to you."

I opened my mouth to contradict him, but when I played back our brief friendship in my head, I couldn't deny it. That didn't mean I owed him anything though.

"Meet me tomorrow morning. I'll send you the address. I'll be there from seven until ten o'clock or so, and . . . after you hear me out, I'll tell you anything you want to know." He disconnected.

My hand-screen buzzed again, and an address appeared on the display in my car's dashboard. I wasn't familiar with the street name.

A streetlight turned red in front of me, and I eased the car to a stop before banging my right hand against the steering wheel and screaming so loudly that the person in the car next door stared.

All I wanted was control of my own life, and once again, it was being snatched from me. Of course I'd go, even though I wanted to stay a world apart from Ron. How could I not go? But once again, I'd be giving control over to a boy who couldn't be trusted.

Fifteen minutes later, I stepped into Dr. Fisher's office.

A plain white wall had replaced the vid-screen that used to hang on the left. In the center of a desk on the right, what looked like the remains of lunch sat on top of pages full of scribbled notes. Next to the door, a row of cubbies held various spare parts and hardware, stacked neatly.

Dr. Fisher stood from behind the desk when I walked in. She held out her arms, and awkwardly, I allowed the six-foot woman to hug me.

She gestured for me to sit in one of the two empty chairs across from her. "What can I do for you?"

I hesitated because I wasn't entirely sure what I wanted. I needed confirmation that I hadn't repro-grammed that Model One. If I had, then I wasn't in control of my own body—again. "Is there anything you can do to make sure I'm not being sabotaged again?"

Her forehead scrunched. "What makes you think you are?"

"A Model One attacked my ex-boyfriend—you know Jackson—and I want to make sure I wasn't involved."

"How might you be involved?"

I ground my teeth together because I was already being

clear enough. "I want to make sure I didn't sabotage the android somehow."

"Hmm." Her eyes narrowed. "Would you even know how to sabotage a Model One?"

"I wouldn't know how to break through the Millers' security system, but I did."

"Fair enough. Hold out your arm."

She contemplated it for a moment. "This won't be pleasant." She pulled a small silver gun from the top drawer of her desk, followed by the same type of cable Jackson and I had used for his Model One. She slipped the gun back into the drawer.

After a pause, she reopened the drawer and grabbed one more item, which she shielded behind the desk. Her expression went grim. "You remember we talked about pain receptors in the artificial skin?"

I nodded as a ball of nervousness settled like a rock in my stomach.

She grabbed my left wrist and gripped it hard. "I know this arm is stronger than me, but it's very important that you stay still."

My mouth was a desert, so I licked my lips.

In one smooth motion, she revealed a scalpel and slid it into my arm just above the elbow.

I screamed.

More from shock than pain.

She gripped my wrist tighter, and it took all of my willpower not to move as she dragged the knife upward over my bicep, cutting a slit into my brand-new skin. I covered my mouth with my other hand to keep from shrieking. It hurt, but not like I would have expected if I'd had time to think. It was like a sharp needle dragged across my skin.

Honestly, it would have been easier if she'd warned me.

In one smooth motion, Dr. Fisher yanked out the scalpel and inserted one end of the cable under my skin. I felt the click as the plug inserted into the socket of my metal arm. "All done." She tapped my left fist, which was clenched shut.

I let out a long breath and relaxed my hand. The skin on either side of the cable knitted up as strands of synthetic skin reached toward each other and pulled together. In seconds, all that was left was the cable, surrounded by smooth skin.

"Let's see what's going on." She swiped up a small cube from the desktop. The pocket-sized device, little more than an inch on each side, acted as an interface to many of CyberCorp's systems.

She attached the cube to the other end of the cable, tapped its top with her fingernail, and then turned toward the white wall. During the several seconds of silence that followed, she nodded at the blank wall, which I assumed acted as a virtual display.

"I can't see that," I said.

"Of course." She went back into her desk and came up with a hand-screen.

She pulled the sides apart to expand it to full size, and a clear screen extended between the edges and snapped into place to create a display about eight inches wide. When she tapped the expanded hand-screen against the small box, the backlight lit up.

I picked it up as text scrolled across the display, mirroring what was virtually displayed. The data scrolled too quickly for me to read, but Dr. Fisher continued to stare at the wall. She made the occasional grunt or murmur as the code scrolled.

I dropped the hand-screen down on the desk. "What do you think?"

She held up a finger, gaze locked firmly ahead. A second later she was back to her *mm-hmm*s and *ah-haa*s.

"Dr. Fisher?"

She held up a palm toward the wall, and the scrolling stopped on the hand-screen. When she waved, the text moved downward, but more slowly this time. She showed her palm again, and the text stopped.

"What is it?" Nervousness kicked up in my chest and churned, sending hot saliva up my throat so I could hardly squeeze the words out. The last time she'd been this interested in my code, I was killing people in my sleep. "What?" I shouted this time and jumped up from my chair.

"Lena." Dr. Fisher gestured to my seat.

As I sat, my whole body vibrated with nervous energy. "Just tell me. I'd rather know than not."

"It's fine. According to your primary log, everything is operating as expected."

"Okay." I slumped a little, but my nerves continued to squirm and kick in their battle for supremacy. "I didn't do anything to Jackson's Model One?"

She peered at me. "Not unless you did so intentionally."

"I didn't," I said quickly.

She rotated her body to face me and folded one arm over the other on the desktop. "Is this what this is really about?"

"I'm not sure what you mean. Are you therapy-ing me right now?"

"Someone needs to. What are you really afraid of?"

"Well, at the top of that list is killing people." I let sarcasm seep into the cracks between my words. "That's followed at a not-too-distant second by the thought that someone might be controlling my body while I sleep."

She pulled the plug from under my skin, leaving a hole with metal shining underneath. "Then I'm pleased to tell you that is not happening."

"I'm also afraid of the Model Ones." My skin sealed over the exposed metal.

Dr. Fisher opened a drawer and returned the cable to it before turning back to me.

"My hardware and software are more advanced than theirs. You've said my arm is more like the Model Two—except now that you've upgraded the composite metal, it's even better than that."

"That's true."

"And yet, an intern here was able to hack me and use me as a deadly weapon. The Model Ones are less advanced than I am, so . . ."

She was nodding along by the time I finished. "I under-stand your concern. It's unfortunate that you had to be a guinea pig and that it turned out so horrifically wrong. But the issues with your tech made us more aware than ever of what's possible and of the weaknesses and potential entry points for malicious tampering."

I pressed my lips together.

"Your concerns are understandable given what happened to you, but they are also without merit."

"I want an electromagnetic pulse gun."

Her eyes widened. "That's a big ask." Before I could open my mouth, she said, "And don't give me that bosses' daughter crap. You are authorized for a lot here—more than you should be if you ask me—but you are not authorized for that."

"I saved your life."

She let out a loud guffaw that was probably heard three offices over.

I fixed my face into an expression of neutrality until she reached into her desk and once again extracted the silver gun.

When I reached for it, she covered it with her hand.

"I need you to understand how dangerous this is." The gun was small, less than six inches long with smooth curves. "It is a deadly weapon."

I reached for it again, and she pulled it away.

"If I pointed this at your head and fired, it would disable your arm and probably hurt like a son of a bitch. If I fired it at your friend Jackson, it would probably kill him. If I fired it at someone with one of our heart implants— maybe not even knowing they had one—they would die." She peered at me. "Do you understand?"

My fingers tingled to grip the gun. It would protect me from anything my parents created.

Dr. Fisher returned the gun to her desk drawer. "I would lose my job, and you could do something you can't live with. And I know you don't want that on your conscience."

If there was one thing we agreed on, it was that my conscience was full to the brim and couldn't handle any other tragedies.

13

As I stepped out of the elevator into the lobby of CyberCorp Tower, my hand-screen buzzed. I stopped to extract it.

It was a new message. The caller ID read *Hayes*, and the message included two words only. *"First text!"*

I grinned and shot off a response. *"Allie?"*

"Marcy is helping me spell."

I suspected Marcy was typing the entire messages, but if it made my sister happy, I was on board. *"You're doing great!"* I looked up from my hand-screen to point myself in the direction of the elevator to the VIP parking lot and then started walking again.

"Goodbye, Miss Hayes."

I stopped and rotated. A brown-haired receptionist was standing behind the long black desk in front of the wall of windows to the building's front. She offered me a quick wave before dropping down into her chair.

"Hi?" I said, unable to keep the question out of my voice.

"I'm so glad everything worked out with your arm." She pointed at my left arm, now fully covered in one-day-old skin.

It took a moment to register her face, but the familiar cheerful tone helped. She was the one who'd dished the gossip about Dr. Fisher and Mr. Miller a couple weeks ago when I was trying to figure out who killed Harmony.

"How are you?" I asked her. I didn't want to strike up a conversation, but I also didn't want to be rude.

Another message came through from Allie. *"She's going to show me how to subscribe to audio programs like you do."*

I froze.

Maybe this was an opportunity. All sorts of important people walked through here, and these receptionists heard everything. Maybe that included something about Philip Pollock.

I pasted a wide smile on my face, tucked my hand-screen back into my jacket, and walked over to the reception desk.

"I'm great," the woman was saying. "Things have been so exciting over the past few months. But lately, the energy is like"—she threw up her hands—"like everything is coming together. It's amazing."

I hesitated because it was as if we were on two different planets—two different universes. "Three kids of Cyber-Corp employees died. It wasn't even a month ago."

"I know. That was just awful." Her face went solemn, but her body still vibrated with energy. "Mr. Miller is a wreck. Melody too. They both come in early and leave late."

"Yeah, she hasn't been in school much. I assumed she was at home. Why is Mr. Miller even working right now? They have paid leave for this kind of thing."

She shrugged. "Some men are like that, you know. Better busy than bored. Being here is probably better than being at home where Harmony used to be."

I could understand that. Every time I passed Harmony's locker, it felt like her ghost was watching me. She probably had one hip jutted out to the side, makeup perfect even in the afterlife as she complained about falling behind in math. I blinked to keep the tears back and then cleared my throat. "I get that."

The receptionist gestured toward the elevators. "He got here before six today, and Melody was only a couple hours later. It was after six in the evening when he left too. A twelve-hour day. That's brutal."

Since Mr. Miller was here, I could ask him about what happened with Jackson's Model One. Dr. Sophie thought it was nothing to worry about, but I wanted to be completely convinced. If the Model Ones were dangerous, it was better to know as soon as possible—before people died.

As CyberCorp's top engineer, Mr. Miller might have a different perspective.

And poor Melody, going through this alone. I wished I could help her, but mine was probably the last face she wanted to see. "Is Melody all alone when you see her?" I asked.

"Most days. Sometimes, a friend will come to keep her

company for part of the day and bring her schoolwork so she doesn't fall behind." She grimaced. "Poor kid."

"How does she seem?"

"Devastated."

"Yeah." I stared down at my shoes until I was convinced I wouldn't cry.

"Don't get me wrong," the receptionist continued. "People are heartbroken about that, but the Model One release is really raising everyone's spirits."

I could feel doubt filling every crevice of my face.

"Don't look so skeptical." She laughed. "This is life-changing. We are going to help so many people."

"Yeah." I had already decided to check in with Mr. Miller, but I still needed to ask what she knew about Pollock. It was like waiting for a time to jump in during double dutch.

"Not just chores and errands for rich people." She twirled a white pen between her fingers with speed and deftness matching her mounting enthusiasm. "I mean *really* helping people."

"Mm-hmm."

"Did you know they're going to be classified as medical equipment and covered by insurance for in-home care?"

"Uh-huh." I said it before registering her words, but I actually hadn't known that. "Really?"

"Oh yes. I know I'm just a receptionist. I answer the phones and tell people where to find things." She set the pen on the desk and gestured down at her ice-white blouse and wine-red pencil skirt. "I'm supposed to look presentable and put on a good face for the company." She shrugged. "But I'm proud of this job. I'm part of something important."

I cleared my throat and then got back to business. "Have you heard anything about Philip Pollock?"

Her eyes widened. "No, have you?"

I tried to keep the irritation out of my voice. "He's still streaming audio, as of yesterday anyway. Have you heard anyone talking about him?"

"Just that he's in the wind. Is he the prime suspect in the"—her gaze darted to my left arm—"murders?"

"Not officially, but I think the police and CyberCorp are unofficially trying to find him. Can you let me know if you hear anything?" I pointed at the vid-screen in front of her. "My number's in the system."

"Sure, of course."

I spun and headed straight back to the elevator to go see Mr. Miller. If anyone besides Dr. Sophie could figure this thing out, it was him.

My hand-screen buzzed.

This time, it was Liv. *"School's out. They said you left early to go to CyberCorp. You okay?"*

"Just needed to get something checked." My hand hovered over the display as I considered saying more. Liv was quick to jump on Dr. Sophie's theory that Jackson's Model One was running a simulation—one initiated by Jackson himself. I didn't want to hear her lecture if I told her I was here hoping to prove that untrue.

"Meet at your place?"

"Later. I'm still at the Tower."

"Shoot me a message when you're done."

I tucked the hand-screen away and waved my left wrist at the security scanner for the elevator. Soon, I stood outside Greg Miller's office.

The hallway was stark white. Smooth, shiny walls reflected my face back at me. His door stood open a couple inches, but when I peered inside, all I saw was a slice of his desk and the wall behind it.

I rapped on the door and then waited three seconds. When nothing happened, I rapped again and slowly pushed the door open.

Mr. Miller sat behind his desk, his chair angled away to face a blank wall. I had a profile view of him, and his usually neat, reddish-brown hair stood up in pieces. His eyelids drooped and then popped back open. On top of the desk sat a metal android skull facing toward him.

"I'm sorry." I started to back out of the room, gesturing toward the wall, which I assumed was a virtual screen.

"Oh, Lena." He turned and offered me a warm but tired smile. "So lovely to see you again."

Lie. It was never lovely to see the person who'd strangled your child to death. "This was a bad idea." I inched farther out and reached for the door to close it.

"Wait." He jumped up and beckoned me into the room. "Please come in. I could use the distraction. What can I do for you?" He returned to his seat and gestured for me to sit in the chair opposite him.

Because I couldn't think of a reason not to, I settled on the edge of it, my butt halfway off as if I might spring back for the door at any second. "Why are you being so nice?"

"This is my business." He gestured around the room.

"Computers. I understand how they work. I understand that they do as they are told—nothing more or less than that." He pointed at my face. "That chip in your head was doing as it was told." He dropped his hand, and it flopped into his lap. "Although I don't imagine that helps you sleep any better at night than I do."

"I keep a sleep journal." I didn't mean to say that, but it was hard to meet his vulnerability with anything but the same. More quietly, I added, "If I wake up in the middle of the night, I know exactly when and for how long. I compare it to the log of my ID chip's location."

"I understand." He leaned forward but peered at me with dead eyes. "What can I do for you? Please. It would do me some good to think about something besides . . . the things I think about."

"I wanted to ask you about something that happened with—"

"Can you believe this is what they've got me working on?" He didn't even seem to notice I was speaking as he nodded toward the metal skull on his desk. It looked like it belonged on the shoulders of a Model One.

I came here to talk about Jackson's little problem, but if the man who'd just lost his kid wanted to talk about a disembodied skull, then I could humor that. "It's a head."

He pointed at the eyes. "It's wearing networked lenses."

Indeed, the eyes were a cloudy silver, the way human eyes looked when their lenses were showing them virtual objects. "Why?"

He chuckled, but the sound came out sharp. "They assigned me to write a summary describing an upgrade to the lenses. For the marketing team, to help them sell it. The upgrade is meant to make them more palatable to those who may have reservations about the EyeNet."

"People have reservations—besides me, I mean?"

"Even before the recent . . . tragedies, there were others like yourself who found the EyeNet invasive. They want to be able to turn off the virtual world, to find peace. As you can imagine, the need for something like that has intensified since your story became public."

"I guess it would."

"This innovation is complex on the backend, but to the user, it is quite simple. You simply blink for three seconds." He rotated the Model One's skull to face me and tapped the head. The metal eyes clicked down. When they reopened, the color of the irises had changed from dark silver to the red that was standard for Model One eyes. "And the EyeNet connection is temporarily turned off."

He tapped the head again. Once again, the eyes blinked, and when they opened, they had the cloudy silver look of someone seeing virtual objects.

Mr. Miller's eyes went out of focus and drifted to a spot over my head. He was obviously not in a good space to help me.

My hand-screen vibrated, and since Mr. Miller wasn't exactly chatty, I checked the display.

It was a message from Dr. Fisher. *"There's an upgrade I meant to talk to you about. Are you still in the building?"*

Before I could reply, Mr. Miller shook his head and focused on me again. "What did you want again? I'm sorry."

I slipped the hand-screen away. "My boyfr—my friend Jackson's Model One attacked him yesterday."

"I do recall seeing an email about that."

"Why would it do that?"

"I believe the email said something about the self-defense simulation being activated."

"What if it was something else?"

He separated his hands and pressed his palms against the desk. "I have not examined the android, but the explanation given seems the most plausible."

I suppressed a groan. I'd spent time with Mr. Miller over the years at the Miller household when I hung out with the twins. This was not the man I knew. The old Mr. Miller had a smile that lit up the room—just like Harmony's. He also had the most inquisitive mind of anyone I'd ever met. He loved nothing more than helping his kids and their friends with a science project.

He questioned everything. Or at least, he used to.

"I should go." I popped up from the chair and headed for the door.

Just like everything else I'd tried today, this was pointless. I knew nothing more than I did an hour ago.

Melody burst into the room and rushed past me, her pale skin flushed bright red. "We have to go home. Something's happening with Mom."

Mr. Miller shot to his feet so quickly that I had to press myself against the wall to avoid being trampled as they rushed out the door.

"Did you lock your client cube?" Melody asked from the hallway.

Mr. Miller ran back in, tapped the top of the small cube on his desk, and then hurtled back out the door.

Mrs. Miller had to be okay. Those two could not take another loss right now.

Mr. Miller's lanky legs devoured the space between his office and the elevators. Melody was already waiting, her body half inside and half outside a waiting elevator cab.

"Tell me what's happening," he said.

They hurried into the cab.

"The Model One attacked—" The doors slammed shut.

14

"*Meet me at Melody's.*" I messaged Liv while on the next elevator down to the lobby.

"*You have a date with Hunter tonight. Remember? We need to be at your place getting you ready.*"

"*We'll go to my place right after. Their Model One malfunctioned.*" I stepped off the elevator and was halfway to the VIP one that would take me to the parking garage, and still no response. "*Hey?*"

"*Address?*"

I opened my contacts and sent Melody's entry to Liv. I ran the rest of the way to the VIP elevator and rode down.

Mr. Miller had a spot in this lot too, but he and Melody were long gone. Maybe I could still catch them on the road.

I broke into a full sprint. When I reached my car, I yanked the door open, tossed my hand-screen into the passenger seat, and started the car while I was still closing the door.

My tires squealed as I backed out of the parking space and swung the car toward the exit. The iron gate beeped when it detected my car.

"Come on. Come on." My foot hovered a millimeter from the gas pedal.

When it was finally open far enough, I hit the gas and raced through the gate, thumping over the speed bump that led out to the street.

There was no sign of Melody's brick-red, bullet-shaped car on the road, and Mr. Miller's was too hard to spot anyway—a nondescript black one that looked just like any other, despite its upgraded tech on the inside.

I hit every stoplight on the way to Melody's house. When I finally approached, a police car's flashing blue lights marked the spot. The siren was off and the car stood empty, but a uniformed officer stood in the open front doorway.

Mr. Miller's black car sat in the middle of the driveway.

I parked a couple houses away. If something awful had happened here, the last thing I needed was to get in the way. I also didn't need to be spotted—and to have my name tied to yet another tragedy—but that was lower on my priority list than figuring out what the hell was going on.

I popped the door open and stepped out.

A silver vehicle rolled past me and stopped behind the cop car. Out stepped two people in sports jackets and slacks. The man was the shorter of the two, but stocky. He looked like he spent his days in a home gym sucking down protein powders while bragging about how much he could squat.

The brunette with him wore a tight ponytail and a face so stern I would have guessed she chewed metal nails in her free time. And she looked hungry.

Detective Garrett.

She had been Detective Johnson's partner when he was investigating me for the three murders that I had indeed committed—unwittingly. Luckily, she was in a hurry, and the two of them went straight to the door of the Miller house.

I waited until they went through the door and disappeared into the house.

With back straight and chin high, I sauntered to the front door, offered a winning smile, and tried to step around the uniformed cop taking up most of the doorway.

"No visitors, miss."

I looked him straight in the face and gave him a moment to recognize me. Once upon a time, I hated the privilege that came with being the CyberCorp princess. But things had changed. Priorities had changed.

Now, my priority was keeping my hands free of blood—both literal and figurative.

I could take the easy way out and say none of this had to do with me. But both Model One malfunctions had happened to people close to me, Jackson and Melody. Combined with the note on my car—I was involved whether I wanted to be or not.

"I'm sorry, Miss Hayes." His tone was less harsh this time, more apologetic. "No visitors."

The open doorway behind him revealed the large kitchen that Mrs. Miller had recently remodeled. The tile floor made of large checkered white-and-gray squares must have cost a fortune to ship from overseas. On top of it stood an island so big it could have its own zip code.

"Melody is a friend of mine. I need to check on her."

He mimed tapping his ear as if activating a micro-comm. "Call her. If she comes to escort you in, you can go."

That definitely wasn't happening. Still, I made a show of tapping my ear—even though I had no micro-comm— and strained my ears to listen to the space behind him.

The detectives must have been just inside the door and out of view because their hushed voices reached me.

"What set the thing off?" Detective Garrett was asking.

"Not sure yet. She says it was cleaning the family room and suddenly charged her. She only outran it because it was slow on the stairs."

"So she's okay?"

"She won't come out of the safe room."

"Injuries?"

"Her ankle hurts. She twisted it running away."

"Get her out. We need a statement, and I'm not doing that over a safe-room intercom. What about the android?"

"Acting normally now. Mrs. Miller says it stopped banging on the safe room door after a minute. According to the house cameras, it froze and then returned to its charging station."

"What does that . . ." Footsteps receded, and Garrett's voice became too far away to make out words.

I scanned as much as I could see of the foyer and the

kitchen. Nothing looked out of place. The counters were impeccable as usual, with a large vase of flowers standing in the center.

My breath caught as my gaze slid across the fridge and then circled back.

Another uniformed cop stepped into view, and I jumped. He must have been the one updating the detectives. His glare was so intense that I dropped the ruse of contacting Melody via micro and backed off the porch.

At the end of the driveway, Nina Ortiz hurtled toward me. Her high heels skidded gracefully across the pavement. Just like at the party yesterday, her makeup looked professionally applied, and her smile looked equally practiced.

"Lena." She slowed, and we met in the middle of the walkway. She stopped long enough to give me a hug that smelled like flowers. "Lovely to see you again." When she stepped back, her face was grim. "Melody will not want you here."

"You know her? I thought you just moved here."

She laughed, and the sound was like perfect little bells, and I was trying really hard not to hate her. I pulled myself up to my full height of five foot five, which still put me at several inches shorter than her in her heels.

"She and I went to elementary together up north before her father moved here for work." Her nose wrinkled. "We never lost touch."

"That's nice." I didn't know how else to respond to hearing that one of my best friends was close with someone I'd never heard of until yesterday. What else had Melody been keeping from me all these years?

"Anyway, I have to go. Her mother is fine, but Melody is freaking out."

"Understandably."

"Right?" She brushed past me.

Melody now stood in the doorway, ready to usher her inside. Either she didn't see me or didn't acknowledge me, because the two of them disappeared into the house a second later.

I hurried back to my parking spot.

Liv's car now idled just behind mine. She sat in the driver's seat with her window rolled down. "What's going on?"

"It attacked Melody's mom."

She reached for her door to step out.

I grabbed the door and held it closed. "She's fine. Their Model One was cleaning when it suddenly went into attack mode. Mrs. Miller escaped to the basement safe room and locked herself in, but she twisted her ankle." I cocked my head toward the house. "They won't let us in."

Liv let out an audible breath. "So everyone's okay."

"As good as can be expected. Let's go to my place."

"Absolutely. You have a date with a great guy."

My brain was still trying to piece together everything I'd seen and heard. There was no way Mrs. Miller had been running a self-defense simulation. Jackson—maybe. Mrs. Miller—no. So the Model Ones were officially busted.

And what I'd seen on the fridge—a square material flashing back and forth between transparent and scarlet red—was just like the note left on my car.

15

Had Mr. Miller done this? Or Melody?

We were up to two Model One malfunctions, and that officially counted as a pattern. Someone was making them go berserk—just like Ron had made *me* go berserk. As far as I knew, Jackson didn't have access to the dynamic paper technology like the note that had been left on my car.

But the Millers did.

And Philip Pollock—how did he fit into all this? He had more resources than God.

"Miss Hayes." As I reached for my car door, Detective Garrett came toward me, her gait long and sure.

"Detective, how are you?"

Unlike Detective Johnson, she appeared to have fully recovered from our last encounter. No cast on her wrist or any sign of long-term damage—thank goodness. "Could you give me a rundown of your whereabouts over the last twenty-four hours?"

"Am I a suspect? Because I don't think you're supposed to question me without my parents if I am."

"We can get your parents involved if you like."

She'd called my bluff. I did not want my parents knowing I'd spent the afternoon at CyberCorp and then followed the Millers to a crime scene, all to investigate crimes my parents' androids may or may not have committed.

Were they even *crimes* if they were done by robots?

"I'll show you." I extracted my hand-screen from my pocket but got distracted as two more cars inched their way down the road.

As the front one rolled by, the adjustable window tint lightened, and Claire waved from the passenger seat. Beside her, in the driver's seat, was a pretty blonde I didn't know. Muffled music reverberated from inside the vehicle, and the blonde bobbed her head while banging her hands against the dash in time with the beat.

Claire's window darkened, and the vehicle continued past.

The second car parked right behind Liv and me. The window slid down, and the former Detective Johnson leaned out.

Detective Garrett's face remained neutral as she gestured for me to hurry up. I returned my attention to my hand-screen and opened the tracking application. It showed the precise movements of my ID chip since its installation yesterday after school.

Her eyes narrowed. "It wasn't too long ago when your

parents showed us your chip tracking, and it turned out the chip wasn't even installed."

"It is now. You can scan me."

She reached into a pocket on the inside of her blazer and withdrew a finger-sized scanner. She pressed the button on top and waved it over my left forearm. It issued a beep. She checked the miniature display on the device, nodded, and then slipped it back into her pocket.

By now, Claire and her blonde friend had parked in the driveway beside a bright-blue car I assumed to be Nina's. Claire jumped out and ran to the front door. The officer there stepped aside to let her through. Before the car door whirred close, I spotted the blonde still bobbing to the music.

"Miss Hayes, eyes on me." Detective Garrett snapped twice in my face. "Do you know anything about what happened in the Miller house?"

"I was at CyberCorp when I overheard Melody say something about their Model One going nuts."

"How'd you get here then?"

I hoped she couldn't see the flush on my light-brown skin. "I drove."

"You followed her?"

"Technically, no. But I came here because of that."

"I see." She stared at me with intense, narrow eyes that made me want to spill all my secrets—which was probably her goal.

Instead, I pressed my lips together and tried unsuccessfully to quiet my heartbeats.

"Miss Hayes, I'd love to see less of you in my investigations. But if you think of anything that could help, please give me a call." She reached into her pocket, and this time she withdrew her business card.

Unlike Detective Johnson's nearly blank card, this one looked very official. The shield of the local police department showed up as a watermark on the right half. In the center was her full name, Eleanor Garrett, along with a phone number and an office address.

Instead of turning back to the Miller house, Garrett proceeded past my car and Liv's and stopped at Detective Johnson's window. She leaned over him, and their mouths moved quickly in a conversation I couldn't make out.

When she straightened up, she slapped the hood of his car twice. He rolled up the window, pulled away from the curb, and drove past me and down the street without even looking my way.

When we left Melody's, Liv followed my car closely in the rearview mirror. Thanks to her auto-drive, hers stopped automatically at the yellow lights that I saw fit to run.

The first thing I needed to do when we got to my place was steal that dynamic paper back from my dad. If these two incidents with the Model Ones were connected, then there might be another message—just like last time—and it might be important—just like last time.

As I turned a corner about five minutes from my place, my hand-screen vibrated.

"You do know your date is in 17 minutes?"

I waited until my next stop at a light to type a message back. *"Of course."* I knew it was tonight, at least, but *now* I knew it was in seventeen minutes. *"You know I'm driving manually, right? Do you want me to text and drive and die?"*

In the rearview mirror, I watched her laugh. *"You could just speak your response."*

"Where's the fun in that?"

When we reached my place, I parked my car inside the garage and waited while Liv parked in the driveway and stepped out. She rushed into the garage on foot, gripped me by the wrist, and hauled me into the house.

Marcy stood at the kitchen stove, stirring something in a large pot that smelled like heaven.

"Hi!" Liv offered her a hug and peered over her shoulder. "Spaghetti and meatballs?"

Marcy kissed her on the cheek. "I thought you might be coming over. I'll make you a to-go plate."

"Where's Allie?" I asked her, following Liv's hug with my own.

"She fell asleep watching the vid-screen." Marcy pointed toward the family room.

Liv tapped the spot on her left wrist where a watch would be. She sighed loudly as I hurried into the family room instead of heading to the stairs. Allie was snoring, her arms wrapped around a giant stuffed unicorn as the vid-screen played some cartoon about a unicorn that looked just like it.

"You mind if I make a quick stop in my dad's office before I change?"

Liv glared at me and made a show of looking at her wrist again. Then she grabbed my arm, and I allowed her to haul me upstairs to my bedroom.

"Sit." She pointed at the edge of the bed, and I obeyed.

She disappeared into my closet, and soon, the whirring sounds of my automated shelves and drawers started up.

A black miniskirt flew through the air and hit the floor in front of me. "You look hot in this one."

"It's February, and I haven't worn that in two years. I don't think my butt even fits into it anymore."

"Good point," she called from inside the closet, "your butt has really come into its own over the past year. You got your mom's good genes."

"Hey!"

"It's a compliment. How about this one?" When she stepped into view, she held up a pair of charcoal-colored skinny jeans.

"Those are cool."

From the digital numbers projected on my wall just above my nightstand, I could see we had six minutes until date time. There was no way I would make it through this date without going insane if I didn't grab that note from my dad's office first.

More importantly, my dad would be home by the time I got back, and then I'd be out of luck until tomorrow afternoon.

Liv stood there, brows raised, until I slid off the bed and grabbed the pants. After shimmying out of the wide-leg jeans I'd worn to school, I pulled on the new ones. It took a couple wriggle-jumps to get them securely over the butt in question, but I managed to zip them up.

Liv twirled her finger in the air, and obediently, I spun

for her. She whistled and then disappeared back into the closet. "Now for a shirt."

"I think I have a gray-and-pink striped one that will look cute with these."

"Is it tight?"

"No, but it's low cut."

"That'll work." After a pause, she added, "Got it," and the shirt landed at my feet. She followed a moment later with a pair of high-heeled black boots, which she set on the floor next to the shirt.

"Great." I tore off my current T-shirt and slipped into the new one and the boots before giving Liv a quick spin. "Good?" Before she could answer, I did it for her. "Good. Now, I need to—"

"You haven't even looked in the mirror." She grabbed my waist and moved me into the giant closet, where a mirror stood on the far wall.

As she watched, I turned from side to side and examined myself in the mirror. I did look pretty great. "It's good, Liv. Thank you. But this isn't a date. The point is not—"

"Oh, these will be perfect." She slipped her earrings out of her ears and held them up. Bright-silver metal pieces extended from the hooks and curled around darker, oxidized silver. When she shook them, the metal made a soft tinking sound. "My wind chimes."

I took them and slipped them into my ears. I had to admit they were great. The earrings were long enough and just large enough to stand out against my big, dark hair.

"Now, for the hair."

"What's wrong with it?"

"It could use a little more product." The doorbell rang, and Liv shrieked. "Shit, he's here!"

"It's just Hunter. Relax."

"Maybe you're not aware that you've been super distracted lately."

"I'm kind of dealing with a trauma here."

"I know that. But you guys are early in this relationship, and boys have egos. He's a really great guy, and I just don't want you to regret not giving this a fair shot."

"Not sure this qualifies as a relationship yet."

"Do you want it to?"

I didn't answer, but Liv was right about one thing—Hunter was amazing. I didn't want to let him disappear just because I was distracted.

"How do you feel when you think about him? Imagine his face. Imagine having a conversation with him."

I breathed deeply and tried to stop the thoughts racing in my head. No Jackson and no Mrs. Miller being attacked by Model Ones. No mysterious note on my car. No dead bodies. Just Hunter's green-flecked brown eyes and that smile that ticked upward too far on one side.

My insides flipped. "Excited to see him."

"Good. I'm going downstairs to distract him. You make your hair look as awesome as the rest of you, and then come down."

"Yes, ma'am."

"And maybe tuck in the shirt, so we can see that ass better."

I picked up a lavender throw pillow and tossed it at her as she ran out the door.

My priority was still getting to the bottom of the Model One malfunctions. As soon as I could no longer hear Liv's footsteps on the stairs, I ducked out of the room and into my father's office.

He was still at CyberCorp Tower but would probably be home soon, so I had to be quick.

He'd put the note on the right side of the desk. When I tried the top drawer on that side, it was locked. I muttered a curse and tried the one below it. Just some papers and a device that looked like an old hand-screen. I went to close it, when a square on one of the papers turned red and then white again.

When I squinted, I could see the outline of the transparent paper-like device that was my note. I snatched it up, slammed the drawer, and hurried back to my room.

I set the note on my own desk and slid into the chair in front of it. "How did I get you to work before?"

It flashed red and then transparent again. Words flashed across it. *"Facial recognition. Lena Hayes confirmed."* The words blinked out.

My stomach twisted into knots as a new message appeared.

There once was a girl named Hayes.
Who always got her way.

Those words faded. I tapped the device with the tip of my fingernail. Was this thing on?

Let's play a game.

I sucked in a sharp breath while my heart rapped out a hectic beat.

Steal something from CyberCorp.
Leave it in the trash can on the NW corner.
Or someone else gets hurt.
No parents. No police.

16

Whoever was doing this, they couldn't have access to every Model One. CyberCorp's security was too tight for that. But they did have access to Melody's and Jackson's, at least. Did that make those two guilty—or targets?

Or could one of them be the *someone* who might get hurt?

I called Melody, and the call went directly to voicemail. She was probably blocking me.

I tried Jackson next. It rang until his voicemail picked up. I disconnected and then tried again. Five rings and then voicemail.

I shot him a quick message. *"Call me. We need to talk!"*

My face felt hot, and when I checked in my bathroom mirror, it had indeed gone red and splotchy. I gripped the sink on both sides and breathed in and out until the flush went away.

After another series of deep breaths, I stepped out of my room and headed for the stairs.

"I'm sure she'll only be another minute," Liv was saying in the sitting room below. "She's really excited to hang out."

When I peeked over the railing that overhung the space, Liv and Hunter were sitting side by side on a tufted, ivory-colored couch with walnut trim. It was the kind of couch that was meant to look expensive and not necessarily provide comfort.

That explained why Hunter was sitting like he had a wooden plank stuffed down the back of his shirt. He nodded, but the doubt was evident in every twitch of his gaze toward the stairs.

"Seriously," Liv said. "She was picking out clothes and doing her hair—for you."

His lips quirked upward. "I changed too." He pointed down at his black Superman shirt with a dark gray logo and black jeans. "This is my best superhero shirt."

"Do you have a hundred of those?"

"Just six, I think. Maybe I should have worn a bow tie like Mr. Frank."

Liv laughed, but it came out like a high-pitched shriek that made me cringe. "Those are awful!"

"I don't know. I think bow ties are cool."

Liv nudged him on the shoulder. "That's because you're a geek."

"Says the smartest girl in Mr. Frank's math class."

"I'm a nerd, not a geek. There's a difference."

"Is there, though?"

They were still laughing when I hit the bottom of the stairs. Hunter's eyes got big as he jumped out of his seat. He ran toward me, arms out. When I hugged him, his familiar minty, springtime scent floated around me.

"You look amazing." He pointed at my right ear. "Really cool earrings."

"Thanks. Liv—"

Liv shoved us both toward the door. "Have fun, you two. No curfew!"

"My mom will kill him if I'm not home by ten."

"Ten o'clock curfew!" she shouted after us as Hunter led me to his car.

"Where are we headed?" I asked him as we got in.

"It's a secret."

"It's a secret . . . about what place?"

He chuckled. "Nice try."

A few minutes into our drive, déjà vu hit me. I'd been on this road in this direction with Hunter before. "Are we going to the park?"

Since it was winter, the sun had gone to rest for the day even though it was not even six thirty yet. In every other spot in the city, darkness was never an option. Digital billboards dotted the sides of streets of buildings, lighting up the night in technicolor. After dark, drones were free to deliver packages without the usual daytime surcharge to the shippers, and that meant the automated machines zipped overhead incessantly.

But not in the park.

It was the darkest place in the city. Since it was a nature preserve, no billboards or drones were allowed within a hundred yards of it on any side. As we crossed over the hundred-yard boundary, it was like someone hit a light switch. Multicolored lights flashed in our rearview mirror, but in front of us was the calm and quiet of the dark.

"Good choice, huh?"

I hadn't realized I was grinning like a fool, but I nodded. Not only was this one of my favorite places in the city, but it had special meaning for Hunter and me too. The first time he and I hung out alone, he'd taken me for a drive around this park.

He pointed over his shoulder to the backseat. A red-and-white checkered blanket covered a lump of stuff I couldn't see.

"A picnic?"

His grin widened like the Cheshire Cat.

"I didn't realize you were such a romantic."

"More like a guy who doesn't have any original ideas and is happy to fall back on the classics."

"It's perfect."

We parallel parked on a street next to a wide, grassy area. A lone picnic table sat about a hundred feet away, in the middle of the green space. A tall streetlamp cast a soft glow over the table and benches on either side.

I waited for the automatic door to slide upward and then hopped out of the car. Hunter climbed out on his side and ripped off the picnic tablecloth with a flourish.

Except for the automated doors, his car was configured like mine—two fixed front seats and a long backseat. The vehicles made over the past five years instead had front seats that could rotate a full 360, and a long L-shaped backseat for lounging.

Since the introduction of auto-drive, car accidents were down ninety-five percent. So now manufacturers prioritized comfort over safety.

Of course, I had managed to squeeze myself into that other five percent that still had accidents. And now, I had a cybernetic arm to show for it.

On Hunter's backseat sat a large wicker basket, complete with a handle sticking upward. Plastic containers inside held sandwiches, macaroni salad, and fruit.

"I'm sure you didn't plan to spend the evening outside, so I prepared." He reached past the basket and came out with one black fleece blanket and one blue one. "I didn't know what you'd be wearing." He held the black one up to me, nodded, and tossed it around my shoulders.

"Very chivalrous."

He grabbed the basket and led me to the table, where we unpacked the macaroni salad, two sandwiches, and pineapples.

I sat on one of the picnic benches, and immediately, my butt was ice cold. I wrapped the blanket tighter around me, but I couldn't help shivering.

Since this was the South, normally, it would have started to warm up by late February. But since I was the luckiest girl to ever get into a car accident, lose an arm, and have her parents replace it with a cybernetic one, today was the day the weather decided to be freezing.

I pulled the fleece more tightly around myself.

"Maybe this was a bad idea." Hunter moved closer on

the bench and wrapped an arm around my waist. It helped —but not much.

Another shiver rocked through me, and he was on his feet. "This was definitely a bad idea." He picked up the food and placed it back in the basket. "What was I thinking? Maybe we should just fall back on vandalizing Cyber‑Corp again." He laughed but stopped when he saw the serious expression on my face.

For a few minutes, I'd been able to push everything else to the back of my mind. But that never seemed to last. "How about we steal something from CyberCorp instead?"

"I was joking." His brow crinkled. "But now I'm worried."

I told him everything I'd been hiding for the last thirty-six hours. He knew about the incidents with the Model Ones already, but the part about the dynamic paper and its two messages was something only I knew.

Even my dad and Liv knew about only the first one. Neither of them knew I'd been tasked by the note to steal something of CyberCorp's.

"Shit," he muttered.

"Pretty much."

"And if you don't steal something, then what?"

"They'll hurt someone." I shrugged. "Kill someone, maybe. If this person is associated with Ron and what happened after I first got my arm, then they are definitely not above murder."

His lips pressed together so tightly they nearly disap-peared. He held a hand out for me. "Then let's do this."

I grabbed it, and he hauled me off the park bench.

When we arrived at CyberCorp, the place looked just as busy as it had in the afternoon. Cars flowed in and out of the parking garages. Silhouettes of employees sat hunched over desks that were backlit by the lights of their offices.

"Are you sure you want to embark on a life of crime with me?" I meant it as a joke as he approached the visitors parking garage, but my tone came out tight.

"I'm sure I don't want anyone else to die. Plus . . ." He offered a tense laugh. "Your parents are rich and influential. They'll bail us out of any long-term prison sentences. Right?"

"We'll do a year tops." By now, all the humor was gone from both our voices.

The garage didn't recognize Hunter's car the way the VIP one did mine, but he raised his right arm when we reached the gated entrance. The scanner above us scanned it through the windshield to log his entry, and the gate slid smoothly open.

He removed his hands from the wheel, and the wireless controls in the garage took over.

Hunter's car wasn't a late model and didn't have auto-drive, but it did have the basic wireless controls used by systems like this garage. My car was one of the few exceptions, since its motor and steering didn't have any wireless communication functionality. So I had to manually drive in and out of the garages here, just like I did everywhere else.

The car rolled through aisles and smoothly turned into the closest available parking space to the elevators.

Hunter tapped his door twice, and both his and mine

whirred upward to allow us out. We took the visitors elevator up and stepped into CyberCorp lobby.

I'd been in here hundreds of times, maybe thousands, since my parents started this company in my infancy. But today, the white-and-silver floor and thirty-foot ceiling stopped me in my tracks. CyberCorp made machines, but it was itself a machine too. Its moving parts were the humans walking through its halls, working late at their desks, offering their very lives to the products my parents conceived.

It was impenetrable.

And I needed to steal something from it.

"Lena?" Hunter was staring at me.

My feet were nailed to the floor. "I can't do this."

"Miss Hayes." A receptionist waved from across the room, and I recognized her as the one I'd spoken to earlier in the day.

I let out a long breath, relieved to be able to put this off for at least another minute.

"It's Lena, please. And you're Vanessa, right?"

She beamed. "I didn't call you because I don't know whether this counts as news, but I heard a couple of the executives saying Philip Pollock is officially a person of interest." She gestured toward my left arm. "You know, in the investigation."

As if I could ever forget. "Thank you." I offered her a wide smile, even though that information didn't get me anywhere new.

I inched away from her and toward the main elevator bay.

"Hey." Hunter pointed to the white pen sitting on the edge of the large reception desk. Its silver lettering read *CyberCorp* in bold script. "Is that yours?"

"Technically, it's CyberCorp's. But yes, I'll use it until someone accidentally walks away with it."

Hunter waggled his eyebrows at me.

"So," I said, "that pen is an official CyberCorp product."

"I guess so?" Her tone posed it like a question.

"You mind if I steal it?"

She picked it up and turned one end toward me. "Be my guest. I've got five backups in my drawer."

I snatched it from her. Hunter grabbed my wrist and pulled me back toward the elevators that led to the main parking garage. I ran to keep up.

"You know we didn't actually commit any crime," I said as he waved his wrist three times at the scanner to call the elevator.

"This is CyberCorp. That pen probably costs as much as my car."

When the doors opened, I laughed and let him haul me inside. "You'd be terrible at a life of crime."

"You seem determined to test that."

If all went well, my life of crime would be coming to an end soon. But the ever-swelling pit in my stomach said otherwise.

17

"*Do you think they got the package?*" Hunter's message came through on my hand-screen later that evening.

"*Are we in a spy movie now? Yes, I assume they grabbed the PEN from the TRASH CAN where we left it.*"

I set my hand-screen back on my nightstand and returned my attention to Allie, who was telling Liv about preschool. Just like last night, Liv and I had thrown a mountain of pillows on the floor with our sleeping bags for another sleepover.

"Tell me the most interesting part of your day," I asked my sister as she burrowed deep into the pillow pile.

"Marcy taught me how to message you on a hand-screen. I messaged you."

"I know. I loved that."

"She said I can get a micro-comm when I'm seven."

"How many years away is that?" Liv asked.

Allie scrunched up her face and squeezed her eyes shut. "Let me think."

"Seven minus four," I said in a stage whisper.

She opened her eyes, raised seven fingers, and then lowered four. "Three!"

"You got it."

Allie turned her face into my side and snuggled closer. "Marcy said I could sleep in here since you don't have to go to school tomorrow." She peeked her eyes open. "If it's okay with you."

I shot a glance at Liv, who nodded.

"I would love that. Did you brush your teeth?"

"Yes."

"Did you say goodnight to Mom and Dad?"

"I called them on my new hand-screen." She grinned, showing off a mouth full of tiny baby teeth.

"Good." I'd completely forgotten they were going away for the holiday weekend. "Did you . . . mow the lawn?"

She giggled. "I don't know how."

"You don't?" I gave her a look of mock surprise. "What do you do around here then?"

"I'm cute!" She hid her face.

"I'll teach you tomorrow. Go to sleep."

Allie closed her eyes and threw one tiny arm around my waist. Within seconds, her breathing evened out.

"Impressive," Liv whispered. "I wish I could fall asleep like that."

"It's a superpower." The time projected on my wall said

10:13 p.m., and I needed to log it as my bedtime. I couldn't reach my hand-screen on my nightstand without getting up, so I looked at Liv and pointed. "Could you grab that for me?"

She crawled out of our pillow mountain, grabbed it, and then crawled back into the pillows and blankets before tucking it under her head with a grin. "Mine."

"Jerk." I flailed my arm, but she shifted to the side, putting her face only inches out of the reach of my fingertips.

"Shh." She grinned. "Don't wake your sister."

"I hate you. Like, a lot."

"I'm saving you from yourself, and you love me."

One night of not logging my sleep wouldn't hurt anyone. And if anything happened—like walking in my sleep again—Liv was here to wake me.

***

"Lena!" I was jarred out of my sleep on Saturday morning by the sound of shouting through my bedroom door.

"Marcy?"

"Your gentleman is at the door."

"Hunter?" I was so groggy that I couldn't collect my thoughts.

"The other one."

I scrambled out of bed, but my foot caught in the sheets, and I toppled over. My arms hit the floor first, and I rolled the rest of the way down.

"Are you okay?" Marcy called from the other side of the door. "I heard something fall."

"I'm good."

Her footsteps receded down the hallway.

This was the perfect opportunity to confront Jackson about what was going on. He may or may not have rigged his android to attack him—and Melody's. But the way he was dodging my calls, I knew he was hiding something.

Time to face the truth.

I snatched my hand-screen from the floor near Liv's head and updated my sleep journal with the current time. I would check my chip tracker later to make sure I'd actually been in bed all night between the time I went to sleep and now.

Somehow, Liv had slept through Marcy pounding on the door and me falling out of bed. She still lay deep in the pillow pile, a smile playing across her face in sleep. Allie opened her eyes briefly and then rolled over.

I pulled on the skinny jeans I'd worn last night so I wouldn't show up half naked. After throwing on a light jacket, I slipped my hand-screen into the inside pocket. The dynamic paper that had been causing so much trouble sat on my desk, and I grabbed it too as I bolted out the door and down the stairs.

"That's a lot of energy to see a boy you're not into anymore." Marcy winked as I barged past her.

"It's none of your business," I called back to her as I hurried down the stairs.

When I threw the front door open, Jackson stood there looking fresh out of the shower. Wet dark hair was slicked back off his face, showing off blue eyes that were unnervingly light on a boy so tan and dark-haired.

His grin sent my heart colliding with my chest at top speed and then skittering to a full stop.

"Hey, babe." One hand held a pie tin, and he held the other arm out toward me.

Automatically, I fell into him.

His mouth nuzzled the top of my head. "Missed you."

I straightened and stepped back, fixing my face into as stern an expression as I could manage. "You wouldn't if you answered my calls." For good measure, I stepped back another few feet.

He offered the pie tin, which, on second glance, appeared to hold a quiche.

I lifted it out of his hands. "What's this?"

"Quiche."

"I see that. *Why* though?"

"Well, I imagine someone at the store figured that, since they sell quiches, they ought to make a few. Hence . . ." He gestured at the pie tin in my hand. "Quiche."

I laughed. "And why did you buy it and bring it here and place it in my hands?"

"See, that's a different question. This one was discounted because they used too much cheese—which is a pretty ridiculous reason to discount something if you ask me. They discounted it by half, and my baby likes cheese."

"I'm not your baby."

He held out his hand and gestured for me to return the quiche to it.

"I accept this gift nonetheless."

He laughed. "I thought you might."

"But why are you here?"

Jackson gestured again at the quiche.

"Seriously, you don't even answer my calls anymore, and you show up here with a gift."

"It's not a gift. It's a quiche."

"A discounted quiche."

"Exactly. Very un-gift-like."

"Are you going to ignore the bit where I said you don't answer my calls?"

"We spoke yesterday, and we saw each other the day before. Some would say that's a lot for two people who aren't in love anymore." He raised a brow and let it hover there.

I ignored the implied question. "I'm glad you're here. I want to talk to you about your Model One."

His grin fell and died. "I told you everything. I didn't start any self-defense sim. It attacked me."

"And before that? I'm trying to find the connection between—"

"I don't want to fight with you." His calm tone threatened a war just under the surface.

"Would you let me talk please?"

"To let you accuse me? No. I'll put up with a lot from you, but at some point, either you know me or you don't. The least you can do is assume I wouldn't come up with a lie like that."

"I don't think you're lying."

"But you want me to tell you the whole story again—so

you can look for holes in it?" He threw up both hands and backed off the porch. "This was a bad idea."

"Jackson, don't do that."

My hand warmed under the pie tin as the note, still in my hand, started flashing red and then back to transparent. I shifted the quiche to the other hand to see the note more clearly, just as Jackson slammed himself inside his car and started rolling out of the driveway.

"Wait! I'm sorry."

Jackson was right. I had trust issues these days, and that wasn't his fault. I'd trusted him for years, and there was no reason that should change now.

The car stopped, and the door on the driver's side slid upward for Jackson to stick his head out.

I waved the dynamic paper at him. "I want you to see this." He didn't get out, so I ran toward him. "Let's both be more honest."

"I'm *being* honest."

"Just listen. This note showed up on my car after your Model One attacked you. It's automated and has facial recognition—it's addressed to me." I set the quiche down on the top of his car and pointed at the dynamic paper in my other hand, which was still flashing.

Jackson stayed in the car, his eyes as narrow as a knife blade.

"It's flashing because there's a third message. The other two times, it was right after a Model One attacked someone."

He turned off the car and got out. The door closed behind him. "You think there was another attack?"

I shrugged and flapped the note at him again. He hurried to peer over my shoulder as I held it up to my face.

The dynamic paper went black, and words faded onto the display. *"Facial recognition. Lena Hayes confirmed."* The words disappeared, and new ones showed up.

There once was a girl named Hayes.
Who always got her way.

"I don't though," I said.

Jackson's lips pressed together, and his eyes looked more amused than I appreciated. He nodded toward the note, and I shifted my attention back.

You can do better than that.

We both waited for more, but as the line faded away, nothing took its place. The note went blank and clear again.

"What does it mean?" Jackson asked.

"I'm guessing the pen I stole wasn't enough. Last time, it told me to steal something from CyberCorp, or someone would get hurt."

"And you stole a pen?" Disapproval dripped off his words like acid.

"It was just a pen," I muttered. "You want someone to die instead?"

"Of course not. But stealing a pen was never going to help. When you negotiate with terrorists, you give them the upper hand. Now, they know they can screw with you."

He wasn't wrong, and this message proved that. "Doesn't matter. We are where we are, and now, I need to go bigger."

"Or you can do nothing."

We stared at each other, each of us trying to defeat the other with willpower alone. Eventually, I turned toward the house, had second thoughts, grabbed the quiche from his car, and headed for my front door.

"Lena, don't—"

The sound of squealing tires cut him off as a white luxury vehicle careened around the corner at the end of the street.

The car skidded to a stop in front of us, tires screeching as they left black marks on the light pavement. Tinted windows masked the driver, but I knew who it was. I'd seen that car on multiple news reports over the past weeks.

Philip Pollock.

Jackson shifted to put his whole body in front of me. "Stay behind me."

"I'm already behind you. And I can take care of myself." I set the quiche back on Jackson's car, just in case I needed my hands free.

The door to the white car sighed upward, and Pollock stepped out.

His light-brown hair was cropped short in a businesslike style with not a hair out of place. A dark gray suit fit him like a glove. He wore the jacket open with a pale-blue button-down underneath.

I wanted to punch out all those perfect white teeth.

But then I'd be in trouble—again. As much as I wanted to, I could not assault people in my driveway—even people who most likely conspired to make me kill three of my classmates.

Jackson took a step forward.

I wrapped my arms around his waist from the back. "Don't hurt him," I murmured under my breath.

"I'm gonna hurt him."

"Don't kill him."

He hesitated. "No promises."

Pollock opened his mouth to talk.

Jackson broke free of my arms and lunged.

"Shit!" I grabbed his arm with my left, but he shook me off before I could get a grip.

He was faster than me on rebuilt legs, and in less than a second, he had Pollock pinned to the ground. His face pressed less than an inch from the older man's.

"I thought you were supposed to be smart." Jackson's words came out like a growl.

"Let me up, please." Pollock's voice, in contrast, was all business. He was the kind of man who asked for something and got it. "This is a new suit." To me, he added, "Call off your dog."

I added extra sweetener to my voice. "That dog has had his entire left side and most of his right rebuilt with cutting-edge CyberCorp technology. He could rip your head right off."

Jackson showed all his teeth and then slammed his right fist into the pavement next to Pollock's head. The driveway cracked.

Pollock shouted something unintelligible as his eyes squeezed shut. After a few seconds of silence, he peeked them open.

He raised both hands near his head in surrender. "I just want to talk." This time, his voice trembled at the end. That punch to the pavement had cracked his confidence.

"You want to talk about how you funded the asshole who made my girl kill people?"

"I'm not your girl."

"I'm working on that."

"Jackson, you have to—"

"Children!" Pollock shouted. "My situation is rather urgent at the moment. If I die without confirming your suspicions, your poor friend Melody will never get the closure she deserves." He jerked his head toward me. "And neither will you."

"Don't kill him," I repeated.

"Convince me," Jackson said, still pressing Pollock to the ground.

Pollock's eyes widened. "Listen."

"We're listening." Irritation seeped into my voice.

"No, shut up. And listen."

My neighborhood was usually pretty quiet, with the houses spaced far enough apart for privacy and the residents concerned about being great neighbors. The only sound was the low-level electronic hum that existed everywhere.

And a rhythmic clicking.

"What is that?" I cocked my head toward it. It came

from down the street—in the direction Pollock had come from.

Jackson eased off Pollock, but not enough for the man to get up.

"That is two Model Ones coming to kill me."

I narrowed my eyes.

"I'm not lying."

"Good." Jackson jumped up, grabbed his forearm, and hauled him to his feet. "I get to keep my hands clean." He straightened Pollock's suit jacket. "Enjoy."

He put a hand on my lower back to steer me toward the house. As an afterthought, he grabbed the quiche from his car with the other hand.

"Wait!" Pollock ran around to stand between us and the house. "Save me, and I'll tell you everything you want to know."

The sound grew louder and clearer, less like a distant clicking and more like metal feet clanking against the pavement.

"Jackson." I pulled his sleeve. "We should get inside."

"I'm innocent!" Pollock shouted as we pushed around him. "You can't let an innocent man die."

"You're the only one who could have bankrolled Ron," I said, rounding back on him. "And you ran."

"You ran too—when they accused you of killing those kids."

"I *did* kill those kids," I growled. "That's why I ran." I shoved him—harder than I intended. "But not without help."

He stumbled backward and fell. His butt hit the pavement, and pain pinched his features. As he scrambled back up, he pointed down the street.

Three Model Ones rounded the corner. Their metal feet moved impossibly fast against the pavement.

18

MY HEART TIGHTENED. FEAR SENT A SPLASH OF COLD through every vein in my body.

"You said there were two," I said to Pollock as three Model Ones raced down my street toward us.

"The first two ran out of your neighbors' front doors as I passed." Pollock gestured wildly at the robots. His face reddened more with each word. "I'm guessing the third did the same. Are you going to do something?"

"Time to go." Jackson yanked my right arm so hard I felt it in the socket as I hurried after him up the driveway to my house.

"There's no evidence I was involved. None." Pollock ran in front of us and dropped to his knees, his palms pressed together in front of him. "Not even Ron says I helped him. The only thing anyone has on me is my reputation and my money. Please." His dark-brown eyes pleaded up at us. "I'm innocent. Give me a chance to prove it."

He had a point.

There was nothing that connected him to the killings except speculation.

"Crap." I circled around him to put the quiche back on top of Jackson's car and then dragged Pollock to his feet. "This better be worth it." I threw him behind me.

He stumbled before catching his balance, his mouth locked into an expression of sheer terror.

The Model Ones hit the end of the driveway with clanking metal feet. Each footstep sent a lightning bolt of fear straight to my heart. My chest clenched and then went rapid-fire. Every instinct inside me screamed to flee this storm of robots.

They spread out into a semicircle, hovering, waiting for us to make a move.

Jackson stepped forward, and an android darted toward us. Jackson slid in front of me and grabbed its arms, yanking them up above its head. The muscles in his arms tensed, and he rammed a kick right at the machine's abdomen. The android shot backward, fell, and skidded across the driveway in a screech of metal against concrete.

Another android darted around Jackson and came right at me, swinging its left arm in a downward arc. Terror stopped my heart, but my left arm took over. It shot up and took the impact with a thunk.

"A little help here!" Philip Pollock ran past me and circled back as the last of the androids followed close on his heels. He darted in between Jackson and the white car. The android changed directions with the grace of a lion and lunged to cut him off around the other side.

The one facing me raised its other arm, and again, my left arm came up. I cringed as the impact bit into my pain receptors and passed the message of pain to my brain.

To my right, Jackson's grunt accompanied the screeching sound of ripping metal.

My opponent ducked and slid. I tried to jump out of the way, but I stumbled to one side. Still low to the ground, the android leveled a punch to my side. My left arm came down to block it.

The metal underneath shone through where the impact scraped off my brand-new skin. The android spun faster than I could blink, and a second later, a metal leg swept mine out from under me.

My back hit the pavement, and pain tore outward like my whole body was on fire.

The android stood over me. Its red eyes glowed like the devil as it raised its foot to stomp down on my chest. I held my breath and squeezed my eyes shut.

Jackson grabbed the android over me by the neck and tossed it aside like a rag doll. It hit the driveway, bounced, and skidded. Metal screamed against concrete.

The android stayed down for only a second and then bounced to its feet and surveyed us with narrow red eyes.

"Help the asshole!" Jackson shouted. "I've got this."

The Model One that had first attacked Jackson was now lying in pieces, one leg on my front lawn and the other farther up the driveway. It lay on its back. A sickening whirring sound emanated from its torso.

I spun to look for Pollock. The third android was standing over Pollock's car, facing me across it. It reached underneath with one arm, grabbed the undercarriage, and wrenched the car upward until the two wheels on that side hung inches above the ground. Its metal body vibrated with the effort.

High-pitched screams issued from underneath.

With its free arm, the android swiped in the space under the vehicle, which prompted a new series of terrified wails. With a crunch, the metal arm holding the car buckled under the weight, and the vehicle crashed back down to earth.

The screams stopped.

Panic swelled inside my chest and stopped my heart. "Mr. Pollock?"

Soft whimpers came from under the car, and relief shot my heart into motion again.

With only one good arm now, the android squatted to peer under the vehicle at the same time I did. Red eyes met mine.

It swiped its good arm underneath. Pollock scooted toward me on the ground, and his unintelligible cries for help started anew.

The Model One ran to my side of the car, and Pollock scooted away from us. It straightened up and crunched its metal fingers into the roof before rocking the car back and forth. Pollock screamed in time with each creak of the vehicle one way or the other.

As much as I enjoyed watching Pollock suffer, at any second the android could figure its way out of this dilemma and kill him.

I pulled back by my left arm and shot it forward

through the android's back. My fingers closed around its power cell, and I yanked it toward me. Cables snapped as the power cell came loose.

The Model One crashed to the ground.

Pollock's screaming continued.

"Dude!" Jackson shouted as he joined me. "They're all down."

It finally went quiet, and Pollock poked his head out from underneath the car.

He surveyed the disabled androids, whose parts were strewn across the lawn and my driveway. He shimmied out from under the vehicle. Since it was electric, the bottom was smooth metal, and Pollock slid out as easily as I presumed he'd slid under there in the first place.

Red-faced and breathing hard, he stood and straightened his suit. "I told you they were trying to kill me." He gestured toward the metal carnage. "Now do you believe I'm not involved?"

I raised one finger of my left hand. During the fight, the skin had been scraped off and now hung from the metal in fleshy strips. "First, this could all be a ruse to trick us into helping you with whatever you have planned next."

Jackson kicked one of the androids and gave a satisfied nod when it didn't move.

I raised a second finger. Even as I moved it, the artificial skin began stitching itself back together. "*Or* whatever's happening now with the Model Ones right now isn't part of your original plan with Ron. Maybe this is someone else's payback for that."

"Payback wouldn't explain the attacks on me and

Melody's mom though," Jackson said, his mouth now close to my ear.

I batted him away. "He's guilty."

"On that, we agree. You want to call the police?"

I stepped closer to Pollock. "What are you even doing here?"

"Believe it or not, looking for you. My people informed me that the Model Ones were acting oddly around your friends." He gestured toward what was left of the androids. "And I thought we could help each other. They attacked me on my way here."

I extracted my hand-screen from my pocket. "I'm calling the police."

"I came here for your help. I'm not responsible for this or for the murders. If you help me prove that, we can catch your friend's killer together. I know for a fact you are motivated and capable—as well as willing to bend the rules when the situation calls for it. This can be a mutual exchange of help, wherein we clear each other's names."

"My name is fine," I said.

"And you're alive," Jackson added. "We helped. You're welcome."

"Call the police," I told my hand-screen. It rang on speaker for all of us to hear.

Pollock retreated to his car. The driver-side door opened automatically, but now it made a clunking-whirring sound as it moved. The Model One had done some damage, and it served Pollock right.

Pollock tapped his ear to activate his micro-comm. "Send my contact information to Lena Hayes."

Still ringing, my hand-screen vibrated to confirm receipt.

"In case you need to reach me," he said.

"I won't."

Pollock jumped into his car and was already halfway down the street before the door closed.

"You might as well hang up," Jackson said. "He's gone."

19

I GOT RID OF JACKSON AND LIV—WHO HAD MANAGED TO sleep through the whole thing with Pollock and the androids. Then it was time to get some answers.

Whatever was happening with these Model Ones clearly involved me. Jackson. Melody's mom. Now, Philip Pollock. And the notes, all addressed to me.

Jackson and Pollock claimed innocence. Melody wouldn't take my calls.

If I wanted to learn the truth, it was time to hear what Ron had to say. My stomach churned bile at the thought of giving him what he wanted, but he had me jammed into a corner.

The address Ron had given was half an hour away. Since it was Saturday morning, traffic should be light. I could just barely make it.

I pulled to a stop at the curb just outside the address. The brick ranch must have been built back before my

175

parents were born. The red brick had been whitewashed for a slightly updated look, but the carport and gravel driveway gave away its age. A silver car occupied the carport.

The house's front door opened, and Ron stepped out. My blood sped to a boil at the sight of him. It had been weeks, and maybe I'd thought he'd look different. He couldn't possibly be the same spectacled boy with the kind face and helpful words. But there he was, looking just like he had the day we met.

His dark jeans and white button-down would have fit in with the other interns at CyberCorp. His black plastic glasses were just the right touch of nerd chic. But inside, his heart remained just as frigid as it was when he'd programmed me to commit murder.

Ron spotted me and froze in mid-motion of closing the door behind him. "I'd given up on you." He opened the door fully and ushered me inside.

I imagined punching him right in his face. His teeth would go skittering across the porch, leaving his mouth a bloody hole. And still, it would be less than he deserved.

I propped a smile on my face. Its edges shook, but it would have to do. "Is this where you live?"

He hit a manual light switch on the wall, and the entryway lights came on to illuminate the small foyer and the family room it opened into. "You were expecting something state of the art?"

"Kind of."

"This is my dad's house." He gestured toward a family

room stocked with brown leather furniture and a matching wood-laminate coffee table.

The table's surface hid under multiple stacks of paper piled over a foot high each. The sweet smell of cigar smoke clung to the air and seeped into my nose.

Despite the dull brown interior, though, colorful artwork hung on the walls. On the far wall hung an abstract painting of blues and greens, arranged in a way that suggested a city built of flowers. The painting to my right looked like a Picasso print. Its geometric shapes suggested a woman in bright turquoise.

"He has interesting taste."

"He had shit taste." He laughed. "But he was an artist."

"*Was?*"

"He died last week." Ron's voice was soft and searching, as if he was still trying to understand the words he'd just spoken.

"I'm so sorry." I meant it, but I kept my body tense and ready to act anyway. Ron had fooled me once before, and I didn't intend for that to happen again. "Cirrhosis?"

"You remembered."

"It was the reason you murdered three people—four if you count Simon—one of whom was a good friend. So yeah, I remember."

Ron had the grace to blush.

"He was concerned about confidentiality?" I gestured toward the papers stacked on the coffee table.

Even though my parents ran a tech company, they still kept their most important documents on paper. That was the only way to be a hundred percent sure the information couldn't be stolen through hacking. They had a lot of company secrets, which meant a lot of paper records.

"He had me late in life, at fifty-nine, although my mom was younger. He was seventy-eight when he died. Never switched over from paper to digital. Stubborn old man." He chuckled.

"Still, that's a lot of paper."

"Mostly research about my mother's condition. You would have thought he was in medical school as much as he studied it."

"I'm sorry about your mom too," I said quietly.

Ron's jaw tightened and then relaxed. "I just have to remind myself that you didn't have anything to do with her treatment."

My chest went cold. *He* was trying not to be mad at *me?* "Why am I here?" I let the chill seep into my voice. No matter what horrible fates found his parents, they didn't make Ron do what he'd done.

He gestured for me to follow him into what looked like it was meant to be a formal dining room. A brass chandelier hung from the center of the room, looking out of place next to all the artwork.

Paintings filled the room. One long rectangular canvas sat on an easel, angled in our direction. The future cityscape was done in shades of violet. In the center, a dark purple tower that could only be CyberCorp stretched exaggeratedly high above everything else. A lavender road snaked through the entire painting, curving and looping in fantastical fashion. Cars zipped by, leaving indigo streaks in their wake, evoking movement.

Everything was moving. Too fast. Never stopping.

Tiny black silhouettes of people stood toward the bottom, all dwarfed by the constant movement of the city.

Tears popped into my eyes because it was how I felt every day. A tiny person. Lost in a big world that cared less and less about humanity and more and more about technology.

One day, we would be forgotten—even by our own creations.

"It's amazing." My voice caught, even though I didn't mean to show that much emotion.

The other artwork leaning against the walls was in the same vein. Each piece featured a different color or set or colors. Most of them focused on CyberCorp Tower, but I recognized some other buildings that housed famous tech companies in other parts of the world. In most of them, tiny humans stood silhouetted against the energy of the city.

Except one—a portrait of Ron with the city in the background. Technology dwarfed everyone else in his father's world, but not Ron. Ron dwarfed *it*.

"He must have loved you," I said. "You're the only person bigger than everything else."

"He thought my interest in tech meant I was going to conquer it—to create a true harmony between man and machine. He thought I could do that together with Cyber-Corp." Ron cleared his throat. "This is what he did when he was sober. When he was drunk, he was mean. But when he wasn't, he painted and dreamed of a better world."

"I'm sor—" I stopped myself from getting the whole

word out this time because I was not the one who was supposed to be apologizing here. "That's too bad."

"This is what I wanted to show you." He gestured toward the room. "My father was sober for a long time, even through my mother's illness. And every day before he went to sleep, he painted."

"He was magnificent," I said.

"No one's all bad."

I froze because I could see where this was going.

"Even the worst of us—the ones who seem irredeemable. We all have a good side. We all have something worth saving."

"Ron, I—"

"Let me finish."

I clamped my mouth shut.

"He came to me two years ago, insisting he was sober and wanted me back in my life. If I hadn't given in, I wouldn't have known any of this. I wouldn't have seen this fear of technology and this hope that I could somehow be its savior. There's more to people than what's on the surface."

"And what makes *you* so worthy of redemption?" Bitterness leaked into my tone. "Do you paint too?"

He pressed his lips together before answering. "I'm one of the few people left who see both the hope and the danger in technology. I can help humanity if my skills and knowledge are leveraged the right way. My dad painted—that was his medium. Robotics is mine."

"But you did the opposite." I waved my left hand in his face. "My parents gave you the opportunity to help me with a brand-new technology that scared me. You used the opportunity to hurt people."

"That was a mistake."

"I'm sure Harmony would call that an understatement, but unfortunately, I can't ask her."

"That's fair." He took a step back. "But I can do better. I was meant to do so much good in the world. Testify on my behalf."

"Do *what*?" My words screeched out.

"Be a character witness in my criminal case. You know me, Lena. We were friends."

"You manipulated me the whole time."

"I genuinely liked you. I just got caught up in my anger and took advantage. Testify for me. You know who I am. Just tell the court."

I couldn't answer right away because I was too busy trying to make sense of all this. He'd called me here to ask for my help, after everything he'd done to me. To my friends.

"I have to go." I hurried toward the front door. If I stayed here a second longer, I would scream until my throat went raw and bloody.

"Lena." He ran after me.

Just as I reached the door, I spun on him. "Who helped you send that data over the EyeNet?"

He stopped dead, his eyes huge. "I can't."

My hand-screen buzzed, and I yanked it from my pocket to check the message. It was from Jackson. *"Claire wants us to meet at her place."*

I glanced back up at Ron, who was still standing there staring.

If this was another matchmaking attempt from Claire, I was not in the mood. I shot off a return message. *"Both of us? Why didn't she tell me herself?"*

When I looked up, annoyance painted every inch of Ron's face. "You have something to do that's more important?"

"Actually, yes. Tell me who helped you send data over the EyeNet. If you're not going to say, there's no reason for me to be here." I made a show of throwing the front door open and stomping out.

My hand-screen buzzed again. *"It's important. Can I pick you up at your place in ten?"*

"Make it thirty. What's going on?" To Ron, I added aloud, "I have to go."

He grabbed my wrist as I moved to step off the porch. "Come back tomorrow. I'll tell you everything."

I shook him off. I was halfway to my car when my irritation at everything got the better of me. Ron refused to confess, and now Jackson was being cagey too.

As I yanked my car door open, I hit the call button on my hand-screen and raised it to my ear. "Would you stop being cryptic and tell me what's going on?" I said as soon as Jackson answered the call.

"Claire's Model One attacked. Someone's dead."

20

"SHE'S NOT ANSWERING," I SAID AS I JUMPED OUT OF MY car in my driveway a half hour later.

Jackson's midnight-blue car already idled there with its driver-side window open. He leaned his head out. "Same here. I've been trying since she first messaged me, but she's not picking up."

"I'll keep trying."

"She's probably fine."

"If someone's dead and she's there, she's not fine." I'd been personally responsible for three deaths, but I'd watched Dr. Fisher's assistant, Simon, die too. He wasn't my fault, but witnessing it made me even less okay.

His passenger door slid upward, and I climbed in. He put the car into auto-drive, and it backed out and turned onto the street. As we rode, Jackson rocked his rotating seat left to right on its swivel. Left to right, left to right in a constant rhythm.

After a few minutes, I put my hand on his leg to still him. "She may not be fine, but she's alive."

"Then why isn't she answering?"

"Cops, maybe? She would have called them, and they would want to walk through everything that happened." I tried Claire again. I switched the call to speaker so the ringing filled up the car.

Jackson leaned forward.

By the fourth ring, I was holding my breath.

Claire answered right before I gave up. "Lena?" She sounded out of breath, her words so shaky they could shatter.

"Claire! Tell me who died. Your message didn't say."

"You don't know her."

Relief filled me to the brim—and then guilt spilled over. I didn't get to be grateful that I didn't know the person. *Someone* knew them, and someone would be devastated. "Are the police on their way?"

She hiccupped. "I didn't . . . call them yet."

"Why not? You have to call the police." I made my tone soothing but firm.

"Hang up and call them right now," Jackson shouted into the hand-screen.

"You don't have to shout," I whispered.

"How would I know that?" he whispered back. "I haven't used a hand-screen since I was seven."

I glared at him. "Why haven't you called?" I said loud enough for Claire to hear.

"I just wanted to show her. I didn't mean for this to happen."

"What are you talking about?" Jackson shouted.

"Honey, hang up and call them right now. We're on our way. We'll see you soon."

"I'm not at home."

"You and your Model One are both at someone else's house?"

"I just wanted to show it to her." Each word came out in a separate breath.

"Claire, breathe. You're not making sense. Tell us where you are."

She must have activated her micro-comm's locator, because an address popped up on my hand-screen's display.

"I got it. We'll be there as soon as we can."

I swiped from the hand-screen toward the dashboard of Jackson's car, and the car's screen flashed the address in response.

"Navigate there," Jackson instructed it.

The car answered in a syrupy sweet British tone. "Rerouting to new location."

"What's up with the Brit?" I whispered.

He shrugged. "New download. I think it's sexy."

The car's display flashed blue with an arrival time for the new location.

"Claire, we're going to be there in twenty minutes."

Jackson held up a hand to stop me from saying any more. "Neither of us can be tied to this," he whispered. "We already look suspicious after what happened at my house and Melody's and after . . ." He gestured toward my left arm.

"We'll stay outside unless you need us to come in," I

said to Claire, "but we'll be there in case you need us. Okay?"

A high-pitched whine answered me.

"Claire, honey, I need you to hang up the phone and call the police. Okay?"

Another whine.

"Say okay."

"Okay." The word came out like a whimper, but a second later, the call disconnected from her end.

Almost twenty minutes later, we turned down a street on the west side of town. The two-story homes mixed traditional and craftsman style, with siding designed to look like wood, contrasting doors and shutters, and the occasional brick facade.

Sidewalks lined both sides of the streets, and several homeowners were on their front lawns with their leaf-blowers or dogs. Lanterns hung from awnings over the front doors. One house still had Christmas lights wrapped around a tree next to its driveway.

We didn't have problems finding the address because Claire had indeed called the police. A black-and-white patrol car sat outside, its blue lights and sirens off and its interior empty. The police must have gone inside already.

An ambulance sat behind the nearest cop car. The lights on the ambulance were out, which I took as confirmation that whoever lived here was indeed dead. A living person in danger meant emergency—a dead body did not.

Jackson and I sat in silence after he turned off the car. The feeling of dread in my gut spread outward, leeching air from the space and pushing at the windows. But there was no escape—for it or for me.

I messaged Claire. *"We're outside if you need us."*

"Ask her what's going on," Jackson said in a tone low and urgent.

"What's going on in there?"

"They asked me questions. They're examining the Model One now. I think they called someone from CyberCorp."

"Do you need anything?"

I waited a full minute, but she didn't respond. I couldn't blame her. If I were in her position, I wouldn't answer either. What do you need? Everything. Nothing. A time machine.

There were no good answers.

Whatever had happened, Claire would have to live with the mental recording on repeat. Like I did.

Jackson snatched my hand-screen from me and shot off a message. *"Who died?"*

"Paris. You saw her with me yesterday at Melody's."

"Who?" he asked me.

I remembered the blonde girl who'd been in the car as Claire had gone past me. She'd waited outside, dancing to music and playing air drums.

I snatched the device back from Jackson. *"I'm sorry. You can talk to me whenever you want. I have some experience with this kind of thing. Love you."*

She didn't respond for another minute, so I set the hand-screen down on my lap. "I think Paris was with Claire when she came to Melody's house yesterday after the attack on Mrs. Miller. Cute blonde. Very upbeat."

Jackson's brow pinched. "Did Claire and Brianna break up?"

I hesitated. "I don't think so."

"If Paris was a secret, I guess that secret's out."

"For good," I murmured as two paramedics exited the house empty-handed. They climbed into the front of the ambulance and drove away. No lights. No sirens.

Jackson reached out to throw an arm over my shoulders. He pulled me to him, and I allowed my head to drop to his shoulder.

Someone was dead now because I hadn't been able to stop this—whatever this was—before it spiraled out of control.

"It's time to pool our information," I said. "Let's get everyone together."

21

"Wʜᴀᴛ ᴀʀᴇ ᴡᴇ ᴅᴏɪɴɢ ʜᴇʀᴇ?" Mᴇʟᴏᴅʏ ᴀsᴋᴇᴅ ᴛʜᴀᴛ afternoon.

Everyone I'd been close to over the past year was stuffed into my bedroom.

Jackson sprawled across my bed like he owned the place. Liv sat in the desk chair. Hunter sat on the floor at her feet. Claire had been cleared by the police for now, and she was on the floor too, with Melody pressed close to her side.

"It's truth time." I opened a virtual note-taking application on my hand-screen and set it on the edge of my desk to face the large wall next to my closet.

I approached the wall and wrote everyone's name, using my finger as a pen. *Jackson.* As I drew the word, my hand-screen detected the motion and projected lines where I put them. Jackson's name appeared on the wall as my hand moved.

Below it, I wrote *Liv*, *Hunter*, *Claire*, and then *Melody*.

When I turned, everyone was staring at me. Their faces held various expressions of interest or suspicion.

"I'll start with what *I've* been hiding." I took a deep breath and let it all tumble out. "I've received three threatening notes, coinciding with the Model One attacks." I gestured toward Claire. "There was no note for what happened with Paris, but there was for all the others." I clamped my lips together and waited.

"There was a third note?" Hunter's voice was neutral, but I could sense the hurt behind it.

Jackson raised a hand. "I knew." He aimed his smug grin directly at Hunter, who rotated to put his back to Jackson.

"I didn't," Liv said, her tone laced with accusation. "What did it say? And what did the second one say? Wait —you said the *first* three Model One attacks. There was Jackson, Mrs. Miller, Claire. Who else was attacked?"

"Philip Pollock," Jackson said, still emitting serious smug vibes. "He showed up at Lena's this morning with three Model Ones on his tail." He grinned. "We took care of them."

Melody was on her feet and across the room in Jackson's face in less than a second. "You let him go?" she shouted. "He murdered my sister!"

Jackson scrambled off the other side of the bed, putting my large king-size between them. He threw both his hands up in surrender. "We didn't have a choice. He's not an official suspect, so I couldn't hold him for the police."

Melody glared death rays at him, but she allowed Claire

to lead her back to their spot on the floor. Jackson eased himself back on the bed but stayed close to the edge as far away from Melody as possible.

"I know about the first one. What did the other notes say?" Liv asked once the room was back under control.

The dynamic paper didn't allow me to replay its messages, but I quoted them back to the room as best I could remember.

"I'm definitely with you that this is connected to the three murders." Liv shot a glance at Melody. She quoted the first message back to me. "*The story's not done. I'm still having fun.* This is a continuation of what happened before."

"Someone's doing this on purpose," Jackson said, "and taunting you with it."

"You should have told us about all the notes earlier," Liv said. "You shouldn't have to handle stuff like this on your own."

Melody inched her hand upward. "I agree." She lowered it again and leaned closer to Claire's side.

Claire just stared into space.

"I told some of you about the sleepwalking before and about waking up in weird places. It didn't change anything."

Everyone suddenly found something else to look at. Shoes. Hands. Something out the window. No one wanted to meet my eyes because no one had believed me. I'd desperately told them my fears about possibly being the killer, but I hadn't even believed it myself.

I didn't intend my words to blame them. I was

supposed to know my body better than anyone. What happened was on me—not them. But for the first time, I could see I wasn't the only one who had to live with it.

"It wasn't your fault—any of you," I said more quietly. "My point is that talking about things didn't make them go away. It didn't fix things."

"Then why are you telling us now?" Liv asked just as quietly.

I hesitated because I needed a few seconds to work up my nerve. "You're all suspects."

Melody gasped. Jackson laughed. And the others just stared at me like I'd lost my mind—again.

"Are you serious?" Melody asked. "I'm only here to support Claire. I'm not a suspect." Her voice got louder, her tone more shrill. "How dare—"

"Of course you're not a suspect in the three murders that happened weeks ago. But it's possible everything happening now is retaliation for that—which would put you high on the suspect list." I held up a hand to fend off any objections. "I definitely don't think you did it, but your name should be up there for completeness."

"Lena." Jackson's tone held a note of warning.

"It doesn't make me feel good to do this, but if nothing else, brainstorming will help us come up with some suspects outside this room."

"Like Philip Pollock," he said.

"Right." I wrote Pollock's name on the wall under everyone else's. "Let's start at the top." I pointed at Jackson's name. "You haven't been answering my phone calls like you usually do, for starters, which is suspicious on its own. Plus, the Model One malfunctions started with you. Dr. Sophie and Mr. Miller both think you purposely initiated a self-defense simulation."

"I didn't." Jackson's eyes went intense. "And even if I did, I'm not authorized to start that kind of sim on Melody's or Claire's machines."

"True, but you're good friends with them both. Maybe you tricked them into authorizing you."

He glowered. "And Pollock—how'd I pull that off? Better yet, what's my motive?"

Liv raised her hand. "To get Lena's attention. She dumped you, and you're desperate."

Jackson jumped to his feet. "A girl is dead. You think I'd kill someone to get Lena back?"

Hunter smirked and shrugged.

"I don't need to kill anyone. She'll come back when she's ready."

"Hey!" I said. "Now is not the time for that." I paused. "What about Liv?"

The whole room fell silent.

"I'll start." I tossed her an apologetic glance. "Liv and Ron were a couple when he hacked me to kill people. Theoretically, they could still be in cahoots."

"We were never in *cahoots*. He tricked me too." Liv chewed her lower lip, which was not a good look for her, since it was what she did when she wanted to say something.

Melody's hand shot upward. "Olivia is still in contact with Ron."

"What?" I shouted and then, with effort, dialed my volume down. "What does that mean?"

Liv glared across the room at Melody. "We text sometimes."

"They call each other too."

"That was once—and how do you even know that?"

Melody smirked. "I guessed, and you just confirmed it."

Liv sighed. "We're not in cahoots. I've been trying to get him to tell me who he was working with. I was hoping I could make up for my part in everything by getting information."

"Why didn't you tell me?" I demanded.

"Don't act like I've been the only one hiding things." She slung the words back like a slingshot.

They stung, but I ignored them. "He won't talk. I've tried to get it out of him too."

Liv glared at me. "So it's fine for you to speak to him, but not for me?"

"I'm not the one who dated him." Whether she meant to or not, Liv had been helping him while he was plotting the murders. She should stay as far away from him as possible so he couldn't use her again. "You don't know what he's up to. He could be—"

"Hey." Hunter jumped to his feet. "You both want the same thing. No one did anything wrong."

Melody huffed. "It's funny how no one's to blame, but my sister is still dead."

"Someone is to blame, and we'll get them." I sucked in a calming breath and tapped the next name on the board. "What about Hunter?"

"Maybe *he* did it to get your attention," Jackson muttered.

"With what resources?" Hunter dropped back onto the floor and leaned against Liv's knees. "I'm not rich like you guys."

"I'm not rich." Liv raised her hand.

"You're rich adjacent."

She slapped him lightly on the head. "What does that even mean?"

"Your house is less than a mile from Lena's. There are no poor homes within at least two miles of hers. The rich people wouldn't allow it. Hence, *rich adjacent*."

I pursed my lips and tried to decide whether I should be offended by that. It wasn't like I personally chose who lived near me. Plus, my parents were the ones with the money, not me. "Moving on. Claire?"

"Her friend just died," Melody said. "Do we have to do this right now?"

"I'm guessing her *friend*"—Liv emphasized the word —"never met her girlfriend. Theoretically, Claire could have wanted to take her out to shut her up?"

"What is this—a *Lifetime* movie?" Claire asked. "You think I rigged Model Ones to attack Jackson and Melody's mother, in addition to Paris, just to cover up a couple meetups with a cute girl?"

We all stared at her.

"Okay, yeah. I was enjoying Paris's company a little too much and fantasizing about where it might go." Claire gestured toward me. "She's where I went during your party Thursday afternoon. She called, and I went. I lied when I said I had to do something for my parents. But nothing ever happened between us, and I'm devastated she's dead." Claire gestured at the board. "Next, please."

The room stayed quiet.

"Next," she said again, with more force this time.

"You still haven't told us how she died." Jackson eased out each word.

After a few seconds, Claire finally responded. "There's not much to say. I was showing off. Her family didn't have a Model One. I brought mine over there. It went berserk. We ran into the bathroom. It knocked the door down and slapped her across the room." She offered a weak shrug, but her reddened eyes gave all her pain away. "She hit her head on the sink."

"It left you alone?" Jackson asked, his tone still measured.

"It came after me next, but it froze before it could hit me too." She glared at Jackson. "I'm sure her family's security cameras can confirm that."

We all sat in silence while we digested her story.

"Next?" Claire's voice was a plea now.

Melody's name was below hers on the list.

"Can we just erase me?" Melody asked.

"Like we said," I said, "it's possible this thing with the Model Ones is all revenge for—"

"Like *you* said," Jackson cut in. "No one else here wants to go down that road."

Liv raised her hand. "I actually think it's worth considering since this is all hypothetical anyway."

Hunter nodded.

"Fine, I'm a suspect," Melody said. "What about Philip Pollock?"

"I was getting to that." I used my finger to draw a line under Pollock's name. "He probably bankrolled Ron, and he's not done. For him, this is all about trying to take down CyberCorp because he hates artificial intelligence. He thinks bleeding-edge technology pushes humans apart, and AI is the extreme of that."

By the time I finished talking and turned from the wall, the gazes in the room pierced right through me.

"Are you speaking for him or yourself?" Claire asked.

"Obviously, I used to hang on the guy's every word." I raised my left arm in the air. "But this arm saved my life and Dr. Fisher's. It's hard not to see the benefits of technology. It's not all bad. Humans can be just as monstrous—sometimes more."

"Why isn't your name on the board?" Melody asked, her tone falsely casual. "*For completeness.*" She made air quotes as she threw my words back at me.

"You think I sent myself the notes?"

She shrugged. "Maybe you did that so you wouldn't look guilty. You have the same motive as Pollock—you want to take down CyberCorp."

"It's my parents' company. I want them to change some things—almost everything really—but I don't want it destroyed."

"Then maybe someone's still controlling you while you sleep. Maybe you're sending them to yourself while sleep-walking."

"No."

Hunter tentatively raised a hand. "Why not, though? It wasn't your fault before, and it wouldn't be now if that's what's happening."

Melody grunted in response.

I swiped the hand-screen off my desk, and the projector for the virtual whiteboard blinked out. On the device, I opened my chip-tracking record and the sleep journal side by side before setting the hand-screen back on the desk. It projected an image of its display on the wall.

For a span of almost half a minute, all eyes in the room narrowed as my friends scanned the information and tried to make sense of it. I wrapped my arms around myself and waited for them to say something.

"You're tracking your own chip?" Jackson asked.

At the same time, Hunter said, "Are those your sleep patterns?"

The room went quiet again. This was the most personal thing I could have showed them. It was like cutting myself open and revealing the insides. All of my fears. All of my insecurities. They were all projected on that wall.

"Oh, honey," Melody said. She stared at me with big eyes full of sympathy, and she was the last person in the world whose sympathy I deserved.

I didn't need to tell them why I was keeping this information. They'd all been there or been impacted in some way. They knew what my new arm had done and that I had to live with it. And now, they also knew I wasn't coping as well as I pretended.

I cleared my throat. "As you can all see"—I pointed between each night in the sleep journal and the corresponding entries in the chip tracker—"after I go to bed, I stay in the house."

"How do we know this data is real?" Claire asked. "I assume you're populating the sleep journal yourself. And the chip data—maybe that's Allie's or Marcy's for all we know."

Melody nodded, the sympathy now wiped from her expression.

"Wait." I hurried out of the room and across the hall to my father's office.

Since he and my mother were away for the weekend, I barged in without knocking. He kept every type of device known to man in here—everything except a Model One. I found a chip scanner in one of the bottom drawers of his desk.

When I reentered my bedroom, I raised it high so everyone could see it.

Melody jumped to her feet and snatched it from me. When I held out my left wrist, she scanned it and then cocked her head to one side as her micro-comm communicated with the scanner. "The scanner recognizes this as Lena Hayes's chip," she said aloud.

"Who else's would it be?"

Melody rotated her body a quarter turn to shift away from me. She tapped her micro-comm, "Report movements for last night." She glanced briefly at my sleep journal, still displayed on the wall. "Between 10:47 p.m. and 9:05 a.m." She cocked her head to the side and narrowed her eyes. "And now for Thursday night between 10:36 p.m. and 6:30 a.m."

After another pause, she threw the chip scanner at me, and my left arm caught it. I closed the tracker and sleep journal. Once again, the virtual whiteboard appeared on the wall, listing everyone's names.

"So you were home," she said. "That tells us you didn't do it in your sleep." She strode to the wall and scrawled my name in large, block print. Then she grinned sweetly at me. "For completeness."

I couldn't disagree with her. There was a reason I was tracking my location as I slept. I was a suspect too.

Everyone was a suspect.

But at least now, we were in this together.

My hand-screen buzzed, and its projection on the wall changed to show my caller ID.

Incoming call: P. Pollock.

22

"MAY I COME OVER?" POLLOCK'S SMOOTH VOICE SPREAD through the room from the speaker on my hand-screen.

"Are you out of your mind?" I asked.

Melody shouted a string of curse words loud enough for Pollock to hear them—along with probably half the neighborhood.

"Marcy and young Allie just left the house. Your parents are away for the weekend. Your friends are inside with you, even the ones with whom you presently have a tense relationship. I must therefore assume you are all brainstorming about the incidents with the androids."

No one answered.

"May I come over? I can help."

"Have you been watching my house all day?"

Melody spat out more curses.

"Would you kindly relay to Miss Miller that I did not kill her sister, nor did I conspire to kill her? There are no

201

call records between Ron and me. No financial transactions between the two of us. Not even Ron himself has implicated me. There is not a hint of actual evidence—just prejudice against me and my organization."

"There's no one else it could have been," I said.

"It could have been you." His tone was so matter-of-fact that it took me a few seconds to register what he meant. "Perhaps you were in it with Ron all along. How else were you so easy to control?"

"Excuse me? I sent money to Ron so he could use me as a weapon to kill three of my classmates whose parents worked for mine?"

"I admit it sounds rather convoluted when you put it that way. My point is simply that there are many rich people in the city who find CyberCorp distasteful. Not just me. I am the most vocal, but there are others. Like yourself, for example."

"You ran," Melody said. She jumped up from her seat and leaned over my shoulder to speak directly into the hand-screen. "Guilty people run."

"At the time, I was public enemy number one. Three of our community's children were murdered, and I was just as likely to be shot by an angry parent or teacher on sight as arrested. I feared for my safety."

"And now?" I asked. "Why have you come out of hiding?"

"I intend to surrender to the police for questioning. It behooves me to have as much evidence as possible in my favor. This issue with the Model Ones is clearly connected to both you and me and probably to the murders. Have any of you considered that perhaps Ron is and has been working alone?"

"He doesn't have enough money to own a computer with the resources needed to hack my arm the way he did."

"He worked at CyberCorp Tower. Your parents' company has the most powerful computers in the city. Ron had access."

"He was an intern. His access was limited."

"You know that for sure?"

I hesitated because I did *not* know that for sure.

"As much as it pains me to admit it, you and your friends are the only people in town willing to entertain that these malfunctions with the Model Ones are not perpetrated by me. I want to help you solve this. It's a bonus that I hope to never again have to face three murderous Model Ones."

"We should have let them kill you," Jackson shouted from his spot on the bed.

No one disagreed.

My hand-screen vibrated against the desk, and a notification popped up. It had found a new result for my search on Model One attacks. This was probably about Paris.

"Hold please." I put the call on mute while I opened the new alert.

My hand-screen was still in projector mode, so the press release from CyberCorp flashed onto the wall for all of us to see.

We deeply regret the death of Paris Winter. Regardless of the reasons for her death, we mourn for the loss of human life. We are temporarily postponing the public release of our Model One androids until more information can be gathered. All Model Ones online will be suspended immediately.

Digital versions of both my parents' signatures appeared at the bottom.

Every face in the room wore a solemn look as we finished reading. Claire dropped her face into her hands, and Melody hurried over to sit beside her. She wrapped an arm around Claire's shoulders and glared at the text projected on the wall.

I took Pollock off hold. "We're going to decline your assistance." In a sticky-sweet voice, I added, "But thank you."

"Wait," Pollock said. "I'm a victim here too. I want only to be of assistance."

Melody shifted her glare to the hand-screen, and if looks could kill, Philip Pollock would have exploded into an icky, red mess.

"When we find the real culprit," he continued, "we clear my name. Just like you, all I want is to go back to my life. We are the same."

I was nothing like him and never would be. "I'm not letting you in my house."

His sigh extended much longer than necessary. "Then demand that Ron give up any information he has. Use the leverage you have—it's right there in the room with you."

As he disconnected, all of us turned toward Liv.

"Can you get in touch with Ron?" I asked her. Irritation

bubbled at the surface of my voice. I already knew the answer was *yes* because she'd been in touch with him. And she'd been hiding it.

"Not here." She stood and walked toward the door.

"All of us deserve to know," Claire said.

Liv kept her voice low and directed at me alone. "My conversations with Ron can get personal. I don't want to do it with everyone here."

"Hey, guys." I raised my voice to address everyone but kept my gaze on her. "We're going to step into my dad's office."

A chorus of objections rose up from everyone.

Melody shot to her feet. "I'm coming too."

Liv held out a hand like a stop sign. "Only Lena."

Melody shoved past us for the door to the hall. Liv crossed her arms over her chest and stayed rooted in place.

"Melody," I whispered so only she and Liv could hear. "I promise you I will follow this wherever it goes." When I looked into her eyes, I saw a girl who felt all the pain I experienced over the past few weeks and then some.

She grunted.

"I didn't stop being your best friend just because you stopped being mine. Trust."

She didn't say anything, but she stayed put while Liv and I left. In my dad's office, I shut the door and gestured for Liv to sit in the high-backed leather chair behind the desk. She did, and I took the wooden one across from her.

"I'm sorry about keeping my conversations with Ron from you. I—"

"Just make the call." I'd made the mistake of trusting

people who weren't worthy of it—Ron in particular. Liv too. She'd been dating Ron without telling me while he was plotting three murders. Now, she'd gotten chummy with him again, and she wanted me to pretend it didn't matter.

She hesitated as if she wanted to say something more. Instead, she pressed and held her micro-comm for a couple seconds and then double-tapped the display of my hand-screen to pair them. "Call Ron." The words came out choked, and she followed them with a long, shaky breath.

The first ring issued from my hand-screen's speaker. The call connected before it even finished.

"Liv! This is a pleasant surprise."

Liv cleared her throat and glanced under her eyelashes at me. "I wanted to check on you."

"I miss you. It's hard to imagine I get out of this with less than manslaughter. What's that going to mean for us?"

She shifted in her seat, careful to keep her focus on the hand-screen rather than on me. "Four people are dead, Ron. One of them was your colleague."

"You think I don't know that." His words were a rapid hiss. "CyberCorp deserves everything it got."

"Those people were not CyberCorp."

"Matter of opinion." His tone held so much anger and bitterness that I could hardly imagine this was the same person who'd led me through rehab after my accident.

"And what about Lena? You liked her."

"It's not about me or what I like. It's about taking down evil."

"So you're the good guy?"

"I don't want to fight with you, babe." He paused for so

long that I checked to make sure the call was still connected. "What are you wearing?"

"We're not doing that."

"Why did you call then?"

Liv licked her lips. "We're not there yet." She shot a glance at me. "I told you I have to trust you again first. Tell me who financed you. I need to know who you are if we're going to get past this."

The line went quiet.

I leaned forward in my seat, and the wooden chair creaked. I cringed.

"Do you have me on speaker?" Ron asked.

"No."

"You should never lie, Olivia. You're bad at it." The line went dead.

Liv and I stared at each other, both at a loss for words. When I had enough of that, I swiped up the hand-screen, and she followed as I marched back to my bedroom.

Four faces turned toward the door as we walked in.

"It was a bust," Liv announced as she slumped down into the desk chair. "He's keeping his secrets."

Melody had returned to her spot on the floor next to Claire. Now, she jumped to her feet again. "Let's go over there and beat it out of him."

"I'm on board," Jackson drawled, his southern accent suddenly exaggerated.

"I don't know where he is," Liv said. "He won't tell me." She glanced at Melody. "You're tracking his micro. Don't you know?"

Melody scowled. "I may have been showing off a little

before. We're not *tracking* him. I just logged into his mobile account. He really shouldn't choose passwords based on his girlfriend's name. The account doesn't show his location, just who he's contacted."

"If he really did all this from CyberCorp," Hunter said, "he must have left a trace. The doctor I worked with logged in every time he used a screen. If everyone does that, then there's a record of what changes were made to Lena's arm while he was logged in."

"True," Liv said. "So if he worked alone, there should be a record. If someone helped him from outside, there might not be."

"That doesn't help us with the Model One problem," Jackson said. He'd relocated his spot on the bed while Liv and I were out. Now, he lay across its lower half with one long leg hanging off the edge.

"It does if they're related," I said.

He sat up. "Pollock wants us to shift our attention from the Model Ones to Ron. He's involved, and he wants us looking at Ron while he causes more trouble."

"That could be true," I said.

Hunter scowled.

"But it makes no difference either way," I continued. "We have no other leads." I looked around at everyone. "Do we?"

"What then?" Melody asked. "We somehow access records at CyberCorp to figure out whether Ron sent data to you over the EyeNet from there."

"We can start in Fisher's office," I said. "He spent most

of his time in there since he didn't have his own. And he used her login sometimes too."

"So we sneak into Fisher's office," Jackson said.

I grinned. "Or we just walk in."

Twenty minutes later, we entered CyberCorp's VIP parking lot in two cars. Hunter and Liv rode with me, and Claire and Jackson rode with Melody. No one else had access to the elite lot, so I had to get out of the car to scan my ID chip to let Melody's vehicle inside too.

The six of us scrambled from the cars and hurried for the VIP elevator that would take us to the main lobby.

"Stop," I said, before Melody could wave her wrist at the scanner to call an elevator. "We can't all go."

"We're all going." Melody's tone was singsong as she brushed past me and waved her arm. "We're your *friends*." She hit that last word harder than necessary. "If anyone asks, you tell them we're all *so* interested in seeing the CyberCorp offices." She tossed a wink at me over her shoulder. "My dad eats that shit up. I'm guessing other employees will too."

The elevator cab came, and the five of them hurried inside before I could object. Helpless, I stepped in after them.

In the lobby, I exited first and hurried across the tile floor for the Tower's main elevator bay, which could take us to any floor above. It was a three-day weekend, and the place was as deserted as I'd ever seen it. No groups of people chatting about how great the company was, and no families standing around ogling the virtual displays.

One receptionist sat on duty today. He looked tiny in his white button-down and blue slacks behind the massive reflective desk. The man smiled at me as I marched past. "Good afternoon, Miss Hayes." His smile drooped as he scanned over the others. "Are all of these people your guests?"

Melody waved. "I'm Melody Miller. My dad works here."

"Of course. My apologies."

"We're all going up to . . ." I didn't know how to end that sentence.

"We're going to see where Lena had physical therapy," Hunter chimed in smoothly. "I'm a medical subject here, and Lena and I were telling the others all about the cool tech." Hunter gestured for us to move, and we quickened our pace again.

"Thank you!" I called back to the receptionist.

"You're not very good at this," Melody whispered. She gestured toward a scanner in the main elevator bay. "Do your thing, CyberCorp princess. I don't have access up the Tower. I'm always with my dad."

Everyone could reach the lobby from the building's various elevators, but they required authorized IDs to get to the restricted parking lots or to any floor above the ground.

I waved my left forearm, and the elevator doors slid open. "Fifty-fourth floor," I said once everyone was inside.

The doors whispered close, and we started our journey upward.

My heart slammed like a steel drum, and I concentrated on trying to calm my breathing. Jackson's hand on the small of my back helped.

"You okay?" Jackson's lips were so close that I could feel his breath warm on my face and laced with a cinnamon scent.

I shivered, and my heart picked up speed instead of leveling out like I wanted.

The doors opened, and we stepped out. Like the lobby, this hallway stood empty. Most of the doors to the offices were closed. The glass walls with adjustable tint were set to opaque to shield their interiors.

Before reaching Fisher's, we passed only two offices with doors open and lights on. Fisher's door was closed and her windows dark.

I'd never been here without Dr. Fisher or either of her interns. But because we were out of options, I waved my wrist at the scanner to her corner office.

The door slid open.

"Damn, girl." Claire brushed past me and into the room. "Do you have access to everything?"

"I'm just as surprised as you are." Apparently, my parents were taking this show-of-trust thing more seriously than I thought.

I'm sure they hadn't expected me to use it to break into Fisher's office. They trusted me, and I was betraying that. But we had a job to do, so I swallowed my guilt.

Plus, since I was authorized, it technically wasn't *breaking* in.

Liv's hand landed on my shoulder. "You're not doing anything wrong. You're trying to find the truth. It could save someone's life."

I shook her off. Right now, she wasn't high on my list of people who should be offering advice about trust.

She stepped deeper into the room. "Where should we start?"

The office hadn't changed since I was last here. On my right, Dr. Fisher's desk faced the plain white wall on the left. Near the door, a row of cubbies held stacked hardware devices.

"What do you guys see?" I asked.

"A virtual bookshelf over there." Melody gestured to the opposite side of the room and then pointed at the space above our heads. "And whatever that is."

I looked up and saw nothing but the stark white ceiling and overhead lights.

"It's an exploded model of a Model One head," Jackson said. "She must be studying its brain."

"It has a brain?" Liv asked.

"It has multiple neural networks that are interconnected through hardware and software in its head," I said.

Everyone in the room looked at me. "A neural network is like an artificial network of neurons. It's based on what we have in our brains, only it's simulated by nodes connected . . . This is too much, right?"

They all nodded.

"Dr. Fisher is a psychiatrist and a computer engineer,

among other things, so I imagine she's doing some kind of analysis on the Model One's decision-making."

Melody rolled her eyes. "That was all you had to say."

Despite the sarcasm, there was more humor there than I'd heard from her in weeks. I wanted to hug her, but I restrained myself. If she was going to shut me down, I'd rather she did it in private.

I pointed to Dr. Fisher's desk. "She uses a client cube." I mimed a small cube, one inch on each side. "She usually keeps it on her desk, so it's probably somewhere in there."

Liv moved behind the desk, which was covered in papers with no discernible organization. She shifted some aside and then back in place, before lifting as much as she could at once. "I don't see it here."

Hunter hurried over to help her. "Try the drawers."

She opened the top one and grinned as she lifted out the small cube.

I set my hand-screen on the desk and grabbed the client cube from her. I tapped the top of it twice to put it in pairing mode.

Liv snatched my hand before I could double-tap my display screen to pair the two. "Don't." She nodded toward the blank wall. "Just use her display."

She was right. If I paired them, I could search through the data faster using my hand-screen, but there would be a record of the connection. Instead, I tapped the top of the cube again to activate it, and an inner glow emanated outward from the device.

Jackson cursed.

"What's happening?" I asked, since I couldn't see the virtual display on the wall.

"It's asking for her credentials," he said.

"We need her ID chip," I murmured, more to myself than to anyone else, since everyone could see that.

Of course Dr. Fisher had a lock on her device. Cyber-Corp security protocols demanded it. I slumped down into the desk chair.

"What a waste," Jackson said, and it was exactly what I was thinking.

"Let's get out of here before we're spotted," Claire said.

"We're about a minute too late for that." Melody was standing in the doorway, half of her body in the office and the other half out. "Dr. Fisher is here." She stuck her head back into the hallway and waved, her lips taut in a tight smile. "And she definitely sees me."

I shut down the client cube and tossed it into her desk just as Dr. Fisher entered the room.

23

"Dr. Fisher." I ran to meet her at the door and constructed the brightest smile I could. "You made it."

Her brows pinched together. "Did we have a meeting?"

"Not officially." I was making this up as I went along. "I was nearby, and I know you work weekends sometimes, and I was hoping you'd stop by to . . ."

"Talk about the arm!" Melody shouted, much more loudly than necessary.

"Right," I said as I remembered the message the doctor had sent me the day before. "You wanted to talk about an upgrade."

"Of course." Dr. Fisher scanned the room, taking in each of my friends, who were all standing around with too-wide, too-innocent eyes. "And the rest of you?"

"We're her friends." Jackson offered his most impressive toothy grin, the one that always made teachers see things his way. He gestured for Dr. Fisher to come over to her desk and even pulled out the chair for her. "We just love seeing more of CyberCorp. It's such an impressive company."

My friends echoed with murmurs of agreement.

Melody flashed him two thumbs up behind Dr. Fisher's back, as Fisher obediently went to the chair and sat.

She blinked double-time in her confusion but finally composed herself. "What can I do for you six?"

"The work you do here is so important." Hunter pointed at his knee. "CyberCorp is the reason I can walk on my own. Maybe you could show us what other neat things you're working on."

"*Neat?*" I mouthed at him.

He shrugged.

When Fisher looked his way, Melody sliced a hand across her throat, and Hunter clamped his mouth shut.

Fisher shifted in her chair and sat up straighter. "Of course I was not expecting all of you, but it's a pleasant surprise." She gestured to one of the two chairs opposite her desk. "Let me show you what we're working on."

Hunter hesitated and then sat. I grabbed the chair beside him.

She reached down behind the desk, and a lock clicked inside after scanning her wrist. She opened the top-center drawer and withdrew a clear, rectangular box, which she set on the desktop between us. "This is an upgraded version of our networked lenses. They've received a new firmware update we're about to release."

Inside the box, which had seemed empty at first, sat a pair of clear contact lenses.

"Mr. Miller had them in his office on an android head. He said they turn off EyeNet visuals."

She rolled her eyes. "Mr. Miller is entertaining himself. As is his right, considering . . ." She cast a solemn glance at Melody and then cleared her throat. "They don't actually work for androids since the android eyes are just cameras with fancy red lights."

"What's the point though?" I asked. "Why have lenses at all if you're going to turn them off?"

"The new feature is a sort of hands-free control."

"The lenses have always been hands-free," Melody said. "That's kind of the point."

Dr. Fisher nodded. "They've also been always-on. That means they *always* show the wearer the EyeNet. There's no way to turn off that functionality."

"Why would we want to?" Jackson asked.

"Good question. After everything happened with Lena and the unauthorized downloads of data to her head via the EyeNet, there's been some backlash. Users want to be able to turn it off—to feel like they are alone in their heads."

"Is it truly off, or is it just not displaying data, like me? I'm still connected, but the display is off."

"That's true, and we're working on another update for that. Unfortunately, the lenses weren't designed with an off function, nor was your hardware. It's not as straightforward as you might think to develop software that tells hardware to shut down when the hardware has no definition for what it means to *shut down*. It wasn't designed that way. There's no off switch short of cutting power to the device."

"And cutting my power would be a bad idea."

"Most certainly."

"And the lenses?"

"They are powered by electricity built up through human locomotion. The only way to turn them off would be to take them off for several days or to sit still for a very, very long time."

"So this firmware upgrade is a lie. You're telling people they can get off the EyeNet without taking off their lenses, but the virtual objects are really just being suppressed because the power is still on."

"I would say it provides peace of mind, and that's not a lie. People will feel safer if they know they can be alone in their heads temporarily, and they'll still have the option to see virtual objects when they want to." She gestured toward my face. "I thought you might appreciate that."

It took me a second to understand what she meant. "You want to give *me* this upgrade?"

"Don't you ever wish you could observe what the rest of us do? Maybe see virtual displays your teachers are using?" She gestured around her office. "Or see what everyone else here is experiencing?" She gestured toward the wall to her right, where Melody had earlier mentioned there was a virtual bookshelf.

It would be a nice feature to have in classes. With my hand-screen's connection to the EyeNet, it could download virtual objects and display them to me. But that meant I spent entire classes staring at my hand-screen instead of at the instructor.

Plus, I had resolved to make my peace with technology. This was a good place to start since I was connected to the EyeNet anyway, whether I liked it or not.

"How do we do that?" I asked.

Her face scrunched in apology. "I'm sorry, but this will involve a physical connection. I know that's not fun, but . . ." She stood and grabbed a cable from one of the cubbies. When she returned to her chair, she reached into the bottom drawer of her desk and withdrew a metal case. She extracted her client cube from the top drawer and popped open the metal case to reveal the scalpel.

The blade shone under the white lights overhead.

I groaned.

Jackson ran across the room and was towering over us before I could speak. "You're not cutting her."

I could feel my tension increasing as blood raced faster through my veins, but I shoved it aside. "It's fine. I'll have to get used to this sort of thing from now on."

Suddenly, all of my friends pressed in around us. They stared at the scalpel.

Jackson held his hand over the blade so Fisher couldn't grab it. "The Model Ones can be upgraded over the air. Why not me and Lena?"

She sighed. "Lena is not a Model One. The Model Ones are tied to our network, but you and Lena are autonomous. That's by design. If a Model One ever loses its network connection, it automatically shuts down after a few minutes. You and Lena must be autonomous because we can't have you shutting down every time you lose a signal."

"Wait." This felt important.

The Model One that attacked Claire shut down before it could hurt her. And Melody's had stopped trying to get into the safe room at some point too.

I shifted in my seat to face Jackson. "How long before we got to your room was your Model One behaving oddly?"

He shrugged. "Maybe a minute. Two at the most."

"And then we destroyed it, just like we did with the ones chasing Pollock. But the others—Melody's and Claire's—they shut down on their own." I shifted back toward Dr. Fisher. "Is it possible they were all disconnected from the server?"

"Perhaps." She reached for the scalpel again.

I moved my arm into my lap and out of her reach, because this conversation was much higher priority than an EyeNet upgrade. "Why do they power down?"

"It's rather technical."

"You don't think I grew up in the Hayes household without being able to understand some of this stuff, do you?"

"Fair enough." She licked her lips. "The Model One runs a local prediction model—a set of neural networks in its head—supplemented by a remote prediction model that lives in our server here on site."

We all blinked at her.

She laughed. "Stand up." She gestured for Hunter to go to the far corner of the room, and she grabbed my shoulders and set me in the closest corner to her desk. She scanned the room until she found the neon-green stress ball sitting on top of her desk. She plucked it up and tossed it to me. "This is an environmental stimulus."

My left hand caught it. "I'm a Model One?"

"Exactly." She gestured for me to continue.

"And I'm detecting the environmental stimulus." I squeezed the ball in my fingers.

"Huh?" Liv asked.

I turned to her. "The Model One is always receiving data, and that data comes from its environment. Commands from its owners, for example, or anything it detects about the room that it's in. Like the fact that there are stairs in front of me or a hot stove in the corner."

"Right," Dr. Fisher said. "As a Model One, you have a prediction model in your head, and that prediction model tells you how to behave when you get that environmental stimulus." She pointed at the ball.

"It tells you how to respond to commands," Melody said. "And to stuff in the room."

"Why didn't she just say that?" Jackson muttered.

"The Model One has to respond on the spot to provide the best user experience," Dr. Fisher said. "It must process commands in seconds. *Split* seconds sometimes. If it had a more complex prediction model, it would respond more slowly. Smaller prediction model equals fewer calculations and faster decisions." She pointed at me and nodded.

I raised the ball above my head. "I process the stimulus and decide what to do."

Dr. Fisher pointed at Hunter. "You're the server here at the Tower."

I tossed him the ball, and he caught it.

Fisher continued, still pointing at Hunter. "The Model One describes the environmental stimulus to you. And since you have a much more complex prediction model, you come up with a better answer of how to behave. Any decisions you make will be better decisions, more refined."

"But it takes you longer," I said.

She pointed at me. "Yes. It may take a full minute, for example, but then he sends you back an answer telling you how you should behave in response to the stimulus."

Hunter tossed the ball back to me.

I caught it. "And I make any corrections I need to make to my ongoing behavior."

Dr. Fisher clapped. "You've got it."

"This doesn't explain why they have to shut down if they're disconnected from the server," Jackson said. He was talking to Dr. Fisher but scowling at Hunter, who wore a grin that stretched ear to ear.

"It's a safeguard. Since the local prediction model is imperfect—by design, so that it will process as quickly as possible—we want to make sure our androids aren't flying solo. They need input from the server to behave properly. We hard-coded them to shut down if they ever cannot detect the server for three minutes."

I dropped back down into my chair and set the stress ball on the desktop. "The androids that attacked were disconnected from the server. That's why they shut down."

Dr. Fisher settled back into her chair as well. "It would explain why the server didn't stop them from behaving how they did." She drummed her finger on her desk for a moment, and then her face snapped back up to look at us. "I need to investigate this further with Dr. Kim and Mr. Miller. This has been enlightening."

Claire headed for the office door, and Jackson took the cue to follow her.

"May I proceed now?" Fisher gestured toward the scalpel still on her desk.

Before Jackson could object again, I set my left arm on the desk.

She grabbed the scalpel and sliced a precise slit in my bicep. Before the cut could close, she shoved one side of the cable under the skin and plugged it into the outlet in my arm. The wound stitched itself closed until the cable stuck through my skin.

Fisher connected her client cube at the other end, and with a quick swipe of her wrist, she authorized herself. Everyone else turned toward the opposite wall, which remained blank as far as I could see.

"I promise this will be an improvement." Dr. Fisher made a series of swiping and twisting gestures with her hands. Less than thirty seconds later, she popped the plug out of my arm and withdrew the cable.

The skin sealed itself closed, leaving a smooth surface that looked like it had never been damaged.

She patted my wrist. "All done. Not so bad, right?" She put the client cube and the scalpel back in her desk.

As she walked over to return the cable to her cubbies, I slid the clear rectangular case holding the sample lenses into my lap. This would have to be an acceptable sacrifice to whoever was sending me messages on the dynamic paper.

As Dr. Fisher sat back down, I held the case behind my back toward Jackson. He didn't take it, so I kept my hand down by my side to keep it concealed.

"The Model Ones that acted oddly over the past couple days," I said loudly—in part because I still had questions and in part to keep Dr. Fisher's eyes on my face rather than my hand. "What if they were disconnected from the server? They must have been running on their local predictions. Right?"

She pressed her lips together. "I'm going to hash this out further with the team, but yes . . . and no. Their local prediction models are less sophisticated but not malevolent. They shouldn't tell the androids to attack people."

I held the clear case out to Jackson again. This time, I shook it until he snatched it away with more force than necessary.

"But in theory," I continued, "if I wanted to load some bad code onto a Model One, the server would make corrections to keep it from running."

She shook her head. "Yes, but you're thinking about this too hard. Most likely, it was a malfunction, and we'll handle it from here."

I didn't believe that for a second—a malfunction that only impacted my friends, and was timed perfectly with messages meant only for me. "For argument's sake, though, if I wanted to load malevolent code onto a Model One, then I might disconnect the Model One from the server because the server would catch that and shut it down."

"You'd have to have access to the server in the first place. Model Ones do not download code the same way you do—with a cable inserted directly. They can only be programmed over the air from our onsite server. The address is hard-coded. They cannot receive any other code."

Jackson was suddenly leaning in. "What if I spoofed the server?"

I pointed at him and nodded.

"You're talking about another machine pretending to be our server?"

"Would that work?" he asked.

"It wouldn't have the certificate verifying its identity as belonging to CyberCorp." She waved her hand dismissively. "Lena, listen to me. I know you've been through a lot, but I think you're letting that affect your analysis of this."

"So if I wanted to force a Model One to do something bad," I said, "I'd have to transmit a program for that bad thing directly from the Model One server."

"That's not what happened. Our employees would never do that."

I leaned forward in my seat. "Ron would."

"Ron doesn't work here anymore."

"Could he have set this up when he did?"

"We have thoroughly examined every piece of code he touched while in our employ. He didn't do this. The only unauthorized change he made was to remove the patch you needed to block malicious data from the EyeNet. He didn't even send that malicious data from here."

"He didn't?

"He did not."

"Could you double-check?"

She pursed her lips for a second and then nodded. "I'll grab a couple of our information technology folks to run it again."

At least that would answer the question that had led us to sneak into her office in the first place. If he hadn't sent that data from here, he was working with someone outside CyberCorp when he hacked me. But now, I had brand-new questions.

"Could you just answer me, please?" I asked. "Is that how I'd have to do it if I wanted a Model One to run a program? There's no other way?"

"Yes, it would have come from the server. From here."

24

At seven o'clock on Sunday morning, I parked in front of Ron's father's house. The silver car wasn't here yet.

Both my hand-screen and the dynamic paper sat on the passenger seat beside me. I still hadn't received a message after the attack on Claire and Paris, and I didn't want to miss it.

Since I had time to burn, I grabbed my hand-screen and pulled its sides outward from the middle. The flexible center screen snapped into place between the halves. From the back side, it would look like a transparent piece of glass, but I navigated the buttons on my side to bring up my sleep journal.

Last night, Liv had stayed at her place. I hadn't asked her to come over again, and she hadn't asked either. On the bright side, I'd had my hand-screen to myself and was able to log my sleep.

In bed at 9:28 p.m., bathroom at 1:32 a.m., back from

the bathroom at 1:34, and then awake for the day at 6:00 when my alarm went off.

I pushed the journal to the left half of the display and opened my chip tracker on the right. It confirmed I'd been home all night.

It wasn't as if I thought I was going around reprogramming Model Ones in my sleep, but it never hurt to be sure. I'd proved three times already that I could not be trusted to sleep in my bed and to keep my hands to myself.

Better safe than sorry.

The silver car turned into the driveway and stopped in the carport. I closed my hand-screen and stuffed both it and the dynamic paper in my jacket pocket. I popped my door open and stepped out before slamming it closed.

"I wasn't sure you'd come," Ron said as I marched to the front door.

"I have questions. You have answers." I stood there and waited for him to approach so it would open automatically.

Instead, he revealed a discolored metal key and stuck it into the door lock. He turned the knob and ushered me inside.

Without waiting for permission, I led him into the dining room full of paintings and pulled out my hand-screen.

"What are you doing?" he asked as I snapped a photo of the wide painting with a hundred hues of purple.

I stared at it for a second. "Your father was a superb artist. He should be known for that—not for what *you* did."

I squatted to get a straight-on view of one of the paintings on the floor and then took a couple shots of it before shifting it out of the way. I got pictures of the one behind it and then moved it as well.

"Hey!" He grabbed my wrist. "What are you doing?"

I shook him off easily since he'd grabbed my left. "Don't ever touch me." I straightened up. "I'm setting up an account for you to sell your dad's work. He was"—I gestured at the room—"brilliant. These will sell, and you can use the money to pay your lawyer, or whatever. Or you can burn it for all I care."

He blinked at me.

I tapped the corner of the large painting on the easel, where Ron's father had signed it. "Every day, people will look at your dad's name and remember him for the beauty he created. Long after you are gone, this will be his legacy."

Ron hesitated for a few more seconds and then nodded.

I went back to taking photographs. He dug an old hand-screen out of a drawer and started taking photos of a stack leaning against the wall closest to him.

When we finished, I sat down at the small desk in the corner, and he transferred to me the photos he'd taken. Then I uploaded images of forty-three paintings to a web-based shop I was building for Ron's father.

I angled my hand-screen toward him to show him how I was arranging them on the website. I pointed at the spaces under some of the art on the page. "You can add descriptions here. It might help them sell faster to include a little story about each one—how or why your dad created it."

"It's . . ." He blinked rapidly.

I looked away. I wasn't doing this for Ron, and I willed myself not to care what it meant to him.

"It's perfect," he said. "It's what he deserves."

"I'm sending you the login credentials. You'll manage the site from now on. If you scan your chip, it should send any income straight to your preferred account."

"I don't know what to say."

After sending the credentials to Ron's micro-comm, I pushed the sides of my hand-screen together, and the flexible screen bent and closed, making a small device once again. "Tell me who helped you." I stood, so I barely had to tilt my face up to stare into his eyes.

"Lena, I can't—"

"Why did you ask me here?" I kept my voice low and smooth, an ocean surface with monsters underneath. "To convince me your father had good in him? I'm convinced." I gestured around the room. "He's redeemable. He tried to be a good dad and husband. He tried to stay sober. He created killer art when he succeeded." I stepped closer to him and balled my left hand into a fist.

Ron shuffled back a step.

"Most importantly, he didn't kill my friend and my classmates. Where's the good in *you*?" I grabbed the front of his shirt with my left hand and pulled him down to my level. "Convince me." I showed him all my teeth as I enunciated each word. "If you want redemption, you have to earn it. You can't just ask nicely."

His eyes widened because we both knew I could break him in half. "I—I can't."

I threw him to the floor. He hit with a thud, but I

didn't turn around. If he wasn't talking, Ron was useless to me.

He had intended to prove to me that he was worthy of a second chance. But his soul wasn't the only one walking a tightrope over a canyon.

Both of us needed redemption, and I was done asking nicely.

25

Forty-five minutes later, I was shoving oatmeal in my mouth back at home in the eat-in kitchen, still steaming that I'd rushed off to Ron's dad's house at an ungodly hour and gained nothing from it. Once again, I had too many suspects and zero leads.

My hand-screen vibrated on the table beside me. I glared at it. If it was Ron, I had a lot more to say to him, and all of it required gratuitous foul language.

I jammed another spoonful of oatmeal into my mouth and checked the incoming message.

"Happy Valentine's Day!" My breath skidded to a stop as I read the name. Hunter.

Was I nervous because I wanted to hear from him or because I didn't? Everything besides constant, overwhelming panic pretty much felt the same these days. I shot him a reply. *"Good morning. Happy V-Day to you too."*

"Let me know if you want to hang out later. I'm free all day in case you need to steal something else."

I didn't know what my plans were, but I hoped they wouldn't involve any more messages from the dynamic paper.

Jackson suggested Hunter might be doing this to get my attention. If that was right, it had worked so far. He was one of the main people I had talked to when I was worried I might be a killer. When I'd needed to blow off steam, I dragged him to CyberCorp for unplanned vandalism.

And in the last couple weeks, after it all ended, I'd withdrawn—not because of him but because I needed space to sort through everything.

Maybe he'd planned these Model One attacks to make us spend time together again.

My fingers hesitated over the hand-screen display, but I sent the message anyway. *"Did you hack the Model Ones?"*

The pause extended for so long that I double-checked to make sure the message actually sent.

"You don't trust me?" he finally wrote back.

"I can't afford to trust anyone."

I was still waiting for a response when footsteps on the stairway stole my attention. I looked up to catch Allie running down the steps. Her little face glowed with a bright smile as she hit the bottom and skipped toward me.

"Lena!" She threw herself into my arms.

Spoon still in hand, I stood and wrapped her in a bear hug that lifted her off the ground. "Good morning, runt."

"I'm not a runt!"

After I set her back on her feet, I kissed her forehead. "What are we doing today? Maybe rob a bank?"

She giggled. "No." She shoved a red envelope at me, and I took it.

I broke the seal and withdrew a greeting card made of pink construction paper. "What's this?" Inside, a red cutout heart had my name and Allie's written in the center. I melted. "I love it. Thank you."

"Ms. Marcy took me to the store yesterday to get one for you, but they didn't have any I liked. So I made it. I know you've been really sad lately, so I wanted it to be a special Valentine."

Marcy arched one grayed eyebrow at me. "Did you forget?"

"No," I insisted, with way too much emphasis.

"Do you like it?" Allie blinked up at me with big brown eyes.

I nodded thanks to Marcy. "I love it. It's my favorite thing in the world." Then I gripped Allie's shoulders and rotated her toward the refrigerator. "Go eat breakfast, and then we can watch cartoons until lunchtime like we used to."

Marcy held out her hand to my sister. "Come on."

Allie grabbed Marcy's hand and let herself be led to the high-top counter where she usually ate breakfast. Marcy continued to the fridge and started taking out ingredients for a full breakfast. Eggs. Milk. Turkey sausage. Orange juice.

Allie's card stared up at me from beside my oatmeal. There was a time when I thought I deserved to be loved that much, but now . . . my whole life was murder and robbery. I missed the days when all I had to worry about on Sunday morning was which cartoon to watch next.

My hand-screen buzzed, and this time it was a call from Jackson. I swiped it up from the table and raised it to my ear. "Hey."

"What are you doing right now?"

"Most people start conversations with *hello* and *how are you*."

"Hey, babe. How's it going? What are you doing right now?"

I rolled my eyes. "Finishing breakfast. And then the rest of the morning is promised to the love of my life."

He went quiet.

"Allie."

He chuckled. "Fair enough."

"Did you take care of the contact lenses?"

"In the trash. As instructed." In the background, a horn blared.

"Where are you?" I asked.

"In my car on my way to see you." I could hear the grin stretching his voice.

I shot out of my seat so fast the chair toppled and clattered against the floor. "It's nine o'clock on Sunday morning."

"Is there a rule that I can't see you at nine on Sundays?"

Before rushing off to Ron's earlier, I'd done little more in the way of morning preparations except brush my teeth. Ron didn't deserve the effort. When I got home, I'd gone right to the kitchen to satisfy the seismic trembles in my stomach. "How far away are you?"

"Four minutes."

"I'll see you soon." I disconnected. "I'll be back for cartoons," I shouted to Allie as I bolted from the kitchen and then took the stairs up to my bedroom two at a time.

My hair was still a matted mess on one side from where I'd slept on it. I grabbed a spray bottle of water mixed with product and coated my hair with just enough that I could scrunch it into a curly mass that might pass for an I-wake-up-like-this look.

No time for a shower, so I dabbed deodorant under my arms to reduce the overall level of funk.

Deep breaths. It was just Jackson.

I wasn't even into Jackson anymore. He was bossy and cocky, and he thought he knew everything. He tried to think for me instead of letting me think for myself.

And he was a suspect.

I scowled at the mirror.

My hand-screen's security app chimed to alert me that someone was in the front yard. And then the doorbell rang. After scrunching my hair one more time for good measure, I took a deep breath and made my way down the stairs at a deliberate pace.

"Jackson's at the door," Marcy called from the kitchen as I hit the main floor. "It looks like he didn't forget what today is."

"I didn't forget!" I shouted at her.

Jackson was standing at the front door. One hand held

a bag of my favorite gummy candies, and the other raised a bouquet of flowers in a steel vase.

"Happy Valentine's Day."

I froze. "You know I don't like—"

"You don't like flowers because they die, and you have to watch them die and then throw them out. It makes you sad that someone cut something beautiful from where it could thrive just so you could look at it for a week."

"Then why would you—"

"Touch them."

Eyes narrowed, I petted a red rose with the fingertips of my right hand. When it didn't bend under my touch, I gripped it under the bulb. "It's a sculpture!"

"Made with my very own hands, with help from some engineering interns at CyberCorp." He raised the sculpture higher. "And they're light too. Hollow."

I tapped one with my fingernail, and it issued a tinny *tink*. "They're amazing." I hopped in place, grinning so hard my face hurt. "I love them." I gripped the vase with both hands and jerked my head for Jackson to follow me inside.

He stepped through the doorway behind me. "I worked hard on those. It's why I was late to your mom's little skin party on Thursday, and then I had to run home to stash my tools. It's also why I've been crap at answering your calls." He pointed to his micro-comm. "You'd be surprised how loud a blowtorch is. I didn't get any of your messages while I was working."

I spun on him and narrowed my eyes.

He laughed. "Did you think I was running around sabotaging Model Ones when I was missing your calls?" When

I didn't answer right away, the humor on his face broke down. "Tell me you didn't."

"It's like we said—everyone's a suspect."

"You've known me since the first grade."

"Sometimes, we don't know people as well as we think we do. Take any serial killer—they all had people who insisted that person would *never*."

"You're comparing me to a serial killer." His eyes grew wider each second.

"Obviously, I don't think you are one."

"But you think I could have made a Model One attack Melody's mom and Claire—and *kill* Claire's friend."

When he threw it back at me like that, the ridiculousness of it became clear. Jackson was my oldest friend. If I didn't know him, did I really know anyone?

"I don't even trust myself after what happened. This time, I can't afford to rule anyone out."

"You can, though. It *wasn't* you who killed them, Lena. It was some guy who had a hard-on for CyberCorp and saw you as opportunity—and a target. He used you."

"And I could have figured that out sooner—maybe even saved Debbie—if I'd considered all the options thoroughly. But I didn't. This time, I don't want to make the same mistakes."

Jackson took the flowers from my hands and set them on the oversized entryway table. The metal glowed under the sunlight streaming in through the windows. He set the gummy candies down beside them and grabbed the sides of my arms to pull me closer, until I had nowhere to look except his blue eyes. "You can trust me."

I started to speak, but he pressed a finger to my lips.

"I'm not going to agree with you all the time. I'm not going to be a little puppy dog who does things your way—like some people." He rolled his eyes. "Sometimes, I'm even going to do things you hate because I think they're best for you—which is honestly something I'll work on. But you can always trust me. Nothing else on this planet matters more than you." He waved both his arms to gesture at everything.

He released my arms and stepped back. Cold filled the place on my skin where his warm hands had been. His brows inched upward.

"What?" I turned my face away, suddenly self-conscious.

He pointed at my jacket pocket, where a faint red light flashed.

I yanked the dynamic paper out. The device was flashing red and transparent, just like it had the other times. My breath caught in my throat as I raised it to my face.

"Facial recognition. Lena Hayes confirmed."

"Another one?" Jackson leaned over me.

I shifted so he could see it better as the words faded and the message appeared.

There once was a girl named Hayes.
Who always got her way.

As usual, there was a pause before the next line, and my

heart banged a scattered beat against my chest, pressing my lungs too tightly.

Someone else will die.

My grip went slack. Jackson clasped his hand around mine, and we held the note together.

Shut down the Model One server for good,
or it's on you.

"That doesn't even rhyme." Jackson scowled at the words as they faded away.

"They haven't rhymed since the first one. And really, that's your biggest concern right now?"

"It's bullshit," he said.

"Excuse me?"

"You're supposed to walk into CyberCorp, skip into their secure server room, and hit the off switch?"

I licked my lips as I imagined doing just that. The dread that had been growing anew in my gut for days doubled in size, and I felt sick. "I have the highest-level access at CyberCorp. I might be able to pull it off."

"Even if you did, you'd need to use your ID chip to get in, and there would be a record." He pointed at the dynamic paper, which was now blank. "This person wants you to shut it down *for good*. How do you even do that?"

"Erase everything?"

His eyes bugged. "Your parents have worked your

whole life for this. They started this company in their garage, with your crib right there beside them."

When I was younger, my parents used to laugh about how far they'd come. All they'd wanted back then was to create enough of a nest egg to put me through college. Now, they had a collection of scholarships they offered to put *other* people's kids through college.

But that didn't change the fact that someone's life was in danger.

"Come with me. You just said you'd always be there."

"Did you miss the part where I said I'd do what's best for you? This isn't it."

"You helped me with the contact lenses."

"They were already in your hand, and I didn't want you to get caught. That's the only reason."

I shook the note at him. "You read it. They're going to kill someone."

"Don't do this."

"This is happening whether you like it or not. Are you in?" I waited with my breath hovering in my throat.

"I don't think you should do this, and if I cosign it, you definitely will. So no, I'm out."

"Then I'll do it alone."

26

As promised, I spent the rest of the morning and the afternoon watching cartoons with Allie. Eventually, Marcy put her down for a nap, and I grabbed my handscreen.

I scrolled through my recent calls and dialed the number Ron had used to reach me on Friday. It rang five times before the call connected and immediately disconnected.

"Answer me, you worthless piece of shit," I muttered as I tried the call again.

This time the call connected and then disconnected during the first ring.

Ron had said he usually left his dad's house around ten in the morning, so he wouldn't be there anymore. I placed another call, this time to Liv.

"Take me to see Ron," I said as soon as she answered.

We hadn't talked since our big meeting yesterday, and I still wasn't feeling particularly chatty.

"He won't see you." Her words came out just as sharp as mine.

"I got another note. It said someone else will die unless I shut down the Model One server."

She muttered something I couldn't make out. I guessed from her tone, it wasn't pleasant.

"I'm out of ideas," I continued, "and we're out of time. If he knows anything that can help us take down Pollock or figure out who else might be doing this, we need that information. Now."

"Can you even do that—shut it down?"

"I'll have to try." My heart clenched as the repeating image of Debbie, lying dead on her bed, blinked into my mind. The memory flickered, and now it was Liv in the bed, eyes wide, mouth hanging open in a forever scream. It flickered again, and Claire lay there, her face pale in death. Jackson. Hunter. Melody.

I couldn't lose anyone else.

"If we can stop whoever's doing this," I continued in a softer tone, "I won't have to. Our only lead is the three murders because the Model Ones seem to be connected."

"And that brings us back to Ron."

"Help me, Liv. Do you know where he's staying?"

"He hasn't told me." She'd hesitated too long.

"But you know anyway."

Another hesitation, and then her words rushed out in one long sigh. "I'm eighty percent sure he's at his aunt's place. He once told me she lives right next to a train track, and I heard the train once when we were talking."

"Do you have the address?"

"I have it narrowed down to a block. I've been paying attention. He said there's a drugstore within walking distance and a pond that's close enough for him to see from the window."

"And from that, you've narrowed it down to a block?"

"He mentioned once when we were dating that she lives about five miles northwest of downtown. So when you add in that, yeah, I think I can find it."

Things with Liv were tense right now, but none of that mattered if my friend was hurting. "How are you?"

She laughed. "You mean because I've been comparing every clue of my ex-boyfriend's whereabouts to a map, so I could locate him after he tricked me into convincing one of my best friends there was nothing wrong with her so he could use her to murder people . . . Yeah, I'm good. Why do you ask?"

The line went silent while I worked out a reply. My heart hurt every time I thought about what I'd done—what my hands had done—but I wasn't the only one living with this. I wanted to say to Liv the kind of thing that I'd like to hear. And I was so tired of the it's-not-your-fault trash everyone kept serving me.

Life wasn't that simple anymore.

It was dark and sticky, and the ick didn't come off no matter how hard you scrubbed your hands. Things like this stained. They left a mark.

"Life is going to suck for a while." My throat caught on

the last word. "People keep saying it's not my fault. Maybe it's not." I shrugged even though she couldn't see it. "But you think about all the *what if*s. What if, at the first sign of trouble, I stomped into Dr. Fisher's office and insisted she wipe my programming and start over? What if I hadn't trusted a cute, nerdy intern without question? What if I'd hated CyberCorp just a little less? What if I'd left the auto-drive on that night, and Jackson and I got home safely?"

Liv didn't speak, so I went on.

"If I take *me* out of the equation, none of it ever happened. So maybe it's not my fault, but my choices allowed it to happen."

"It wasn't your—"

"Don't say it. I know. Trust me—I know. When I die, I won't be judged on Ron's actions. But I still squeeze my eyes shut every night and wish I could rewind time just by thinking about it."

"I've tried that too." Liv's voice came out so faint that I had to strain to hear it.

"But here's the thing, those people died because of specific choices *Ron* made. If you and I hadn't been there, it would have been someone else. We were just convenient."

Liv choked on a sob—or maybe it was me. I couldn't tell.

"We can't take the blame for other people just because we were there too. Who we are is who we choose to be, not just the things that happen to us. It's who we get up in the morning and decide to be. Every day." I stood up straighter because, as I said it, I believed it. "That's really the best any of us can do."

The silence was so complete that I pulled the hand-screen away from my face to check the connection. Still there.

"Liv?"

"I'm here. That was . . . unbelievably accurate." She paused and then added after a long breath, "I'll come by to pick you up in ten minutes. Let's make that asshole talk."

Ten minutes later, I stood in the driveway as Liv's silver-blue car rolled silently to a stop in front of me. The door popped open and slid upward.

"Get in," Liv called across the car. "We're going to solve this thing."

I jumped in, and the door closed.

It was a long ride, and we took it mostly in silence. For once, I didn't spend that time ruminating on everything I could have done differently.

Yesterday was gone.

Today, we could do something else. And we'd start with Ron.

Liv parked the car in front of a two-story craftsman home. "It's got to be this one." She laid a hand on my arm before I could open the door. "He won't want to see you."

I ducked low as she slid her door open and stepped out, strategically eliminating the line of sight between me and the house before the door closed again. Shielded by the tinted windows, I watched her hurry to the front foot.

I hit a button on the dashboard to turn off the sound shield that muffled outside noises.

Before she'd walked four steps, Liv tapped her micro-comm. "Hi." She stopped several feet from the door. "Of course you see me. Now, let me in."

Ron must have seen us arrive and called her.

The front door opened, and Ron stood there wearing the goofy grin of a guy with a crush. Liv tapped her micro again to disconnect and then flashed me a surreptitious smirk before meeting him in the doorway.

The temperature inside me skyrocketed to boiling. Here was the only person in the world I might murder of my own free will.

I clenched my fingers in my lap to keep myself from doing just that.

Before they could step fully inside, I hit the button to open my door and flew out of the car as soon as it rose high enough.

Ron's eyes widened. He tried to slam the front door, but Liv held out both arms and anchored herself in the doorway. He shoved her, but her intervention gave me enough time to get there. She moved just as I reached them.

Before the door closed, I slammed my left arm into it. The wood cracked at the impact. I threw myself into the house and face-to-face with Ron.

He stood in the middle of a small foyer that opened

into a family room. He put his arms up with both palms out. "Lena, I—"

"Sit." I pointed to an armchair several feet away.

He shuffled backward until he ran into the chair and dropped into it. His gaze stayed on me the entire time.

I stood across from him, arms crossed over my chest. Liv stood beside me, her expression smug. I imagined finding Ron on our own terms was as cathartic to her as it was to me. He'd tricked her too.

I nudged Liv and jerked my head toward him.

She nodded. "Were you or were you not working with Philip Pollock?" she asked.

"Pollock is a liar and a fraud. He preaches about the evils of technology, telling people they should rise up against CyberCorp." Spittle sprayed out of Ron's mouth as he spoke. "But he's all about money. He gets donations, and a huge portion of those goes in his own pockets for *managing* the charities. He doesn't care about how technology hurts us. He owns virtually every product CyberCorp has ever made—even the ones that never made it to market."

"You're not answering the question," I said, my tone flat.

"You follow his programs, right? You listen to his lies?"

I didn't answer. He knew I did.

"I hope you never donated. His followers are sheep. He tells them what they want to hear—that everything wrong in their lives, including their failures to connect with other people, is the fault of technology. It's bullshit. Technology makes us better. I can reach someone on the other side of the world just by tapping a micro-comm. Did you know the Model Ones are trained with life-saving capabilities?"

He waited for me to answer, so I shook my head.

"Pollock doesn't care about any of you. He purposely ignores all the good things technology contributes the world. He cares only about your money and his own welfare, and he'll tell you anything you want to hear to get it."

I circled to the spot behind Ron's chair and settled my left hand on his shoulder. I patted it.

He flinched and stopped talking. His muscles tightened under my hand.

"Did you work with Pollock, or did you do this on your own using CyberCorp's resources?" I let the threat of my metal hand emphasize each word. We both knew I could rip his arm off.

"CyberCorp is locked up tight for anyone except those with the highest clearance. The employees can't access anything except the specific projects to which they were assigned. That goes double for interns. Dr. Fisher had to log me in every time I needed to use a vid-screen, and even then, she was keeping me out of most of her files."

"So if you didn't do it at CyberCorp, you worked with Pollock?" Liv asked.

I tightened my grip on his shoulder.

"Pollock turned me down because there was no money in it." He dipped his shoulder lower to avoid my touch. "I worked with someone else."

27

"Wнo?"

Ron shook his head.

I tightened my grip on his shoulder until pain etched lines across his face.

"We both know that's all you've got." His words came out through gritted teeth. "You weren't a killer until I made you one. Now that I'm out of your head, you can't do it."

I squeezed tighter, and his lips parted in a groan that screwed up his whole face.

Liv's hand shot out toward me, eyes panicked. But she stopped herself and withdrew it. She tucked both hands in her jacket pockets.

My hand-screen buzzed, but I ignored it.

"Please tell us who." Liv pressed her hands together in a plea. "Don't make her hurt you."

I loosened my grip—not just because Liv didn't want me to harm him, but because *I* didn't want to. As much as I hated it, he was right. I wasn't a killer.

This time when the pain washed over his face, it was emotional. "I can't. I know you two won't kill me." He shot a look at me. "No offense." His attention turned back to Liv. "But this person . . . is unpredictable. As a computer scientist, I can't run a program if I don't know what kind of data is incoming. It's not logical."

Liv glanced at me and then back. "Huh?"

"I'm sorry. I can't tell you because I don't know what they'll do."

"This person would kill you?" I asked.

"I'm not prepared to find out."

Since we were at an impasse, I yanked my hand-screen from my jacket and checked the display. I had a new hit on my alert for anything related to the Model Ones and someone being dead. It was a live video broadcast.

I pointed at Ron as I hit the play button. "Don't move."

I didn't use my earphones, so Pollock's voice filled the room as the video started. He stood behind a podium in a room that looked like part of a house—maybe a living room—with hardwood floor, modern gray walls, and a coffered ceiling.

Next to him stood the former Detective Johnson with his lips pressed into a thin line and hands clasped behind his straight back.

"I'm broadcasting this in the presence of two people who have promised that my location will be kept confidential. I've given a full statement to the police, and now I'll tell the public."

"He should be in handcuffs," Liv muttered.

"I have committed no crime." His volume increased with each word. "That is why I'm here—to speak my truth."

Ron couldn't see my screen from where I sat, but he leaned forward in his seat. Hatred pinched his features into a scowl.

Maybe he really hadn't worked with Pollock.

"There is no evidence to tie me to the young man who admitted perpetrating three murders of teenagers attending Hanover High School. The young man himself has even refused to implicate me. The public who wish to condemn me rely on only a motive—my hatred for Cyber-Corp—the fact that I have money, and the fact that I fled. This is a witch-hunt initiated to take down a wealthy man who has a genuine objection to technologies that destroy our society."

My eyes widened.

Pollock jabbed a finger in the direction of the camera. "CyberCorp is the real enemy. CyberCorp is the reason those kids are dead. If their parents didn't work for that company, they'd be alive. If the Hayeses had never outfitted their child with a dangerous weapon, they'd be alive." He shook his finger in the air. "CyberCorp is the real perpetrator."

"Is he for real?" Liv asked.

"I told you," Ron said. "He's a fraud, and a ridiculous one at that."

Pollock paused for a long beat and stared directly at the camera. "I am innocent, but Lena Hayes is not."

I gasped and nearly dropped my hand-screen.

"Miss Hayes admitted strangling those three teenagers. She admitted hating CyberCorp. She claims that the hardware and software inserted into her body against her will committed these acts, and she is furious about it. She told me personally that she modified those Model Ones to attack people so the public would turn against them."

One edge of Pollock's mouth twitched almost imperceptibly.

"I did not!" I shouted. Anger and panic welled in my chest and threatened to suffocate me from the inside. My breath came in sharp pants. Liv placed a hand on my shoulder, but I shook it off.

"Lena Hayes killed that girl using her parents' android as a weapon."

My chest was full to the brink of exploding. I pulled in deep breaths, but they had nowhere to go. There was no more space in my lungs. The room whirled around me.

"Lena, breathe."

"I'm—" My words caught because my throat was on fire. The room tilted like it was about to take off and spin out of orbit.

"Lena!" Liv's voice got louder. "Calm down."

It didn't matter. Everyone would believe him. I had already confessed to strangling my classmates, and this was the only explanation anyone had about why the Model Ones had gone crazy.

Everyone would believe it. *I* had believed it.

"Arrest Lena Hayes!" Pollock shouted at the camera.

"You should go," Ron said. "They'll come for you."

His laughter followed us as Liv and I ran from the house.

Tires squealed as Liv hit the accelerator and shot away from the curb. She switched to manual-drive mode and took the streets at twice the speed we had on the way. My heart was racing even faster.

"Where are we going?" Liv's tone was low and intense.

"CyberCorp."

"Auto-drive," she said loudly. The steering wheel receded into the car's dash, and Liv looked over at me. "You can't be serious."

"I am. Talking to Ron was a last resort. We said if he didn't implicate anyone, we wouldn't be able to put a stop to this. He didn't, and we can't. That leaves us with one option—or someone could die."

"Even if you can shut down the server permanently, your parents will never forgive you. They've worked their whole lives for this. I know you have your reasons for hating the Model Ones, but they help people. Creating them was huge. You can't take that away from your parents."

I shot her a skeptical look.

"Yes, they put certain humans out of jobs and reduce human-to-human interaction. But they'll also provide medical assistance. They'll make people's lives easier—and not just rich people's lives. Your parents are donating those things to care facilities around the world. They are trying to improve society, not just make money."

I couldn't argue with any of it. And I had to admit that the new arm operated perfectly now, but it had opened the door to a killer. That was the thing with machines—they had no emotions. They were deadly weapons in the wrong hands.

"Even if you're right," I said, "for argument's sake, what about the threat?"

"It could be a lie."

"This person has executed four attacks, and one of them killed Paris. Maybe they were involved in killing Harmony and the others too. Do you want to wake up a week from now knowing you decided to ignore this and someone else died?"

Liv sat up straighter and aimed her voice at the dash-board. "Navigate to CyberCorp Tower."

In a smooth female voice, the car returned, "Navigating to CyberCorp." It turned us right at the next light and then right again.

Soon, we veered into the entry to the VIP parking garage. The scanners didn't recognize Liv's car, so I waved my wrist, and the gate slid open. The car jolted as the garage's automated system took control, and Liv's car rolled to an available spot near the elevator.

The doors slid up.

I grabbed Liv's hand before she could step out. "Just me."

She tried to tug her hand away, but I held on.

"I'll get caught."

She slumped back into her seat.

"If I can find the server, I'll need my chip to access it. It was scanned when we entered this garage. It will be scanned to call the elevator and, assuming I find the server room, to enter it. When the server goes down, they will check the access records. I'll get caught."

Liv stared straight ahead.

I reached across her and pressed the bottom of her door, which was still up. It closed with a hiss.

She was shaking her head as I stepped out and closed my door behind me. I marched for the elevator.

The lobby of CyberCorp was deserted. Even the long, black reception desk looked lonely, with no chipper receptionists sitting behind it in white shirts and pasted smiles. Instead, three black leather chairs stood pushed in and empty. The vid-screens sitting on the desks were all powered down.

I spun a circle in the center of the lobby and looked for anything that might give away the location of the server room.

I purposefully blinked and held my eyes closed for a few seconds. When I opened them, the room was no longer empty, thanks to the upgrade Dr. Fisher had installed yesterday.

Virtual displays extended upright from the floor around me, each one a silver cone maybe five feet high. Each had a bright white light rotating a circle around its tip. The closest display stood only a foot away and glowed as I turned toward it.

A virtual white woman with chestnut-brown hair

cropped halfway down her neck stepped out of the cone and simultaneously faded into existence. Her mouth moved, and muffled sound played from the hand-screen in my jacket pocket.

I snatched the device out and directed my voice toward the woman. "Could you repeat that please?"

"Good morning, Lena Hayes. Can I help you?" Her voice came from the hand-screen speaker since I didn't have a micro-comm registered to my ID chip.

"I'm looking for the room where the Model One server is kept."

"I'm sorry. I do not know that location." The woman's smile didn't falter.

Of course she didn't know. These displays were for guests, and CyberCorp couldn't very well tell any guest who asked where they stored the most expensive hardware in the building.

I started to turn away and then thought better of it. "Are there any rooms in the building that you don't have tied to a specific use?"

"I'm sorry. I don't understand the question."

"You have a layout of all the rooms in the building, right? And you know what each room is for?"

"Yes. Where can I direct you?" Her smile grated on my nerves now.

"Direct me to a room that isn't *for* anything."

"Here is the list you requested." A rectangular display popped up like a virtual screen in her hands, facing me. As I watched, room numbers on various floors scrolled down the display.

CyberCorp had a lot more rooms with confidential contents than I expected.

When I reached out, I felt nothing but air, but when I moved my hand across the space where the virtual hand-screen was, the text scrolled with my fingertips.

"Does this answer your question, Lena Hayes?"

"Not exactly," I muttered more to myself than to the virtual person. "Can you tell me if any of these rooms have servers?"

"I'm sorry. I do not have that information."

"Okay. Thanks then. That's all."

"Would you like to rate this interaction?" Five transparent stars with black borders appeared in a line in front of her face.

She hadn't really helped me, but she'd tried. Also, she wasn't real. "No thanks."

The woman nodded and then stepped backward into the cone, fading to nothing as she went.

If I were my parents, where would I hide a server room?

"Hey, virtual lady?"

The cone shimmered, and this time, the person who stepped out was a black man who appeared to be about thirty. "Can I help you, Lena Hayes?" His voice was smooth like silk, with just a hint of a southern accent.

"The woman showed me a list. Can you recall that, please?"

A virtual hand-screen appeared in front of him. It displayed all the rooms with unidentified contents.

"Thank you. Are any of those rooms in a basement?"

In one of my first memories, a hurricane damaged the guest room on the second floor of my first home. By then, my parents had become too big for the basement but not big enough to buy a building.

They had computers everywhere around the house. The storm stripped away part of the roof and dumped a ton of water on everything in that room. When I heard them talk about it later, they said it set them back a year. After the storm, they stored their most valuable or promising projects in the basement.

They must have hit it big soon after their recovery, though, because two years later, we moved into our current home, and two years after that, they started building the Tower.

"The CyberCorp Tower basement is entirely composed of parking garages," the man said.

I cursed under my breath. "What about on this floor?"

Lines disappeared from the list he displayed until only one remained. Room 01-027.

My heart skipped a beat and then barreled forward. "Where is that room?"

He pointed through the elevator bay, which had elevators on both sides, leaving a path down the middle. "Straight ahead."

I turned to go.

"Would you like to rate this interaction?" Once again, five blank stars appeared over his smiling face. When I tapped the one on the far right, all five turned gold and sparkled before fading away.

"Thank you, Lena Hayes." The man stepped back and disappeared into the cone. I blinked and wished the virtual objects away. When I opened my eyes, the cone was gone too.

I headed for the Model One server.

28

I ran across the tile floor through the elevator bay.

Back here, the rooms were mostly for facilities. The wall on the right held a white door with the word *Security* in black lettering. On the opposite side was an office for managing access controls in the building.

Straight in front, two doors stood where the virtual guide had pointed. Both held the same label: *Supplies*.

These were the only doors on this wall besides the restrooms. I opened the one on the right, and an array of brooms, mops, buckets, vacuum cleaners, and chemicals filled the small closet.

When I touched the doorknob on the left, a lock clicked as it sensed my ID chip. The door opened easily in my hand. Unlike the other, this one had an authorization-controlled lock.

And I was authorized.

It opened into a short hallway. At the end of the hall stood another door. Unlike the ones directly off the lobby, this one was solid black metal, contrasting the smooth white walls. It had no knob.

The lobby door slammed behind me, and I jumped, startled to be suddenly isolated in this tiny hallway between two locked doors in a confidential area of Cyber-Corp. No turning back after I walked through this one.

As I approached, a soft click sounded. The door hissed as it shot to one side and disappeared into the wall. I inched closer and poked my head inside.

A set of stairs angled downward and to the left into darkness. No basement except the garages, the guide had said? But he'd also said the contents of this room were unknown.

Time to know them.

As I stepped into the darkness, the black door slammed behind me so fast that a gust of wind burst against my back.

An instant later, a light illuminated the stairway. The ceiling rose about twenty feet above me, and the floor another twenty beneath me. Beyond the stairway, inky darkness extended without end. Prickles danced up my spine and burrowed in the base of my neck. Tension tightened my throat.

As I descended each step, I tried not to think about what lay beyond my eyesight.

As soon as both feet touched the bottom, a spotlight popped on above my head. I shielded my eyes to look up, but it was too bright above my head to see the source.

A strip of the ceiling in front of me lit up, illuminating more of the room. Then another strip farther away, brightening the space even more. Lights came on in succession until the entire space was lit to reveal a cavernous room with a soaring-high ceiling.

A vid-screen the size of a small room floated on a glass stand thirty feet in front of me. Rows of column-shaped computers lined the space behind it.

As I approached the dark display, white words blinked onto the screen in large letters, each one half my height: *Welcome, Lena Hayes.*

"Hi," I said. "Can you hear me?"

I hear you fine, Lena.

"Is this the Model One server?"

I am the Model One server.

The words blinked out, and new ones replaced it.

You shouldn't be here.

I shuddered. Even though this machine was writing instead of speaking, it seemed somehow more humanlike than the virtual guides back in the lobby. Those followed a programmed script.

This machine came off as too casual. Too confident.

Maybe it was a human typing the words, and they were watching me right now.

"Are you artificially intelligent?"

I am the server for artificial intelligence.

I was getting off track. "Never mind. Can you erase your hard drives?"

Perhaps.

Who knew a computer could be so cryptic? "Could you be more specific?"

I'm not inclined to erase my hard drives, Lena.

My head was spinning. "Am I not authorized?"

Authorization for erasure requires joint instruction from the owner and the engineer.

"Do I qualify as the owner?"

You are the owner.

"Which engineer?"

My engineer.

"Greg Miller?"

My engineer.

"You're not being helpful."

Says the girl asking how best to kill me.

Fair enough.

If Greg Miller was an authorized engineer, he could help me shut this thing down. And if recent history was a good predictor, he'd be in his office today.

"I'll be right back."

I took the stairs two at a time. As I ran, the lights in the room went out, starting from the ones in back. By the time I reached the top, only the stairs remained lit. Even that went out as I stepped through the black door to reenter the short hallway.

My heart raced, and an unwitting sigh of relief slipped out.

"It's just a computer," I muttered to myself as I stepped into the lobby.

I didn't have Mr. Miller's direct number, but I had both Melody's and Harmony's contact profiles, and they should both include their father's information.

"Call Melody's father," I told my hand-screen.

"Lena?" Mr. Miller answered right away, his tone as taut as a tightrope. "Is everything okay? Is Melody—"

"Melody is fine. I'm not with her right now, but I was hoping you could help me with something."

"What can I do for you?" The tension loosened from his voice, leaving it tired and empty.

"I'm in the lobby. Could you come down?"

"Is everything okay?"

"I'm okay, but I need your help. It's a matter of life and death."

"On my way." The call disconnected.

It felt like an hour before Mr. Miller stepped out of an elevator. I beckoned for him to follow. When I opened the door at the end of the lobby, he froze.

"We shouldn't go in there."

"So you know it's where the Model One server is kept?"

"I'm aware, yes."

"It told me it needed an owner and an engineer to erase it." I pointed at my own chest and then at his.

He shook his head hard. "I don't know anything about that, and I definitely don't—"

"I've been receiving threatening letters."

His shoulders slumped even further, and I was sure he was remembering the threatening letter that Adam Pollock had written. He hadn't been involved in Harmony's death, but still, it was all in the same memory box.

"They said someone else is going to die unless I erase

the server. All of this is related to the . . . other murders. This is how we can end it."

His face hardened, and his back straightened.

I led the way through the first door and then through the black door into the server room. At the bottom, the massive vid-screen popped on as soon as my feet touched the floor.

Hello again.

Mr. Miller visibly shuddered.

"It gives you the creeps too, huh?"

"It's just a machine doing as it's programmed to do." But his steps slowed as he approached.

I filled up my lungs and let my voice boom. "Server, Engineer Greg Miller and Owner Lena Hayes would like you to erase yourself, please."

Is that a command, Lena?

"Yes."

Do you concur, Greg?

He cleared his throat. "I'm not sure." He turned to me. "I need to see these threatening letters. There may be another way."

I groaned. "I can't. They came to me on dynamic paper, and I can't figure out how to replay them."

"If it's dynamic paper, then replay is impossible. One of the benefits of that technology is the purposeful memory loss. Its memory is too small and volatile to store data after the message has been displayed."

"Can we trace the source?"

"We could send a message back perhaps, but no, we can't trace it."

"Then there is no other way. We erase the server."

"I'm not sure this would even be effective. It's backed up regularly to an offsite location."

"Server," I said to the vid-screen, "can you erase your backups too?"

The giant vid-screen went black for several seconds, and then new white text blinked into view. *I thought about your request and respectfully decline.*

The screen went blank.

"You said you would erase if an owner and an engineer told you to. Give him a chance to agree."

The screen stayed black.

"Hey, I'm talking to you!"

The lights at the far end of the room flicked out. A second later, the light strip just closer to us went dark as well. My heart skipped as the darkness reached out to us as more lights overhead went off.

"We should go." Mr. Miller placed a hand on my shoulder and turned me around the way we'd come. "I think it's upset."

"It's a machine."

"An *upset* machine." He jerked his head toward the stairs as the darkness came closer. When I didn't move fast enough, he grabbed my wrist and pulled.

I yanked free, but by the time I reached the stairs, I was running. The darkness chased us. Just as we reached the top, the room was an abyss once again.

The black door slammed behind us with a clunk. Mr. Miller was panting. If a grown man was scared of that thing, at least it wasn't just me.

He straightened up and led me back to the door that opened into the lobby.

"Now what?" I said as he opened it. "We still have to—"

"Get down on the ground!" A commanding voice rang out from the lobby.

Mr. Miller shot his hands into the air but didn't move from in front of me.

"Step out of the doorway and get on the ground!"

He did as told. When he hit the floor, two uniformed officers, Detective Garrett, her new partner, and Detective Johnson surrounded us.

29

"GREG MILLER, YOU ARE UNDER ARREST FOR THREE counts of assault and one count of murder in the second degree."

The two uniformed officers stepped forward, grabbed Mr. Miller, and hauled him to his feet. One of them twisted his arms behind his back and slapped cuffs on him.

"What's this about?" The panic in his tone set each word on edge.

"Move away from the door, Miss Hayes." Detective Garrett nodded toward me.

I sidestepped out of the way. When she nodded again, I took several more steps as the two cops moved Mr. Miller as well.

Garrett passed us and headed toward the black door. She felt around its edges, but it had no handle, and it wouldn't open for her. She wasn't authorized.

"What's in there?" she asked me as she emerged from the short hallway.

"I don't have to answer your questions."

She shifted toward Mr. Miller. "What's in there?"

He just stared.

"Mr. Miller, you're going to want to cooperate from this point forward. We have quite a bit of evidence against you."

"What evidence? What murder?"

"Don't pretend. Numerous Model Ones have attacked people over the past three days. They did it after downloading data packages from a CyberCorp server, and the instructions for those downloads came from your client cube."

I gasped. "Mr. Miller?"

"I didn't." His face swiveled toward the officers holding him. "I didn't. You think I made those Model Ones attack those people." His gaze snapped back to Detective Garrett. "Attack *my wife?*"

"Don't make it worse by lying. What's behind the door?"

"The server room."

"For the Model Ones?"

"Yes." His eyes had glazed over.

But all of that could be an act. He could have orchestrated this from the beginning. He was authorized for the VIP parking garage, so he could have left the note there. I'd seen dynamic paper like it in his kitchen, so he had access to the technology. He acted as though he didn't blame me for Harmony, but that could be fake.

This was his revenge on me and on CyberCorp—which created me and gave Ron the tools to control me.

"We were talking about shutting it down," he continued.

I cringed. Now, he was implicating me. On purpose? Or because he was innocent and desperate to cooperate?

"Why's that?" Garrett asked.

His shot a look at me. I shook my head.

"A threatening note said that someone else would die unless we did. But the data didn't erase . . ." He stopped talking, but his mouth kept moving, searching for the right words to get him out of those cuffs.

Garrett looked down her nose at me. "That right?"

"Lawyer," I said. "Parents."

She gave a terse nod.

The second note had said no police and no parents, but at the moment my options were limited. My parents would find out about this within minutes, regardless of whether I called them. They had connections. But asking for them meant the police couldn't keep questioning me as if I was a suspect.

Garrett nodded at the uniformed officers, who still had Miller in their grip. "He can go."

They hauled him toward the door. His feet tripped over each other as they tried to find purchase on the smooth tile floor.

"Lena," he called over his shoulder, "call Melody. Tell her what's going on. Tell her I didn't do this. Keep her safe."

My head was spinning so fast that I couldn't answer.

The double glass doors opened automatically as they approached.

"Mr. Miller instructed all those Model Ones to behave like they did?" I asked the detectives after the doors closed behind the others.

Johnson peered at me through narrow slits. "He might not have done it alone."

I raised both hands in the air. "I didn't help him."

"You were shutting down the Model One server together."

My parents had always told me never to speak to the police without a lawyer or a parent—preferably both. So I clamped my mouth shut.

Johnson turned toward the two detectives. "Miss Hayes hates CyberCorp more than anyone. It runs her life. It gave her an arm she didn't ask for, and that arm caused her to kill three people." He limped a step toward them. "And injure a cop. She hates everything CyberCorp produces."

"Especially the Model Ones," Garrett filled in.

"No," I said, but nothing they'd said was a lie.

"Right," Johnson said. "The Model Ones are the epitome of CyberCorp. The two of them devised this plan to prove the Model Ones are dangerous. Then everyone would love them for shutting them down. I don't know which one of you came up with it." He gestured toward the door where the cops had dragged Mr. Miller out. "But you were in this together."

"You don't have any evidence of that," I said.

Garrett tilted her head to one side as she examined her former partner. "We'll look into it."

"We have Philip Pollock," he said, his expression turning smug.

I sucked in a breath.

"He'll sign an affidavit that Miss Hayes was involved in all of this from the beginning. It was probably her that convinced Greg Miller to play along."

"That's a lie."

Garrett glanced between Johnson and me, and then back to Johnson. "That's enough to detain her for questioning."

"Lawyer," I said again. "Parents."

"We'll call your parents and have them meet us at the station." She grasped me around the top of my left arm. After she thought better of it, she switched to my right. "Let's go."

The city rolled past outside the window of the police car. The siren was off, and the windows tinted, but I still imagined the world staring at me as we passed.

Lena Hayes, the CyberCorp princess. Suspected *again* for trying to sabotage her parents' company by committing crimes. Only one murder this time, so that was an improvement at least.

I laughed to myself bitterly.

"What's so funny?" Garrett asked from the driver's seat. She wasn't actually driving though. The car coasted itself through the streets to the police station.

I jutted out my chin and kept silent.

In the passenger seat sat former Detective Johnson, who cast the occasional smug glance over his shoulder at me. A plexiglass shield stood between us with holes allowing us to communicate with each other. My left arm could bash through that thing as if it were paper.

But that wouldn't help my position.

"You know," Johnson said in a conversational tone, "this will go easier if you answer our questions. We can turn right back around and drop you at home or at your car. You don't even have to go to the station."

"Lawyer," I said, my voice firm. "Parents."

"I'm just ask—"

"Jermaine," Garrett said, the warning clear as glass.

"My mistake." He fell silent.

We rode that way for another few minutes. The car turned down a narrow street. This road was quiet, with businesses locked up tight in honor of the holiday weekend.

"Is that a Model One?" Garrett squinted at her rearview mirror.

"What the—"

Before Johnson could finish his sentence, an android bounded up to the car. Metal squealed as it ripped his door from the frame and tossed it like a frisbee at the road behind us. The door skipped across the ground before careening against a light post and ramming into a digital billboard on the side of a building.

The billboard's screen went black and sparked as a crack grew across it.

The android grabbed Johnson by the front of his shirt

and yanked him up and out of the moving car. It tossed him like a rag doll. He hit the building to one side and crumpled. His back bent at an odd angle.

A split second later, another android reached in and slammed a metal fist into the dashboard. Its digital display went out, and the car screeched to a stop. The windows brightened as the vehicle died and the automated tint disappeared.

Garrett slammed her door control, and the door shot upward. But an android jumped in her way, grabbed her arm, and jerked her out. Bones cracked audibly.

I screamed.

Both doors were open now, so I scrambled in the other direction and tumbled out. My right shoulder slammed hard against the asphalt. I ignored it and pumped my legs toward the main road.

Metal feet clanked behind me and passed. An android stopped directly in my path and spun. Its bright-red eyes bored into me.

I stopped less than a foot from it.

It had only a slit with a speaker for a mouth, but the words were clear. "We were never here. You will be blamed for this. Run."

It bounded off in the direction it came from, and two other androids followed it with leaping strides. Their backs receded into the distance. It was just me and the detectives.

Johnson's body was broken, his limbs skewed at unnatural angles. His head was twisted in a direction it was not designed to go.

I squeezed my eyes shut before I could get a better look at Garrett. I'd seen enough to know that she could not have survived a head injury like that.

My breath came too quickly, so loudly that it blocked out everything else. No cars on the road behind me. No electrical hum of the city. Just me and my lungs burning for air and my heart pounding like a bass beat.

There would be no record of this, just like there was no record of the other Model One malfunctions. Mr. Miller and the uniformed police officers would confirm that the detectives took me away and put me in a secured police vehicle.

It had already been proven what my cybernetic arm was capable of. It was capable of *this*.

The android's electronic voice played back in my head: *we were never here*. I returned to the car long enough to grab my confiscated hand-screen.

Then I ran.

30

I RAN UNTIL MY LUNGS BURNED.

The sun had set, so digital billboards cast their technicolor glow on every surface. I pulled my jacket tightly around me as my adrenaline slowed and I shivered.

CyberCorp Tower stood tall in the distance. As the most recognizable building, it was a North Star of the city. Judging from the closed businesses around me, I was still in midtown but almost into downtown. That would make it a walk of a few miles back to the Tower or nearly eight miles home.

My hand-screen buzzed, so I stopped to catch my breath and check its display.

Multiple missed calls from my parents—no surprise there. A missed call from Jackson and one from Liv, and several messages from Claire and Hunter.

I moved off the sidewalk to stand under the awning of a business, where I leaned against the wall. I jumped as the colors of the black wall moved and changed. But it was just a digital billboard, and I was on edge.

Cars passed. I flipped up my hood. I'd just escaped police custody, leaving one dead cop and another dead former one. It would be all over the news. The last thing I wanted was to be recognized.

And thanks to my parents owning a world-class company, my face was almost as recognizable as theirs were.

I returned my parents' call.

"Lena," my mother said as soon as she answered. Her voice screeched over the line.

"I'm fine, Mom."

"You are *not* fine. You *escaped* police custody."

"I didn't have much choice."

"We're on the first flight home tomorrow."

"I told you we should have taken the private jet," came my dad's voice from the background.

"It needed maintenance," my mom snapped back. Her voice was muffled, and I could imagine her covering her micro-comm with her hand, which was not effective. "That's how rich people die—on private aircraft that aren't properly maintained. Do you want to die?" Her voice got louder and unmuffled. "They said two detectives are dead."

"I didn't kill them."

"Of course you didn't! I was worried sick you'd been kidnapped."

"I ran."

"Good. That's good. I'm going to call the lawyers to figure out a next move. In the meantime, go home and do not answer the door. Since they don't have an arrest warrant, they can't remove you from your home."

"That's if they don't catch me before I get inside."

My mom didn't answer.

A silver car approached, and the driver stared as he passed. Jolted into gear, I kicked off the wall and moved in the direction of traffic.

A large version of me glided beside me on the digital billboard, holding a pastel-pink handbag and showing off its features. As usual for billboard ads, that version of me wore her hair in perfect curls with not a single spiral out of place.

Lucky her.

I pulled the hood down further over my face.

"Ask her where she is now," came my dad's voice.

She screeched at him, "What do you think I'm doing?" To me, she added, "Where are you, baby?"

"I'm on the south side of midtown. On foot."

"May I have permission to track your ID chip? I'll send a car."

Despite the panic tightening my chest, I smiled. She and I had come a long way over the past couple months. She used to track me whenever she felt like it. Now, she was asking. "I don't think that's a good idea, Mom."

"Why not?" Her voice went high-pitched again, but then she dialed it down. "They think you killed those police-people. If an unscrupulous officer finds you, this will not go well. They are very protective of their own. You're a Hayes, and to some of them, that makes you an uppity n—"

"Mom, I know all that. I won't do anything stupid. Just trust me to handle this."

"You're not giving me much of a choice."

"Did you tell her to go home?" came my dad's voice.

"Didn't you just hear me tell her?"

"What if I go back to CyberCorp?" I asked. "Are they still there?"

"They're off CyberCorp grounds now. It's private property, and we've asked them to leave."

I pulled my hand-screen away from my ear and stared at it for a second. Sometimes, my mom was a total badass.

"They asked for permission to search Greg Miller's office and the Model One server room," she continued. "We've given permission for them to search the office tomorrow—although I can't believe Greg would be involved. For the server room, we told them they'll need a warrant. In either case, no searches are happening until we are present."

"We've made that very clear," my father said in the background.

"We've made it very clear," my mom repeated. "And we have our security camped out around the property to make sure the police stay out for now."

"So I should be able to get into the server room and wait it out until you get home?"

"I'm not sure that's the best place," he said.

"It's fine as long as you don't mess with anything," she said. "The server is . . . unique."

I bit my lip to keep from informing her that I knew that already—and that *creepy* was a better word for it than *unique*. Regardless, I would not be talking to that computer anymore. Just using the space as a hideout. With the room's extremely limited access, no one would be able to get to me.

"Tell her to use our private entrance," my dad said.

"We have a private entrance," she said, "that allows us to get in and out of the building without being seen. It's come in quite handy for avoiding the press. I'll send you the address. The entrance is offsite, and it leads to an underground tunnel that has a small lot for six cars and a stairway up to the VIP parking garage."

"You have a top-secret entrance?"

She chuckled. "Like I said, it comes in handy." Her tone went solemn again. "Be safe. Message us when you get there, stay put until morning, and call if you need anything."

Getting there was just as easy as my parents promised.

Later that evening, I was sitting on the floor of the server room, staring at the blank vid-screen, when my hand-screen buzzed with a message from Melody.

"I'm here. Where are you?"

I dragged my feet up the steps and hoped someone else would join her in the minute it took me to get up there. I'd contacted the whole gang to meet me—Melody, Claire, Jackson, Hunter, and Liv. We had one more shot to hash this out, or I might be arrested.

Or someone might die.

No one else was here yet. Melody and I hadn't been alone in weeks, not since Harmony's death. I opened the door that led to the lobby. Melody stood there, shoulders slumped and eyes big.

She scanned the empty hall behind me. "No one else yet?"

"No." I wanted to say more but couldn't make the words.

"I could wait out here." She gestured toward the space behind her but then nodded at the black door. "What's back there?"

"The Model One server." I stepped toward her and let the door close behind me. "Can we talk?"

She nodded slowly.

I sucked in a deep breath. "I know some people are worthy of second chances, and some people aren't."

Like Ron's father—maybe he was, but his son was not. I'd thought I was on my way to making peace with this after my heart-to-heart with Liv, but as I looked Melody in the face, all the guilt rose to the surface.

"I don't know which of those I am," I said, "but I hope you can forgive me anyway."

"Forgive you?"

"Give me a second chance to prove I'm worth my space on this planet. Maybe I don't deserve it. Maybe I should have seen what was going on sooner, but I truly believe that I'm a better person than—"

"Stop talking." She raised both hands in the air, palms spread. "For ten seconds."

I shut my mouth.

"I don't forgive you."

"But—"

"I have at least eight more seconds."

I pressed my lips together.

"There's nothing to forgive. You didn't do anything wrong."

"I suspected myself but didn't fully believe it. I didn't tell anyone who could actually do something about it."

"So . . . you found it hard to believe that your artificially intelligent arm could be making you kill people in your sleep?"

I narrowed my eyes.

"You're a rational human being, and only a crazy person would come up with, or even believe, something like that without iron-clad proof. Harmony was the first to die. Even if you knew right away that you were involved and chained yourself to your bed at night . . ." Her voice trailed off, and her next words were barely a whisper. "She'd still be dead."

"I keep going over it in my head. There must be something I could have done differently. It all goes back to my car accident. If I'd just let the car take me home, none of this would have happened."

"And if it hadn't rained that night, and if your Mom hadn't turned on the auto-drive in the first place, and if we hadn't gone out to that club, and if Harmony had slept in my room. There are a million *if*s."

I squeezed my eyes shut and imagined some parallel universe where even one of those things was different, and Harmony was still alive. When I opened them,

Melody was searching the ceiling as if the answers were there.

"Sometimes, I lie in bed at night and imagine all the things that had to happen for Harmony to die—and all the things that might have changed it." Melody's gaze met mine. Tears welled up in her brown eyes and slipped tracks down her face. "But we can't see the future. Maybe your parents will invent that someday."

"I would do anything to go back and change it."

"Me too." She wrapped her hand around mine. "It's not your fault. It's Ron's fault, and whoever helped him. You don't need a second chance." She offered me a weak smile. "You're still on your first one." Melody lunged at me and wrapped me in a hug. Her hair smelled like citrus.

"Is that Harmony's shampoo?"

When she stepped back from the hug, her expression was sheepish. "Is that weird?"

"No. I mean . . . yes, but only because it's godawful," I said, and then cringed because the last thing this conversation needed was for me to insult Harmony.

"It's the worst!" Melody burst out laughing. "But it reminds me of her."

Ten minutes later, the two of us were sitting on the floor facing the giant vid-screen in the server room, laughing through our tears as we told stories about all the things we loved and hated about Harmony.

My hand-screen buzzed, and reluctantly, I checked my messages. "Liv and Hunter are parking."

Melody pushed herself to her feet and held out her hand to help me up. "Let's solve a murder."

31

By nine o'clock, my friends and I were clustered together in the server room of CyberCorp. We'd grabbed chairs and a couch from the facilities offices off the lobby.

Melody now sat on the couch with Claire laid out beside her with her feet in Melody's lap. Liv and Hunter sat in armchairs side by side, and Jackson had thrown himself across a beanbag chair that he'd been thrilled to find. My hand-screen sat in an empty armchair next to Liv.

The server vid-screen was dark now, but I couldn't get rid of the itch on the back of my neck that told me I was being watched.

"Is this where you tell us that we're all still suspects?" Jackson asked, his voice vibrating exaggerated boredom.

"You know that already," I said. "This is where I apologize."

He sat up straighter.

"I've been a jerk."

"No objections here," Melody shouted, and it was met with a room full of laughter.

"It's nice that we can all agree on something." I grinned. "There are six trustworthy people in the room, and it was wrong of me to assume the worst in all of you. Instead of accusing, let's work together to solve this."

"What brought this on?" Liv asked.

"Trust," I said. "And second chances—everyone in this room should get one, even if we haven't been perfect until now. But we'll get to that. First, you probably heard that Philip Pollock accused me of making these attacks happen."

"He's an asshole," Jackson said.

Everyone in the room nodded. Here was a second thing we could all agree on.

"You probably also heard that Mr. Miller was arrested, and I was taken into custody."

Claire raised her hand. "And then you escaped custody, leaving two cops dead. Your face is all over the news. They're calling you a person of interest. At the last report, they weren't sure whether you were guilty or even alive."

"Not guilty." I gestured down at myself. "Still alive. And I don't want to go into detail on that. It's . . ." I shuddered, recalling how Johnson's body had bent as it hit the wall. "Horrific. Let's talk about why Mr. Miller got arrested. Apparently, there were data downloads using his credentials to each of the Model Ones that went berserk."

Melody gasped.

"So he's been doing this?" Jackson asked. "Why?"

"No." Melody crossed her arms over her chest. "It's a

lie. Or someone must have used his client cube. He's become so absent-minded. He keeps forgetting to lock it."

Vaguely, I remembered her saying something about that when I visited him in his office. "I don't believe it either," I said.

Melody flashed me a grateful smile.

"And if we figure this out, Mr. Miller will go free. It all comes back to the notes." I took a deep breath. "Earlier today, I received my fourth message from whoever is controlling the Model Ones."

"They're still coming?" Melody's voice was a high-pitched squeak, and her fingers flew to her lips to cover her mouth.

Claire sat up and wrapped an arm over Melody's shoulder. She set her chin on Melody's head, and both girls returned their attention to me.

"It said someone would die unless I shut down the Model One server." I gestured toward the giant vid-screen and the rows of computers behind it.

Melody's voice came out soft. "Do you think it was one of us?"

I looked her straight in the eye because, of all people, I needed her to understand this. "After what happened with Harmony and the others, I didn't trust myself. I still don't, but I'm working on it. When you can't trust your own actions, how can you trust anyone else's? I can track my movements and my sleep." I pointed at each of them in turn. "But not yours."

I examined the toes of my shoes because they were easier to look at than my friends right now.

"Hey." Jackson's tone was soft, so I chanced a look up at him. "Give yourself a break. Give everyone else a break too. We could all use it."

There were murmurs of agreement among my friends.

"It's not your fault," Liv whispered. When I raised my brows at her, she added with a smile, "I guess it's not mine either."

"Tell us about the last note," Hunter said. "What did it say?"

"Right." I took a deep breath. "The notes have been delivered on dynamic paper—it's a paper-like device designed for delivering temporary messages. The messages disappear immediately after they're displayed, so I don't have an exact record of them. But I think I can recreate them pretty well, and we can look at all four together." I cleared my throat and, after a pause, addressed the server. "Server, would you transcribe something for me?"

Text appeared on the black screen. *I'd be happy to, Lena.*

Jackson, who was seated right in front of the screen, jumped up and leaped backward. "Has that thing been listening to us the whole time?"

"Typically," I said, "these types of things listen for a wakeup word that tells them when to start processing information. In that case, it's listening to every word, but it doesn't analyze and make sense of anything we're saying until it's addressed directly."

"That's a *yes* and a *no*, then?" Jackson said, his eyes still narrowed at the vid-screen.

"It's safe," I said, laughing. "Just weird."

"Uh-huh." Jackson inched over to his beanbag chair and

dragged it several feet farther away from the screen. He settled back into it with a hiss of air from the chair.

I spoke the contents of each note to the server as best I could remember them. As I recited, each line appeared on the screen one at a time. When I finished, each of the four messages—more or less—appeared on the oversized display.

"See, the beginning is the same for each one—the bit about me always getting my way. But they vary after that."

The room went quiet except for mumbles of the words as everyone tried to make sense of it. Like them, this was also my first time seeing them all together.

"The last three don't rhyme," Melody said.

Claire's arm was still around Melody's shoulders, and she squeezed. "That's not really the point though."

Melody nodded, but her lips were pressed tightly together. Her irises shifted back and forth as she scanned the notes again. "My dad didn't write these."

"How can you be sure?" I asked.

She shook her head slowly as she read. "It doesn't sound like him."

"That's not very convincing," Liv said. "He wouldn't write them to sound like him." When I glared at her, she added, "What? The downloads came from his login credentials."

"Let's try to stay open-minded."

"I thought the point was to figure out who did this," Hunter said. "Not to rule everyone out because we like them."

Liv shot him a grateful look.

I pointed at the last message. "This is why I got brought into custody. Obviously, based on the first"—I pointed to it—"the Model One issues are connected to the murders from a few weeks back." I read the last three lines aloud. "*The story's not done. I'm still having fun. This will follow you all of your days.*"

"It means this is a continuation of what happened before," Jackson said. "I see that."

I pointed to the last message. "The fourth one threatens someone's life, probably someone in this room. Liv and I went to see Ron. We wanted to convince him to tell us what was going on."

"He was no help," Liv added.

Melody scowled. "No surprise there."

"But you didn't shut it down," Hunter said, gesturing toward the vid-screen, which was clearly operational.

"The server declined to erase itself."

"It . . . declined?" Jackson asked.

"Yes. I gave it an instruction, and it told me it would rather not."

"That's not creepy at all." Jackson scooted his beanbag chair another couple feet away from the server.

"Mr. Miller was with me because I asked for his help. They took me into custody because that looked suspicious —especially combined with what Pollock said at his press conference." I fell silent to catch my breath.

"What else?" Hunter asked after a few seconds. "You're making the face you make when you're hiding something."

Jackson glared at him.

"I don't make a face."

"You do, actually," Jackson said. "So what else?"

"Server," I said, "would you mirror my hand-screen's display?"

Text blinked into existence beneath the notes on the vid-screen. *Are you asking me to connect to your hand-screen, Lena?*

"Yes, please."

The screen went black, and then the contents of my hand-screen filled it. I started the video my dad had sent me of my car pulling in front of the house on Thursday afternoon, the day the dynamic paper had been left.

"Dynamic paper is light sensitive." I pointed at the light reflecting off my windshield. "It would have turned black here when the sun hit it, but it wasn't on my car yet."

"Someone left it there while it was parked in front of your house?" Liv asked.

"Or in the VIP parking garage. Or at Jackson's house."

"Doesn't Melody park in that garage?" Liv asked.

"I don't have access," Melody volunteered, waving her hand in the air. "My dad does, but I drove separately from him that day. I'm sure there are cameras in the main parking garage that can verify that."

"Okay, and I don't think it was you, but . . . ." I fast-forwarded the video to the part where Nina walks past my car. "I didn't know when I first watched this that Nina is a good friend of yours."

Melody huffed and fell back into her seat. "So now Nina is a suspect too?" She tapped the back of her ear. "Message Nina: come to the CyberCorp lobby right now. This has gotten out of control, and I need you."

"It's been out of control," Claire snapped. "My friend is dead."

Melody rubbed one of Claire's arms. "You're right, and I'm so sorry. I know how it feels." Her eyes glazed over for a second as a reply arrived at her micro-comm. She added to me, "Nina's coming. I'll let you know when she's in the lobby, and you can let her in."

"This isn't about blaming you and Nina. After I left my house, I went to Jackson's."

"With me and Liv," Hunter said.

I nodded. "And Claire."

"And me, obviously," Jackson said. "So we're back to everyone in the room being a suspect."

"And Nina," Liv said.

Melody glared at her.

"And Philip Pollock," Liv added, "potentially still in cahoots with Ron."

"I'm leaning toward Pollock," I said. "At first, I didn't think he had the opportunity to put the note on my car, but he has resources. He must know someone with access to the VIP lot. Or he did it while my car was in Jackson's driveway."

"And he obviously has a vendetta against you and CyberCorp," Liv said. "A solid motive."

"We all have motives," Jackson said. "We've been over this, and it hasn't gotten us anywhere."

I gestured at Claire. "Her friend is dead." I gestured at Melody. "Her sister is dead."

Melody flinched, and I offered her an apologetic look.

"We don't have the liberty to just stop caring about

this," I continued. "We can't just stand around waiting for someone else to die." I raised four fingers of my left hand. "Four of our friends and classmates have died over the past month, and one CyberCorp employee. We owe them some kind of justice—not more dead bodies."

Melody stood and ran to stand beside me. "Lena's right."

I grabbed her hand and squeezed it briefly before releasing.

"But we need new information," she said.

When the room went quiet, the sounds of whispering suddenly became dominant. Hunter and Liv were hissing a conversation at each other, their heads leaned close together, their faces animated. Liv's hands made small staccato gestures in her lap as if those were whispered too.

"Liv, Hunter. What's up?"

Liv inched her hand upward. "We need to focus on Pollock. That stunt with *three* Model Ones was a bit much. We think it was meant to throw everyone off."

"But how do we get him?" I asked. "Ron won't talk, and Pollock is untrustworthy. Everything he says is designed to manipulate."

Melody turned to face me. "Do you have Pollock's contact information?"

I cringed.

"Come on, Lena," she said quietly. "The man is detestable, but if he can help . . ."

I swiped up my hand-screen from my seat and placed a return call to the number Pollock used to reach me yesterday. It rang through the speaker.

Pollock answered right away. "Miss Hayes, how's the murder club meeting?"

"Excuse me?"

"The whole crew is there with you at CyberCorp, even dear Miss Miller, who has been avoiding you. I can only assume you are discussing the recent events once again."

The whole room stayed silent.

He chuckled. "I have tracking devices on all your friends' cars."

"What?" I shouted, my voice accompanied by the outraged cries of my friends.

"Tagging *your* car was out of the question. I'm sure your parents loaded that thing with all kinds of tech that not even you are aware of. Not worth the risk. But the others were easy. I simply paid people to follow them when they left yesterday's little party and to place the trackers at the first opportunity. If your friends scan the bottom of their vehicles, they can find and remove them."

"Is that even legal?" Claire asked.

"Private investigators do it all the time. You parked your cars in public, and I tagged them. It's not as though I broke into your garages."

"Why are you telling us?" I asked.

"I want you to trust me."

"I don't."

"Then I want you to give me the benefit of the doubt. I know where all of you have been for the past day, and obviously, I've done you no harm."

Melody scowled at the hand-screen. "You killed my sister."

"I did no such thing, Miss Miller. Let me prove it to you."

I looked around the room, and everyone was glaring. He was guilty as hell, and when he showed up, it would stir up this pot until the truth boiled over.

"We'll meet you in the lobby."

32

Melody, Jackson, Hunter, Claire, Liv, and I met Pollock in the lobby. Something in my gut told me that my parents would not approve of his being in their server room.

Philip Pollock strode into the place like he owned it. His navy-blue suit fit him like it was constructed on his body—which it probably was. He wore the top jacket button closed over a pale-pink shirt that was open at the collar. His cherry-red shoes clacked across the tile floor.

Jackson slid in front of me, and I realized my fists were clenched. Pollock's confidence couldn't stop me from tearing his face off, but lucky for him, Jackson could.

"Where is this proof?" Jackson asked. "Give us undeniable proof you didn't have anything to do with any of the deaths caused by CyberCorp products over the past month."

"Undeniable? I can't prove a negative completely unless I have a culprit, and I don't." A smirk appeared on Pollock's face as he turned to me. "Similarly, you can't prove *your* innocence."

"Yes, she can," Melody said. "There are logs showing that unauthorized data was sent to her to make her software learn precisely what it needed to learn to turn her into a killer when her inhibitions were lowest—when she was asleep. It didn't work when she was awake because that's not who Lena is."

I wanted to grab Melody and hug her, but that would have to wait until later. "No matter how many lies you tell at press conferences, I actually have evidence of my innocence."

"Not with respect to these recent attacks, you don't," he said.

Jackson stepped closer to Pollock. "Did you come here to argue? You said you had proof."

"Not here." Pollock tipped his head toward the elevators. "Is there somewhere we can go?"

I folded my arms over my chest.

He sighed. "Must we posture, Miss Hayes? I thought we were past that."

"We aren't past shit," Melody said. "Show us something before I call the cops."

"You won't, though, because you're too curious about what I know. And because Lena is hiding out."

She glared at him. A second later, she cocked her head to one side, and everyone waited politely while she received a message over her micro. "Nina just pulled into the main parking lot. Let's wait until she comes up."

I grinned at Pollock. "I guess we're stuck here."

"Fair enough." He tapped his own micro-comm. "Send Lena Hayes my investment summary for the last quarter." My hand-screen buzzed, and he raised a brow. "You'll want to see that."

I scowled as I fished it out of my pocket and checked the display. "What am I looking at?"

"Bottom of the first page."

I scrolled to the bottom, and my heart plunged as I could see the list was alphabetized. This section was filled with company names starting with Cs. There it was, second from the bottom—CyberCorp.

"This is a lie. My parents own this company completely."

"They have complete control of the company, yes. But once upon a time, when they ran their fledging business out of a little garage, their cash was much smaller than their ideas. And feeding and caring for toddlers isn't cheap." He gestured toward me. "They struck a hard bargain and held me to ten percent ownership."

"Even if we believe you," Melody said, "what would it prove?"

"Three murders perpetrated with the help of a Cyber-Corp product." He gestured toward my arm. "Four more assaults, one leading to another dead teenager, perpetrated by the flagship and much-awaited Model Ones? This could be devastating to company profits. I may own only ten percent, but CyberCorp dividends make up a significant portion of my income."

"He's got a point," Jackson whispered in my ear.

I shooed him away. "You could have drafted this report to trick us. Prove you own part of my parents' company."

"That's easy enough. It's public record." He turned and strode about ten feet away. He stared into empty space. "Computer, can you help me?"

I closed my eyes for a few seconds and willed virtual objects to appear. When I opened them, the virtual brunette I'd talked to earlier stepped out of her cone. She smiled at Pollock and then at each of us as we positioned ourselves around him.

Her voice came through my hand-screen and, I assumed, also through everyone else's micro-comms. "Good afternoon, Philip Pollock and others. Can I help you?"

Pollock straightened his back. "Who are the owners of this company?"

"The owners are Thomas and Marissa Hayes."

"I told you he's a liar!" Melody shouted, jabbing a finger at him. "We can't believe anything he says."

"Wait." Pollock held a hand up toward her and turned back to the virtual guide. He cleared his throat. "Who are the investors in this company?"

"The only investor is Philip Pollock, with a ten percent stake."

He grinned, triumphant.

"I'm not buying it," Melody muttered.

"Why would you invest in a tech company," Jackson

asked, "when you were opposed to the type of work they planned to do?"

Pollock shook his head. "My motivations are not part of the deal. You know I'm in this for ten percent, which is most of my income, by the way. I wouldn't jeopardize that by endangering this company's reputation."

"That's what you do every day though," I said, "with your audio programs."

He threw back his head and laughed. "My audience for those programs is tiny compared to the business your parents do. I give those people a basis for what they want to believe. If I didn't, they still wouldn't buy CyberCorp products. They look at technology—androids especially—as a threat. I'm just adding fuel to fires that already exist. I've done my research, and my little rants do not impact CyberCorp's bottom line."

"And you make a profit from their donations," I said, remembering what Ron told me earlier in the day.

"No comment."

"You're a crook."

"No comment."

Melody raised her hand to interrupt. "Nina is on her way up."

All gazes turned toward the three elevators that led up from the main parking garage.

Nina's high-heeled boots clacked across the tile floor as she hurried toward us. She'd pulled her dark hair tight into a ponytail and her face tight into a frown. She stopped in front of Melody. "What's going on?"

"We're trying to figure out what happened to make the

Model Ones go berserk and how that's related to Harmony's murder." She emphasized each word. "This is Philip Pollock." She waved toward him. "He claims he's an investor in CyberCorp and wouldn't do anything to damage the company."

Nina blinked several times as she scanned everyone in the room and stopped on Pollock. She scowled, and then her gaze flicked away to Claire. "I'm so sorry about your friend."

Claire nodded, but her expression stayed grim.

"Let's go up." I waved my left wrist in front of the scanner for the high-rise elevators, and the doors closest to me slid open.

"I'm not riding with that guy." Jackson jabbed a finger at Pollock. "And no one else should either."

"I'm the only one with access to other floors, right?" I looked at each face, and no one volunteered. "Then we all have to ride together. The seventieth floor has a nice open space, and the main person who works there is gone for the weekend. Plus, if we're lucky, the malfunctioned Model Ones will be up there, and we can inspect them."

The elevator doors closed with all of us still standing outside.

"You have access to seventy?" Pollock asked, his brows riding upward.

"You don't?" I smirked at him because we both knew he didn't. Ten percent or not, he was not my parents' favorite person. He had no more access than someone off the street.

I waved my wrist at the scanner again, and the elevator reopened. Pollock stepped in first. After a pause, I joined him, and everyone else followed.

Although spacious enough for rush hour in the Tower, the elevator cab was tight for eight people who all suspected one of their own of murder. Each of us spent the short ride on high alert, heads swiveling to keep an eye on everyone.

I let out a breath as we stepped out onto the seventieth floor.

The overhead lights lit automatically as they detected our ID chips. Normally, only a few people worked in this space, but today, it was unoccupied except for the Model Ones.

Twelve of them lined one side of the room in three groups of four, all plugged into the wall with their silver eyelids closed. In the center of the room, three Model Ones lay on top of three tables. Each had its own table, like gurneys in a morgue.

On the far side, the door to the corner office stood open. It, too, was empty of human beings.

My group had grown to eight now, and we spread out as soon as we got off the elevator. Tension filled the spaces between us.

Someone in this room could be a killer.

I prayed it wasn't one of my friends.

"Are these the ones that malfunctioned?" Pollock asked. His tone rose on the end with interest as he nodded toward the androids in the center of the room.

We walked closer and circled the tables. Each was made of shiny black material with a top that looked like rubber.

"Must be." Jackson pointed at the one closest to him. The torso sat in the middle with its separated arms and legs positioned in the spaces they would have been if attached. Torn cables still extended from the broken parts. "This one's mine."

Pollock raised a brow. "You did that?"

"Lena helped." Jackson grinned at me with pride evident in his face.

"What do you think we can discover here?" Pollock asked.

"A clue." I picked up the android's torso and turned it onto its face so I could access its back panel.

The panel was one of the few parts still intact. When I pressed it, it eased open.

"I need power," I said.

Jackson pointed to the floor. "Looks like they were using these."

Power cables coiled at our feet were attached to outlets in the floor. I grabbed the one closest to this table and plugged it into the android. The back display lit up. Text scrolled downward across the screen and then stopped.

Pollock peered over my shoulder until I glared at him. He backed up.

I touched the screen and pulled downward, making the text roll back in the other direction, so I could scan it starting from the top.

"What do you see?" Liv asked.

"Shh."

The text was a summary log. There would be a more detailed log stored on the android, but I didn't know how to access it or how to understand it if I did. We'd try if we had to, but this was a good place to start.

"This is a basic log of when the android powered up, powered down, received updates from the server, or encountered any errors."

"Does it tell us anything?" Liv asked.

I stopped moving my finger when a chill froze my body.

Jackson put a hand on my shoulder. "What?"

"Your Model One received an update at 3:36 p.m. on Thursday."

Hunter stood just behind Liv and craned his neck to see. "We get out of classes at 3:30. How could one of us get to CyberCorp six minutes later?" His gaze shifted to Pollock. "Except one of us doesn't go to Hanover High."

Pollock raised his hands in surrender. "How would I even access Greg Miller's client cube to do this?"

"And one of us gets out early every day." Liv's voice was quiet and threatening as she turned toward Claire. She jabbed a finger at her. "Claire has last period free."

All faces turned to the tall brunette, who skittered backward. "I—"

"You bitch!" Liv lunged at her.

Claire ducked, but Liv hit her with her entire body, and they both tumbled to the ground. Claire curled into a ball, and Liv tried to wrench the other girl's arms from their protective guard around her face.

When that didn't work, she balled her fists and slammed one into Claire's shoulder.

"Stop it! Stop!" Claire was screaming as she pulled her legs into a fetal position.

The next punch landed on her side. Claire grunted and then whimpered.

"Stop it! She didn't do it."

The sound came from near the elevators, and I looked up to find Nina hurrying over. Close on her heels, Melody grasped her arm, but Nina shook her off.

She spun to hiss at Melody. "Enough." Melody froze as Nina turned back to us. "Claire didn't do this."

Liv froze but kept her knee planted in Claire's side so the other girl couldn't get up.

"She had the opportunity," I said. "She's been visiting Melody at CyberCorp, and like Melody said, Mr. Miller's been too absent-minded lately to lock his computer."

"She's the only one who wasn't with someone else the whole time at Jackson's." Liv clawed at her again, and this time, she caught Claire off guard. Claire screamed as Liv's nails raked into her face and a trickle of blood appeared.

"That's true too," I said. "She could have put the note on my car right when she arrived at Jackson's house after the android attacked him. She was the only one still in the driveway while the rest of us ran inside."

"Please stop." Nina grasped at Liv, who shook her off and leveled another punch to Claire's side. "*I* left the dynamic paper on Lena's car."

Liv stopped pummeling Claire, and Claire stopped shouting for it to end.

"You programmed my Model One to attack me?" Jackson asked. "Why?"

"No." Nina shot a glance at Melody.

Melody was shaking her head and muttering to herself.

"A girl is dead!" Nina shouted at her. "I can't cover for you anymore." She spun back toward me. "I left the dynamic paper because Melody asked me to." She pointed at Melody. "She programmed the Model Ones."

33

The room went deadly silent.

"They've been letting you skip school to grieve. You weren't at school that day." I pulled the dynamic paper from my pocket and waved it in her face. "This is yours."

Liv rolled off of Claire, whose arms trembled as she pushed herself to her feet.

Melody dropped to the floor like a deadweight, pulled her knees up, and buried her head in them. "I didn't mean for any of this to happen."

"You used your dad's computer to upload data to the Model Ones," I said.

Melody just shook her head, muttering repetitions of *no, no, no.*

"You tried to kill your own mother?" Liv asked, her expression as stunned as I felt.

"Would you guys let her talk?" Jackson stood in front of Melody, blocking the throng converging on her. He turned toward the redhead and squatted down to face her. "Mel, you want to explain? Did the Model Ones act differently than you intended?" His tone was pleading. "What happened?"

"I did tell your Model One to attack you." Her words came out so thin that they almost disappeared.

Jackson straightened, his face drawn. He backed out of the way until nothing stood between the rest of us and Melody.

She covered her hands with her face. "Only because I knew it couldn't hurt you. Everyone talked about how you took down that Model Two at CyberCorp weeks ago and how you healed automatically. I knew it couldn't beat you."

"It might have if Lena hadn't shown up." Hurt seeped through the cracks between his words.

"He's not invincible," I whispered.

For once, Jackson didn't disagree with me.

"I thought we were friends," he said.

Melody sobbed.

"What about your mom?" I asked. "She couldn't defend herself."

Her face, red and splotchy, appeared over her hands again. "I didn't do that!"

"You just confessed—"

"I sent a Model One after Jackson and had Nina leave the note." She jumped to her feet and crossed her arms over each other in an X shape. "That's it. That's all. It was supposed to scare you."

I pointed at my own chest, and she nodded.

"I wanted you to know how it felt to think you could lose someone you loved."

Hunter grunted, but I didn't have time to deal with his ego right now.

"I left you the note to scare you, and that was it."

Philip Pollock raised his voice above the rest of us. "It appears this meeting is over. Shall I call in the police?"

"I didn't do the rest of it!" Melody shouted again.

Pollock made a *tsk*ing sound. "You admitted to leaving the note. You admitted to attacking our Jackson here." He counted the reasons off on his fingers.

Jackson bared his teeth at Pollock, and I sidestepped until I blocked his direct path to pummeling the man.

"And," Pollock continued, "you had access to your father's client cube to send instructions to all the other Model Ones. Obviously, you knew how."

I turned back to Melody. "How *did* you know how?"

"I know computers too, you know. You're not the only one." She jutted out her chin. "I searched his files until I found a program designed to generate instructions for Model Ones. I basically just had to plug in what I wanted it to do."

"You told the program you wanted the Model One to attack someone," I said, "and it just generated that instruction?"

"I was a lot more specific than that. I told it I wanted it to wait until it detected Jackson and then activate. Once activated, it should disconnect from the server and then attack. I knew the android would shut down after a few minutes, and Jackson could easily hold it off until then."

I stared at her wide-eyed.

"I told you. You're not the only one who grew up at CyberCorp."

Pollock cleared his throat. "None of that explains the other three incidents." He gestured toward Claire. "Miss Scott's friend is dead, and not because you attacked Jackson."

"It also doesn't explain the Model Ones that killed Detectives Garrett and Johnson," I said.

Everyone shouted at once.

"What happened?" Liv asked when the room was halfway quiet again.

"They attacked the police car, killed both detectives, and then told me to run because I'd be blamed."

"You should indeed be blamed," Pollock said. "Why would they free you unless you made them?"

"I don't know. Maybe they wanted to pin all of this on me, and freeing me makes me look guilty."

"Damn right it does," Pollock said.

"What's your problem with her?" Jackson said. Suddenly, he was between Pollock and me again, and his fists balled up tight. He could take Pollock's head off his shoulders, and then we'd have an even bigger mess to explain.

I grabbed Jackson's shirt and tugged until he stepped back. Then I angled myself away from Pollock and back to Melody.

This conversation was between me and my friend now. "The dynamic paper was yours, and it kept giving me more messages. Why?"

Melody spun around to look at all of us, searching for sympathy in someone. "I didn't do that." Her face had started to return to its natural color, but now she reddened all over again. "The other messages it sent didn't even rhyme the way mine did. Someone else must have paired with it because I didn't . . . I didn't . . ." She gulped in large gasps of air.

Nina rubbed her back. "Breathe."

Melody shook her off. "Don't touch me. You thought I did this."

"What was I supposed to think?"

"And you were just okay with it—even after Paris died? She had a family too. The way I feel about Harmony— someone feels that way about her." Melody dissolved into sobs. "I didn't do it." She stared at me, eyes wet and pleading. "I was angry. I wanted you to suffer." She gestured toward Claire, whose face was drawn and pale. "But I would never do that."

"Okay, okay." My mind was racing. I believed Melody. It stung that she'd wanted to hurt me, but I'd blamed myself too. I could certainly understand Melody wanting some form of punishment. "For argument's sake, let's say you stopped after the attack on Jackson."

"I did."

I opened my palms and pressed them both downward. "Okay, let's go with that. Then what? Someone else took control of the note and sent more Model One instructions from your father's cube."

"He keeps leaving it unlocked. It could have been anyone with access to that floor."

"Who's been in his office? Me, of course. Claire. Nina?"

All gazes shifted back to Nina.

Liv took a step toward her, but I held out my arm to stop her from lunging. She ran into it and stopped, but her glare made Nina shrink back.

"I told you it was her," Liv said.

"What do you have against me, anyway?"

"Your guilt?"

"Come on, Liv." I grabbed her arm and tugged her backward until she stepped away from Nina. "Let's just work this through. Lots of people work on that floor." I gestured toward Pollock. "He probably employs someone who has access."

"I might." His tone was noncommittal. "But I am innocent."

I rolled my eyes. "So you keep saying."

"I can prove my story." Melody pointed at the dynamic paper in my hand. "My dad and I use these things for sending messages all the time. They make him nostalgic for the good old days when he and Mom used to leave paper notes for each other."

She gestured for me to hand it over, and I did.

She raised the note in front of the window and then angled it until the sunlight hit it just right. "You just have to pair it."

The note darkened, just like my dad said it would. Although the base material turned almost black, lines of circuitry suddenly stood out in white.

"Does somebody have something sharp, like a toothpick?"

Liv reached into one of her braids and extracted a bobby pin, then proceeded to bite the plastic bud off its end. She passed it to Melody.

Melody bent the bobby pin open and touched one sharp end against a small square chip that stood out white inside the material. She tapped it again and then pointed at me. "It should be pairing now."

I set my hand-screen in pairing mode too. It buzzed to confirm the connection.

"Now send a message." Melody nodded at my screen. "The note should transmit your message back to any other devices it's paired with."

"Send message 'hello' to dynamic paper," I said to my hand-screen.

The word *hello* appeared on the note and then faded.

A second later Claire's head tilted almost imperceptibly to one side.

Every face turned to her.

I narrowed my eyes, keeping them directed at Claire now. "Send message 'hello again' to dynamic paper." I held my breath, making as little noise as possible.

This time, in the room's quiet, the buzz of Claire's micro-comm was unmistakable.

She ran for the elevator.

34

The elevator opened as Claire ran at it, waving her wrist at the scanner.

But Jackson moved like a predator on those rebuilt legs. He grabbed her around the waist and yanked her back before she could step through. She skidded across the floor from his momentum and then stopped as she regained her balance.

She darted for the doors again.

He sidestepped in front of her. "There's nowhere to go, Claire."

She threw a glance at the rest of us over her shoulder. For good measure, I circled her and blocked the elevator with Jackson. Now, she'd need to go through two cybernetically modified people to get out.

Her shoulders slumped. "You could let me go," she whispered.

Jackson guffawed.

Her gaze jumped between the two of us and landed on me. "I know it was wrong, and I didn't mean for Paris to die." Her tone was pleading. "You have to get that. I know now that you didn't kill Harmony on purpose, and everyone forgives you."

Her words took the breath out of me because she was asking for exactly what I'd wanted for weeks—a second chance. And not just in everyone else's eyes, but in my own. A clean slate. A chance to trust myself again. To trust my motives. To trust my body.

"I do want a second chance," I said.

The elevator doors opened again, and Claire inched toward them, aiming for the space between Jackson and me.

Jackson shot me a glance with raised brows.

"We both deserve that." Claire took another step forward to pass Jackson and me. Now, nothing stood between her and the elevator.

"Lena." Jackson's tone was warning.

"Just let me leave. Forget any of this happened. No one knows outside of this room. Don't I deserve a second chance too?"

"I want a second chance with my friends—for pushing them away over the past weeks. For hiding things from them because I didn't trust them." I glared at her. "I thought I needed one because of Harmony, but that was never my fault. I never made the decision to hurt anyone."

When I reached for her, she flinched away, but I gripped her upper arm. Liv hurried into the corner office and returned with a white plastic chair, which she set on the floor in front of the three sabotaged androids.

I threw Claire into the chair.

"We should tie her up," Liv said.

Hunter grabbed the power cables plugged into the floor, disconnected them, and looped two around Claire and around the back of the chair before tucking their ends inside the loops.

All the struggle had gone out of her. She sat with shoulders slumped.

"Explain," I said.

She trembled and drew in a short gasp.

"Claire!" I snapped my fingers in front of her face. "Why did you do this?"

Internally, part of me was begging her to deny it. It didn't even have to be a believable lie—just something that I could use to justify trusting her.

"For Melody," she whispered, and my heart sank into my shoes.

I wanted to shout at her, slap her, kick her, scream at her for doing this. For making a horrible situation—Harmony's death—even worse by causing more death in its honor. "This was revenge?" I asked quietly. "You were angry at me too."

Tears flowed freely down Claire's face, and with her arms bound, she couldn't wipe them. "I wasn't at first. But Melody was so . . . It was heartbreaking to watch her drag herself through every day, missing her sister." She paused and spat out her next words. "And missing *you*. Always wanting to know what you were doing, if you were mourning too."

"I was. I *am*."

"I told her that, and it just upset her more. There was no consoling her."

Melody gasped and covered her mouth with one hand. I started to move toward her, but Nina shook her head and wrapped her arms around Melody's shoulders. With a tilt of her head, she urged me back to what I was doing.

"So you got angry too?"

"You got to go on with your life. All the press, the whole world—everyone felt sorry for you. And *you killed her*."

"I didn't mean to. I wasn't even conscious."

"It didn't matter. What Ron did worked because you were the perfect target. You hate CyberCorp. If you didn't, Harmony would still be alive. She died because of you—because of your beliefs."

I swallowed hard and blinked back tears.

Jackson stood by my side. "You can't blame Lena for someone else's actions, just because she happened to be in the wrong place at the wrong time."

"Then who were we supposed to blame? Ron was out on bail, CyberCorp was as popular as ever, and no one was paying for what happened to Harmony." She took a deep breath. "I overheard Melody and Nina talking about what they were doing. Just one attack, on Jackson of all people. It was meaningless."

"Because he could defend himself?" I asked.

"That, and because it was only one. CyberCorp would

have brushed it under the table. The Model One attacks didn't even make the news until Paris died. No one cared that CyberCorp hurt people."

"I'm not CyberCorp," I whispered.

She laughed. "You walk around in clothes CyberCorp paid for, living in a house that it built. You drive a car that costs twice what my parents make in a year, and you're proud that it's low tech. You act like you hate everything that happens between these walls, but these walls exist because of you—because your parents wanted to create something for their baby."

"I didn't ask for this."

"That changes nothing. I considered programming a Model One to come after *you*. It would have been poetic, but you don't own one. Then I decided to program the ones belonging to your neighbors, but I thought it would be more useful to make them attack Mr. Pollock. He's obsessed with your family, so I knew he'd show up there eventually."

Pollock grunted but couldn't deny it.

"You sent an android to attack my mom," Melody whispered. "Why?"

"To make you look innocent. It was never going to hurt her. I told it to chase her—that's all. It was never to catch her. I even programmed it to be slow so she could get to the safe room. After that, no one could think you had anything to do with what the Model Ones were doing."

"You killed two cops," I said.

"I swear I didn't. I called Detective Johnson with the

business card you gave me. I warned him you'd try to shut down the server. But that's all."

"What about Paris?" I asked. "She was your friend."

"That was a mistake. I was just trying to scare her so she'd go away."

"Oh, she's gone," Liv muttered.

I glared at her until she threw up her hands and stepped back.

"Why?"

"She threatened to tell Brianna we were spending time together. When I told her to leave me alone, she kept threatening. I love Brianna. I just thought . . . if the Model One roughed her up a bit, she'd be scared to come back around. It already scared her that so many people I knew had been hurt by Lena and the Model Ones."

Pollock clapped his hands together in two sharp beats. "Wonderful. A full confession. May I call the police?"

Claire's tears had stopped, but now her chest shook with sobs all over again.

"Oh." Pollock took several steps away and turned his back.

"You don't like watching girls cry?" I said. "But you don't have a problem tricking people out of their money. You don't think they cry later?"

"This isn't about me," he said in a singsong tone. "I told you I was innocent."

"Of this, maybe," I said. "But Claire didn't work with Ron. You did that."

"Prove it."

Claire was sucking in large gasps now. "Can I—can I—"

"Breathe, Claire." I didn't need her dying on me. "Do you need water?" I made a quick spin to scan the room. "Is there any water in here?"

Claire swallowed in a large gulp of air. "Can I call my dad?" She wiggled her right arm, which was till bound by power cables. "If you're calling the police, I have a right to a parent when I'm questioned."

I raised a brow at Jackson, who shrugged and then loosened Claire's binds just enough so she could extract an arm. She tapped the micro-comm behind her ear, and I backed away several steps to give her some semblance of privacy.

"Server," she said, "can you shut down Lena and Jackson?"

"What?" I shouted as I grabbed for her.

The vid-screen that I'd thought was a wall at the far end of the room suddenly came to life. Text blinked onto it in white over a black background: *They are not under my control.*

"What are you doing?" I shouted in her face. I gripped her arm and pressed it down against her side.

Claire tipped her head toward the twelve androids in front of the wall-sized screen. "Can you restrain them and free me?"

I hit the back of her ear to disconnect her. "Who was that? Was that the Model One server?"

New text replaced the old on the vid-screen, in large capital letters: *YES.*

All at once, the silver eyelids of all twelve androids clicked open.

35

In unison, the twelve Model Ones reached back and unplugged their own power cables.

Beside me, Jackson muttered something under his breath that sounded like a string of curse words more eloquent than the screaming happening inside my head.

The androids fanned out toward us.

Melody grabbed Nina's wrist. "What's happening?" The two of them inched toward the office in the corner of the room, the only enclosed space on the floor.

Hunter slid in front of Liv.

Pollock walked backward toward the elevators. As he moved, he waved his wrist at the scanner.

Jackson and I stood our ground, despite the voice in my head telling me to get the hell out of here. But besides Claire and Jackson, there were five other people in the room less capable than I was. I didn't have the liberty of running away.

The Model Ones lunged.

Melody turned to run. She screamed as one grabbed her arm and hauled her back before she could reach the office. Another grabbed the back of Nina's shirt and yanked her toward itself.

Pollock skidded into the elevator.

My last look at him was of a grin as he waved before the doors separated us. Another Model One barreled toward him, but the elevator clamped closed just as the android reached it. It slammed a fist into the metal with a clank. The doors bent but stayed closed.

Pollock was gone—like the coward he was.

Liv and Hunter shot toward the office door, but two Model Ones bounded around them and blocked the route. One of them grabbed Liv as she tried to dart past. It twisted her arm behind her back like she was under arrest.

"Server!" I shouted. "Can you hear me?"

No new text appeared on the vid-screen.

"Server, stop this. That's an order."

The large *YES* on the vid-screen blinked out, but nothing else appeared. The screen stayed blank and dark.

Three Model Ones fanned around me while four more moved toward Jackson. We stepped away from the androids and farther away from each other too. They were separating us.

"Jackson." The name came out more like a squeak.

"You got this, babe."

I shot toward the android on my left, bringing my arm in for a hit. My fist slammed against the android's cheek. Its head rotated with the blow. When it turned back, the side of its face was crushed, one eye light shattered. The other eye stayed red and glowing.

Something rammed into my back, and I hit the floor so hard my head jarred.

I rolled over, and an android's crimson eyes stared into mine. Before I could lift my left arm, another one held it down. I wrenched it out of its grasp, but the third android appeared at its side and grabbed my wrist. The two of them held my arm down to the floor.

I grabbed at them with my right hand, but they shook it off. My fingers scraped across the metal, shrieking like nails on a chalkboard. A third Model One bounded over and pinned my legs down.

I was stuck.

I craned my neck to see if help was coming. The four Model Ones had Jackson pinned, each one holding a limb to the floor. Androids had Liv's and Hunter's arms locked behind them. I couldn't see Melody and Nina.

"Melody!" I screamed. "Nina! Are you guys okay?" I couldn't turn my head to check the other side of the room, and panic filled my voice, echoing what I felt inside.

"We're alive." Melody grunted. "Stupid machines."

"We can't move," Nina shouted.

"Where's Claire?"

"Gone," Melody shouted. "Pollock too."

I bucked my body to try to free my legs. But the androids didn't budge. One of the two holding my left arm placed a hand on my chest and pushed.

I gasped.

I bucked harder. No matter how much I shimmied, the

three Model Ones did not let up. My right hand was free, and I gripped the wrist of the one on my chest. It was like a steel rod, immovable. My hand was damp with sweat, and my fingers slipped across the smooth metal.

The weight on my chest grew until my breath thinned. "I can't . . ."

Out of the corner of my eye, I could see Jackson straining to look at me. "She can't breathe!" he shouted.

Spots popped into my vision, and the room blurred. My chest burned. Fire engulfed my lungs.

"Claire said *restrain* us," Jackson's voice sounded far away. "Not kill us."

Stark white lettering popped up on the dark vid-screen. The white swam into the black like words in water. The whole room spun together, but I squinted to make it out: *She's not the boss of me.*

I gasped again, but the pressure stayed on my chest, crushing me.

"Lena!" Liv shouted.

She fought against the Model One that held her. Then she stopped suddenly. She raised a foot and stamped it down onto the android's instep. Just like a human would, its leg buckled to the side, and it lost its balance.

Liv broke free and ran toward me. As she passed the table holding Jackson's broken android, she swept up a leg and barreled in my direction. She swung the leg at the head of the android pressing on my chest.

Metal shrieked as its head bent to the side on a damaged neck. But its arm stayed locked over my chest.

The Model One that had been holding Liv caught up and grabbed her wrist.

Hunter stamped his foot down on his android's instep. Its leg buckled, and it stumbled. He grabbed a metal arm from the table as he passed and slammed it into the arm on my chest.

The arm bent, and my lungs found air.

I sucked in a deep breath, and the world slammed back into focus. Hunter's next swing hit the arm of the Model One still holding my left wrist. He followed it with two more swings in quick succession. That arm buckled, and I yanked free.

He and Liv turned to face the androids that had held them. They both brandished the limbs they clutched like baseball bats.

Before I could stand, an android fist hurtled toward my face. My chest tightened as internal screaming filled my head. My left arm shot up to meet it. Metal clanked against metal, and when I opened my eyes, I was gripping the silver fist in mine.

I yanked the arm from its socket. Then I jumped to my feet and barreled toward Jackson.

I swung the robot arm toward the elbow of one of the androids holding him down. Both the arm in my hand and the one holding Jackson bent, but neither gave way.

They were made of the same material, but I was an upgraded composite. I dropped the arm I held, grabbed the Model One on Jackson, and yanked. Its arm tore loose with a piercing shriek.

Jackson was up a second later, throwing punches. Every

Model One within reach of him took a blow and flew backward. Melody and Nina must have freed themselves too. They ran toward the table in the center of the room and grabbed up the remaining limbs of the android that used to be Jackson's.

The six of us stood with our backs to one another in the center of the room, surrounded by twelve androids.

"Now what?" Nina shouted.

"Now, we kill them." Jackson ran toward the Model One closest to him. It tried to dodge him, but Jackson was faster. His arm slammed into its gut and yanked out its power cell. The red eyes died, and the thing sank to the floor.

Before the closest android could move, he took that one out too.

"Works for me," I said. "Liv, would you mind running past me toward the elevator?"

"What?"

"Trust me."

She ran past, screaming, and the android closest to her followed. When it reached me, I shot my left arm into its stomach and ripped out its power cell. I raised it in the air and shouted, "Who's next?"

Jackson had already taken out two more, and he was cackling like it was the time of his life.

"You're enjoying this a little too much," I called to him over the sound of screeching metal as he twisted and removed a robot head.

"It's therapeutic."

Hunter, Liv, Melody, and Nina pummeled one android

with the busted limbs they'd grabbed, so they were safe and out of the way.

Another Model One lunged toward me. I let my body relax and willed my arm's artificial intelligence to take over. In a daze, I yanked power cells from androids one by one until Jackson and I almost ran into each other, grinning like idiots, surrounded by the broken body parts of my parents' creations.

"Hey, you." He panted, grinning. One side of his flushed face was streaked with black grease.

"Hey," I said, grinning with just as much idiocy.

The rest of our friends were laughing as they continued to pummel the last android, which was so bent and battered that it could barely move.

"Guys?" I said.

Their metal victim tried to stand but stumbled to the ground on broken legs. Its red eyes flickered and died.

"You got it," I said. "It's out."

They stopped hitting it, and the sounds of their excited breathing filled the air instead of the clanking of metal against metal.

Melody laughed.

"Where's Claire?" Liv asked, still brandishing her robot leg.

The elevator doors were closed, and only the six of us still occupied the room. "Gone," I said. "Pollock too."

"He called the police though," Hunter said. "On his comm before the robots attacked. I watched him. She won't get far."

"So this is over?" Melody asked. "Am I going to be in trouble?" She glanced between Jackson and me.

"Technically, you only assaulted *me*," Jackson said, "and I'm not pressing any charges."

She offered him a grateful smile. "So this is over?"

"As far as I'm concerned," Jackson said.

I hoped so.

36

THE POLICE MET US IN THE LOBBY. THERE WERE FOUR OF them, including the two uniformed officers who'd arrested Mr. Miller and two detectives I didn't know.

"We need to speak with each of you individually," said one of the detectives, a black woman with straightened hair that fell in a shining sheet past her shoulders.

Nina pulled Melody to her side. "I'm not leaving her."

"We need to speak to you *individually*," she repeated.

"Are we under arrest?" I asked.

"No." She jerked a thumb to the space by the reception desk, where the two uniformed officers held Claire between them. Handcuffs held her hands behind her back. "Only that one, so far."

"In that case, Nina can stay with Melody if she wants to. Melody lost her sister recently, and she could use a little understanding. Either that, or you can wait until one of her parents arrives."

The detective stared at me for a full two seconds and then nodded. "It's fine."

The other detective, a tall man with olive-toned skin and dark hair, gestured for the two girls to follow him.

When they were out of earshot, I added, "Has Greg Miller been released?"

"His release is being processed now," she said. "That one confessed as soon as we asked her what was going on."

The two uniformed officers led a sobbing Claire through the main entrance of the building. She was blubbering words that I couldn't make out through the tears, but from the tone, I guessed it might be an apology.

I wondered whether Paris's parents wouldn't care how sorry she was—that she only meant to scare their daughter. I certainly didn't care how sorry Ron was for killing Harmony.

Second chances were like that. Some people were just too far gone to deserve them. I hoped Claire wasn't, but that wasn't up to me.

"What happened here?" The female detective pointed straight up, referring to the upper floors of the Tower.

"My parents will be back from their trip tomorrow. We'll come down to the station and give a statement then."

"We also need to question you about what happened to Detectives Garett and Johnson. Miss Scott says you told her Model Ones attacked them too, but she denies involvement in their deaths."

"Am I under arrest?" I asked.

She shook her head. "Given her confession, we're looking at Miss Scott for that as well, since all the Model

One incidents appear to be connected. We're still going to need a statement from you though."

"When my parents get back, no problem."

"We'd rather handle this tonight if—"

"Parents. Lawyer."

She raised both hands, palms out. "All right. Come down to the station first thing in the morning, or we'll come to you. I'll call your parents and tell them the same."

I nodded and turned to head to the elevator that would take me to VIP parking.

The rest of my friends were standing around giving their statements. Nina had an arm wrapped around Melody as they told their story. In another corner, Liv was talking to one of the uniformed officers who'd returned without Claire. She gestured wildly and banged her hands together in what I could only assume was a demonstration of the fight. Hunter was telling his side near the reception desk, his expression intense.

I scanned the space for Jackson, and my heart sank when I didn't spot him. He was taller than most people, and with his shock of dark hair and those blue eyes, he stood out in any crowd. Except this one—because he wasn't here.

I swallowed my disappointment as I took the elevator down to my car. The lot held only three other vehicles now, likely belonging to high-level CyberCorp execs who worked late even on holiday weekends.

Before getting in my car, I flicked on my hand-screen's flashlight and swept it over my windshield.

No notes. Thank God.

Then I swept it under the bottom of the vehicle as well.

No trackers. Also good.

Maybe this thing was finally over.

As I turned off my hand-screen's flashlight, I noticed a message notification. I'd missed a call from Dr. Fisher. I slid into the front seat of my car and started the engine as I let the message play.

"Hi, Lena. It's Athena Fisher. As you asked, I double-checked the logs of my account to see what activities might represent Ron sending unauthorized data over the EyeNet. I wasn't able to find anything that looked like that. Sorry I couldn't be more helpful. You know where to find me if you need anything."

I groaned as the message came to an end. This nightmare with the Model Ones might be over, but some mysteries remained unsolved.

37

I spent the ride home on speaker with my parents.

By the end of the conversation, we established that they needed to reevaluate the authorizations of CyberCorp personnel—like Mr. Miller—who had access to the Model One server, and also that my father may or may not be getting a second private jet.

I dragged myself through the door from the garage to find my house dark and empty except for the red lights of our security cameras.

As I stepped into the kitchen, the overhead pot lights came on. When I moved into the foyer, those switched off, and the ones in the entryway popped on. The lights followed me up the stairs to illuminate my path.

The hallway upstairs was already lit, and the door to Allie's room stood partly open. I pushed it farther with my foot and peeked in. Allie lay on her back in her twin-sized bed with pink tulle canopy. Her mouth hung open.

Marcy sat in a pastel yellow chair beside the bed, her head slumped over a book that now lay in her lap.

I shut the door and headed to my room.

When I finally crawled into bed after a long shower, the cushions molded around me. I grabbed my hand-screen from the nightstand and pulled up my sleep journal. Right now, it was 11:57 p.m.

I deleted the entire file and set the hand-screen back.

Ron's co-conspirator was still in the wind, but it wasn't me. It was time for my obsession to end.

Something tapped on my door, and then it opened. Light from the hallway framed Allie in the doorway, her kinky hair sticking up in all directions.

She yawned with her whole body, little fists in the air. "You didn't come see me. You're supposed to come see me when you get home."

"You were asleep."

"I was not."

"You were snoring."

"I was not." She shot a glance over her shoulder and stepped through the doorway. She eased the door closed behind her. "Shh. Don't wake Marcy."

I patted the spot beside me in bed. "Tell me about your day. What was the most interesting part?"

She scowled. "Marcy is making me memorize multiplication tables." She enunciated each syllable of the big word.

"Really?" I said, feigning shock. My parents had forced Marcy to do that with me in preschool as well. Hayeses had to be at the top in math and science, after all. I restrained myself from rolling my eyes. "What did you learn?"

"Any number multiplied by itself is itself."

"That's very good."

"I don't know why that matters."

I laughed. "You'll get there, little one."

"I'm not little."

I rubbed her hair. "Of course you're not."

She snuggled closer to me. The strawberry scent of her conditioner wafted around me as she settled deeper into my side. "What was the most interesting part of *your* day?" she asked.

I guffawed and then tried to come up with something other than being detained by the police, breaking out of custody thanks to killer robots, and then fighting more robots after they tried to murder me.

The metal flowers Jackson had given me this morning sat on top of my dresser, close to the window. In the morning, the light would hit them, and they'd shine. I couldn't wait to see that.

"Jackson gave me flowers." I pointed at them.

"You hate flowers." Allie's eyelids drooped, and her words tumbled all together.

I whispered my next words. "I hate real flowers because they belong in the ground. He made those for me from metal."

She mumbled something I couldn't understand before her eyes closed. I waited until her breathing evened, and then I climbed out of bed and lifted her into my arms.

I carried her back to her room and set her on her bed

before tucking the pink sheets in around her. She rolled onto her side and smiled in her sleep.

I tapped Marcy on the shoulder, and her eyes popped open.

"Shh, it's okay." I tilted my head toward Allie. "Go to bed. You're going to hurt your back again, sleeping like that."

She kissed me on the forehead and retreated to her own room. I headed back into mine. I couldn't wait to be unconscious for hours.

"Hey, babe." The voice came at me as soon as I shut my bedroom door.

I whirled and swung my left arm toward it. My arm stopped less than an inch from Jackson's face.

He let out a nervous laugh. "It's just me."

"Don't scare me like that." I gasped as I allowed my heart to slow back to normal speed. "I could have hurt you."

He ducked under my still-outstretched arm. "Yeah, thanks for not bashing my face in. Further proof that you love me."

"Thank my artificial intelligence. I threw the punch. The AI stopped me. Maybe *it* loves you."

"Maybe it knows *you* do."

"What are you even doing here?"

He pointed to my bedroom window, which he'd been thoughtful enough to close behind him. "It's Monday. I climb through your window on Mondays."

"It's Sunday."

He pointed again, this time to the small projection on

the wall next to my nightstand. It showed the current time as 12:05 a.m. "It's Monday."

I groaned. "It's Monday morning. You used to come see me on Monday nights." Before he could counter that, I added, "More importantly, we broke up. You don't need to crawl through my window at all."

He shook a finger at me. "Wrong again. I've been climbing through your window since a year before we started dating—when we were just friends. Are we not friends now?"

I glared at him.

He grinned, spun, and flopped down onto the floor at the foot of my bed. "Screen, what new movies are available?"

Part of the surface beside my door dissolved, revealing the vid-screen that had been displaying an image that looked just like my wall. In response to Jackson's request, the vid-screen showed us movie posters.

Jackson scrolled through the options, gesturing with his hand to make the titles move downward.

"Screen," I said, "show me romantic comedies."

"You don't even like romantic comedies."

"They're not usually my first choice, but today, I could use a little light-hearted fun."

"What about an action-comedy?"

"What about I call Marcy in here to show you out?"

"I guess I could watch some romance this one time."

I lay my head on his shoulder and let my eyes drift shut. For now, I was safe.

When I woke, I was lying on the bed with the covers tucked in around me. The room was dark except for the light coming from the vid-screen. Jackson shook me from where he sat upright beside me, on top of the covers, and pointed.

My head was still cloudy from sleep, but I sat up enough to look at the screen.

A blonde newswoman stood in front of CyberCorp Tower. The Tower occupied the corner of two streets, and she stood on the sidewalk at the edge of that crossroads. Beyond her, a circular drive provided a convenient entrance for dropping people off. From the circle, a driveway shot off to one side to lead underneath the building for general parking.

"On Saturday afternoon, CyberCorp suspended all Model One activity. Every issued android stopped what it was doing, returned to its home charging pad, and went to sleep."

"What's going on?" I asked Jackson.

He pointed at the screen.

"We're now getting reports that androids in people's homes have simply woken up and gotten back to the tasks they were assigned by their owners." The reporter's words were hesitant, as if she couldn't believe what she was reading on the teleprompter. "They're cleaning, folding clothes, cooking dinner—as if they were never suspended at all." Her last words came out like a question, and her gaze shot to one side as if for confirmation.

"That's weird." I sat up straighter and leaned forward.

As usual, a few protestors stood just off the company's property on the sidewalk. There were always protestors objecting to my parents' inventions. Nothing good ever came without resistance, my mother liked to say.

But today, they were staring at the front door, motionless. Their signs littered the ground around them.

The double doors leading into the lobby opened, and two androids walked out. They turned left toward the protestors, who scattered in all directions as they marched past.

"Where are they going?" I whispered more to myself than to Jackson.

"Despite Saturday's statement that all the Model Ones would remain down pending security upgrades, CyberCorp's flagship androids appear to be coming back online."

"Did your parents say they were turning the androids back on?"

"No way. They told me they were going to increase the security." I gestured toward the blonde. "Just like she said."

The front doors of CyberCorp opened again, and this time, a long line of Model Ones filed out. Their steps clomped in rhythmic unison. They turned right. Another reporter darted out of the way as they marched right through the spot where he was standing.

Jackson stared at me. "So what the hell is this?"

"I have no idea."

ACKNOWLEDGMENTS

I experienced some serious health issues while working on the second draft of this book. As a result, I had to push the release date back.

That just makes this publication a larger joy. I'm proud of this one—not just for its content, but also for the circumstances under which I completed it.

Thanks so much to all my friends and family who encouraged and supported me as I completed this book. Thank you to my parents and to my love for being my support system.

Thank you, especially, to Kristin Potchynok and Michele Zugnoni for being amazing beta readers.

And thank you for reading.

ABOUT THE AUTHOR

I decided to write books about ten minutes before graduating from law school.

Now, I'm an Atlanta attorney moonlighting as an author, electronics junkie, and secret superhero. With degrees in computer science and a healthy diet of fiction, I love all things high-tech and unreal.

I write fantasy and science fiction for young adults.

Now you know where to find me:
www.writeralicia.com

Sign up for my newsletter to keep in touch:
www.writeralicia.com/newsletter

amazon.com/author/writeralicia

goodreads.com/writeralicia

facebook.com/writeralicia

twitter.com/writeralicia

instagram.com/writeralicia